Unfinished Business

A Cape Cod Mystery/Thriller

By: F. Edward Jersey

Unfinished Business

A Cape Cod Mystery/Thriller

By: F. Edward Jersey

Copyright © 2010 by F. Edward Jersey
First Edition

Cover photos © 2010 F. Edward Jersey
Edited by Wendy H. Jersey
        Victoria L. Jersey
        Diane Kelley

ISBN: 1450554059
EAN-13: 9781450554053

This book is dedicated to my wife Wendy. Thanks for your inspiration, patience and help.
The story continues.

Unfinished Business

Chapter 1

"Did you ever have one of those years?" Katherine Sterns said to Detective Frank Jenkins.

"Not like the year you've had Kat."

"First my husband died in a freakish fishing accident last year. Then I lost my baby. Then someone stole two million dollars from me. You think it was Charles Chamberlin because he's disappeared. Now I've been accused of attacking my friends. I'm having absolutely no luck with men in my life."

"What am I, chopped meat?" Frank said as he sat back in the chair.

"You're a good friend Frank. You have helped me out in just about every bad situation I've been in."

"I guess I have. But that's only because you live in the town where I work."

"It might have started out that way but you've become something special in my life."

Katherine Sterns and Frank Jenkins were on a long weekend down in Key West Florida. Jenkins was just a Sergeant when Katherine's husband Sam had gone missing during an ice-fishing trip with a friend of his. Jenkins had been one of the policemen in the town of Dennis, Massachusetts to work the case. He came to know Mrs. Sterns from this first incident. Sometime after the death of her husband, Jenkins had gone to the Sterns' residence as a result of a 911 call and investigated an incident where Katherine had fallen down the stairs and ended up losing her unborn baby. Then as luck would have it, Jenkins, who had been subsequently promoted to detective, was one of the officers involved in the widow robberies. It was widely thought that Charles Chamberlin had befriended a number of widows on Cape Cod, gaining their trust and access to the widow's assets. Mr. Chamberlin stole millions of dollars from at least five widows the police were aware of, Katherine being just one. Recently, Katherine had been accused of being involved in the attacks on middle-aged women in the mid-Cape area, most of whom she knew. Because of the age of each of the victims, the cases were called the "cougar attacks."

Detective Jenkins had met numerous times with Katherine, or "Kat" as she liked to be called, to discuss leads and other matters involving the theft of assets and in the attacks on the cougars in town. At some time during one of the encounters, the two discovered they liked each other's company, and Jenkins had finally asked Katherine out for dinner. Now a few months later, they were dating on a regular basis. The relationship was a little strained when Katherine had been accused but ultimately cleared in the attacks. Jenkins had to be careful.

Katherine was also a rather wealthy widow. She had inherited assets from her husband. While Mr. Chamberlin stole two million from one of her accounts, he left another three and a half million in her accounts plus he left her the entire balance of her dead husband's 401k account totaling over five million dollars. When everything was added up, her net worth before being robbed was about ten point two million.

Jenkins on the other hand didn't have much money. He did own a home, had saved a few thousand dollars in a savings account and had a retirement account that was approaching a hundred thousand dollars. Nevertheless, he lived a rich lifestyle being a bachelor. His detective job paid a nice salary of eighty five thousand dollars a year plus whatever he could make on side jobs.

Katherine had picked up the tab for a long weekend in Key West. The two had been sitting at an outside table at the Island Dog watching people walk by. Kat took a sip of her mojito and said to Frank, "Look at those two. It must be nice to be young and in love."

"You don't have to be twenty something to be in love."

"I guess, but I don't seem to have much luck in that department."

"If I remember correctly, you seemed to be doing quite well for yourself last night."

"That was just sex, and I am pretty good at it if I do say so myself."

"It might be just sex to you, but I think you were pretty involved emotionally."

"Frank, you're just being kind."

"No I'm not. You were really into it."

"Maybe so, but I would love to be in my twenties again."

"And have to do all of this over again?"

"Well, I wouldn't want to have to do all of the same things over again. Just some."

"Then let's get the check and get out of here. I'd like to do some of the *just some* again."

"You're on."

Jenkins picked up the check, paid the waitress and the two started to walk down Duvall Street. There were quite a few snowbirds visiting Key West at that time of the year and it seemed like most of them were walking on Duvall. Katherine was dressed in a pair of white shorts with a red knit tight fitting top. She had her hair pulled back into a ponytail giving her a college girl look. Frank was dressed in sandals, khaki shorts and a Red Sox tee shirt.

Walking along, Frank said, "I read in the paper this morning that the influx of people in Key West at this time of year happens because of St. Patrick's Day."

"When do they celebrate it down here?"

"Same day it's celebrated back home, March 17th."

"So why are there so many people here today? The 17th isn't for three more days."

"Probably came down early to do more partying."

"Probably."

The two walked past Sloppy Joes Bar and looked in. The place was mobbed. A band was playing on the stage.

Frank said, "Want to go in?"

"Why not? We're here to get some R and R. And I'd like another mojito."

They found a small table off to one side of the stage and sat down. When a waitress appeared, Frank ordered two mojitos.

"I still want to get back to the B and B before we go to Mallory Square to see the sunset tonight."

"Frank, you just want to have sex and I promise you I'll make it worth your while."

"In that case, we can have a few of these island nectar specials."

"Well don't drink so many that you can't participate in our afternoon activities."

"Oh, I'll make sure I'm up to the challenge."

"I'm counting on it."

The two had a few more drinks and eventually got up and danced along with the other fifty or so patrons who decided to scuff some leather on the dance floor. At around three thirty, Frank paid the tab and indicated he was ready to go. Kat agreed and the two continued their walk down Duvall Street.

Along the way, the two stopped into a liquor store and purchased all the ingredients they would need to make mojitos back in their room.

Arriving back at the B and B, Kat said, "Frank, why don't you make us a mojito while I change into something more comfortable?"

Frank retrieved the sugar bowl from the kitchenette closet and put a half-cup into a small saucepan. He added a half-cup of water and turned on the heat. He stirred the water a few times as it came to a boil dissolving the sugar. When finished, he took the saucepan off the range and put it into the freezer to cool the liquid down quickly. While the sweet water was cooling, he put a few mint leaves into two glasses. He put a half-teaspoon of sugar into each glass and mulled the sugar and mint. "Only in Key West would the kitchen come with a mudler" thought Frank. After a few hearty strokes of the mull the fresh scent of mint reached his nose and he added ice, rum and a splash of soda water. Then he added the now cool sweet water and stirred the drinks. When he turned around, Katherine was standing behind him wearing a sheer nightgown.

"What have you got for me?" she asked in a sexy voice.

"Just what you asked for."

She reached down, "Time for an afternoon delight."

She undid his belt and unhooked his pants. Then she unzipped his pants. She reached, he sighed. Frank was holding a glass in each hand. Kat said, "Why not put those down and follow me?"

Their accommodations in the B and B had a comfortable layout. They had a small kitchenette, a sitting room with a couch and oversized chair, a flat screen TV, a balcony off the sitting room overlooking a pool and a large bedroom with a king size bed.

Frank pulled the drapes on the sliding doors leading out to the balcony but left the door open for the gentle breeze.

Katherine took his hand and led him to the bed. He quickly shed his clothes. In one motion, Kat took off her nightgown. Frank slowly caressed her body. She pulled him down on her. She could tell he was ready. The two kissed slowly at first and then more passionately. As their breathing grew more rapid, they made love.

After what seemed like an hour, Frank laid back and let out a big sigh.

"Does that mean you're exhausted?"

"Not exhausted, but content."

"Now that's not something I've heard after having sex?"

"I don't mean in a bad way. I'm just totally satisfied."

"Frank, if you're like most men I've known, you've reached a level of calmness resulting from an orgasm."

"What? Are you a clinical person now?"

"Kind of. I make it my business to understand men. It comes in handy."

"Do you think it will help you in your legal matters?"

"I'm sure it will. Now, I'm going to take a shower. Care to join me?"

They showered together. Frank lathered his hands with the sweet smelling soap and gently applied it to Katherine's body. Katherine put some of the liquid soap on her hands and applied the soapy lather to his mid-section. He sighed.

"Do you like this?" she asked as she gently turned and kissed him on the cheek.

"What's not to like?" Frank put his arms around her from behind and held her breasts. He started to get aroused again.

"What do we have here?" Katherine said as she reached around to her back. "You'll just have to wait until later. Let's call it desert," she said playfully.

"You're going to let this go. Just like that?"

"You'll want me even more if I put you off. Plus, you had your way with me. I'll be here for you later."

Katherine got out of the shower and dried off. She took the towel and started to dry Frank off. He had relaxed.

"See, you didn't have it in you after all."

"I did. It was your lack of interest that made this happen." He reached down and held out the limp appendage.

She grabbed him, "Limp. This thing is putty."

"You didn't think that way a half hour ago."

"That was then, this is now."

"Oh, alright. I'll be ready to head out whenever you are."

They finished their mojitos while getting dressed in light clothing for the night, and then they walked to Malory Square. It was a carnival atmosphere: a juggler, tumblers, parrots, musicians and everyone had a drink. The sunset was spectacular; to the west was a blue sky with only a few clouds. The clouds turned gold then amber, pink and purple in color as the sunset.

As the sun set below the horizon, Frank put his arms around Kat from behind, "I could get use to this."

"Me too."

"Want to move down here?"

"You wouldn't give up your career would you?"

"I'd look into work down here."

"Do you think you could do this every day?"

"What part are you talking about? The drinks, sunsets, sex with a beautiful woman?"

"Yeah. All of it."

"It might be interesting to give it a try."

"Then why don't we?"

"Because you have those legal matters needing resolving and I have things I need to finish up before I could even begin to look for a job down here."

"If my legal issues get resolved will you consider moving?"

"Let's see how things go."

"You're waffling."

"Maybe a little."

"Frank, you have to commit to something sometime."

"I know. But let's see if we can wrap up these loose ends and then talk again."

"Ok."

After watching the sun set, the two walked back along Duval Street to their B and B.

"Tomorrow we head back home."

"Yeah. I'm not looking forward to going to court."

"Speaking of court, when you had to go there last week, why were you smiling when the bailiff announced the judge's name?"

"Smiling? What are you talking about?"

"You did. I saw you."

"Oh, I don't know. I must have been thinking about someone from my past. What was the judge's name?"

"Benson."

"Oh, now I remember. When I was in college, I knew a guy named Benson. I must have been thinking about back then."

"I thought it might have been something else."

"Not that I can think of. Anyhow, I'm not looking forward to going to court."

"I'm sure you'll be found innocent."

"I hope you're right."

"I'm sure I am."

"Let's change the subject."

"Ok. How about we go to our room?"

"Sounds good to me."

The two turned on to the side street where their B&B was located, and within ten minutes they were back in the sack.

Chapter 2

Early the next morning, Frank and Katherine checked out of the B and B. They got into a cab and headed to the airport. Their flight was scheduled to depart at 9 am with one stop in Atlanta. From there, they had a direct flight to Logan airport in Boston. The process of checking in for the flight was a little different in Key West. The airport isn't as busy as the major airports around the country making check-in less stressful. After checking their luggage and passing through security, Kat and Frank stopped at the airport café and ordered a Cuban coffee.

Sipping her coffee, Kat said, "Frank, this has been a very relaxing trip. I'm glad we came."

"Me too."

"I've been thinking. My attorney says Tom Bowman will be responsible for the physical attacks on the women in the cases you've been investigating."

"That may be, but you were involved, too."

"I didn't attack those women. My only mistake was telling Tom who they were and where they live."

"I think his attorney will say you coerced Tom into committing the attacks."

"How could he say something like that?"

"If I recall correctly, his attorney says you used sex as a tool to convince Tom Bowman to do your bidding."

"I may have slept with Tom, but I didn't attack any of those women."

"But you did collect his DNA and used it at the scene of some of the attacks to identify him. Didn't you?"

"I only followed him after Ann's attack and saw him going after Tina. That was when I got the idea of getting his DNA and making sure he left his calling card to be caught."

"Your actions might be construed as an accomplice."

"But he didn't know I was even there."

"So you're saying you only followed him?"

"Either followed him or went back to the scene where he said he committed the attacks and left the evidence."

"Your actions are crimes themselves. You tampered with evidence. You knew about the attacks and didn't say anything."

"I want him put away forever. I think there was more to Sam's death than what Tom Bowman described. He's a sex predator and he needs to be stopped."

"Look Kat. There are ways to deal with these kinds of things and taking the law into your own hands isn't the right way. That's vigilantism."

"He's no good Frank. The law didn't stop him, so I had to."

"I hope it all works out for you in court."

"Me too."

As they were talking, an announcement came over the intercom announcing their flight boarding. They picked up their things and proceeded to the gate. Once on board the plane, the two didn't talk anymore about Katherine's problems. Katherine had brought along a book. She read for most of the flight. Frank read the papers and then dozed off. When the plane landed in Atlanta, the two had about twenty minutes to make it to the next flight. They hurried along and about fifty minutes later, were on their way to Boston's Logan airport.

At 4:35, their flight touched down at Logan. It took about thirty minutes to get their luggage. Finally, at just before six, they were headed back to Cape Cod. The drive from Logan took just over an hour and they got to Katherine's house around 7:30.

Katherine opened her front door and switched on the lights. She held the door open for Frank. As she started to close the door, she could see her neighbor peeking out of her window. Katherine smiled and waved.

"Frank, can you put my bags in my bedroom?"
"Sure."
As he did, she went to the kitchen and made them each a dry, ice cold martini. She brought the drinks into the living room and set them on the coffee table. Frank was seated on the couch.
Katherine picked up the drinks and handed one to Frank. "To a nice relaxing time."
"I'll drink to that."
"Why don't you stay the night? We can finish off this trip on the right note."
"I thought we did?"
She took off her blouse and reached around undoing her bra. As the clothes fell off her body, she leaned in and kissed him. Frank couldn't resist her. The two picked up their drinks and went into her bedroom. Kat turned off the lights as they made their way down the hall. Her neighbor stopped looking out the window and said to her husband, "That Katherine, she just can't get enough."

"Enough of what?" said her husband.

"Never mind Nick. Go back to your basketball game."

Frank stayed the night. In the morning, he rolled over, "I could get used to this."

"Then get going and wrap up what ever it is you to do. I'll be here."

"I will."

Frank Jenkins wanted to believe Katherine's explanation of her role in the cougar attacks. He knew his involvement with her created a conflict of interest but he had fallen for her. He made up his mind he would do all he could to clear her. He realized he would have to keep certain secrets to himself lest he implicate her with the information he had about her freezer.

Jenkins went to the police station to begin his workday. He went through his in-basket, sorting out the contents and then turned on his computer. There was an e-mail from Captain Tomlinson when he logged in. In the e-mail, he indicated he had received a request from the Olympic Committee asking about officer availability to assist with security matters regarding the 2016 Olympics in Rio de Janeiro. He had asked Jenkins to come see him when he had a few minutes. "This sounds promising," thought Jenkins.

Knocking on the Captain's door, Jenkins said, "Captain, you wanted to see me?"

"Jenkins, come in. How was the trip to Key West?"

"Very nice. The weather was great."

"And Ms. Sterns?"

"She was just great as well."

"You know you might need to be careful with her given her legal matters."

13

"I know. I don't think I have anything to worry about though. From the evidence gathered, it looks like Mr. Bowman committed the actual assaults. Ms. Sterns only provided him with information regarding the home addresses and identity for some of the cougars. She didn't know what he would do with the info."

He didn't offer any information about the condoms he found in her freezer.

"In any event, be careful Frank. You don't want to jeopardize your position."

"I'll be careful. Is that what you wanted to talk to me about?"

"No. Actually, I received a request from the US Olympic Committee for assistance with security at the 2016 Summer Olympics to be held in Rio."

"Really?"

"Yes. Since you had worked on security for the Olympics in the past, I thought you might be interested in helping again."

"Oh I am. What are they looking for?"

"I spoke with a Mr. Travis yesterday. He's on the Olympic Committee. He said they're looking for someone from a law enforcement organization to assist in the planning stage for the Olympic team."

"Fred Travis? I worked with him two Olympics ago. Small world. What would be required?"

"He said they want someone to go to Rio and evaluate the housing, event locations and get a general feel for security issues in Rio. Then make recommendations to the Committee."

"Do you think the department could give me the time to do the evaluation they want done?"

"I think so. This kind of thing goes a long way in helping us secure special funding from the State and Federal Government. I'm told the department can expect to receive a special grant to cover all of the expenses."

"So do you think I should go?"

"Most certainly. When you go to Rio, you might want to even take along some company."

"I don't know. That might be a big expense."

"Mr. Travis said the expense stipend would cover you and a guest."

"Can I let you know tomorrow?"

"Sure."

"Did Fred leave a number where he can be contacted?"

"He left a number and an e-mail address." Captain Tomlinson handed a piece of paper to Jenkins. "They're both here."

"Why are they starting on the 2016 Olympics when the 2012 Olympics in London have not even taken place?"

"I asked Travis the same thing. He said the USOC likes to overlap security teams with the prior Olympic security team. That way, they get to share information and hopefully save themselves time and trouble, you know, learn from past mistakes."

"Anything else?"

"I think Officer Trudy wants to talk with you about the cougar attacks. She has been working with the DA lately trying to get all of the facts and timelines worked out. The trial starts in a few days."

"Ok Captain. I'll see where Trudy stands with the cases."

"Let me know if I can do anything Jenkins."

"Sure thing."

Jenkins went back to his office. He logged on to his e-mail account again and wrote an e-mail to Fred Travis.

"Fred, my boss got your request and has given me the ok to assist. What did you have in mind? Let me know what's the best time to call you and where you are located. Frank Jenkins."

Jenkins thought about the last time he saw Fred Travis. The two of them had just finished up an assignment for the 2000 USOC. They had been out partying with some of the other security people and things had gotten out of hand. Fred had pictures of Frank with a few women naked in the hotel hot tub where they had been staying. Jenkins smiled at the memory.

He picked up his phone and called Katherine.

"Kat, what would you think about making a trip to Rio?"

"Rio might interest me."

"I've been asked by the USOC to help out with the security planning for the 2016 Olympics. If I accept, I can take along a guest, all expenses paid."

"Really? What would I do?"

"See the sights, relax and be there with me."

"Would the duties take up most of your time?"

"If past Olympics are any indication of what to expect, it would be like a regular nine to five job for a few days. Then we can extend the trip for a few extra days and relax together."

"I like the sound of that. Count me in."

"Great. I'll call my contact at the USOC and start the ball rolling. I'll tell you more when I know more."

Chapter 3

Frank had just hung up the phone when it rang. He pressed the blinking button and answered, "Detective Jenkins."

"Frank, it's Fred. I just got your e-mail."

"I just sent it out only a few minutes ago."

"I was on my computer and saw it come in. When I saw your name, I had to call right away. How have you been?"

"Just fine Fred. I'm with the same department I was with the last time we got together only now I'm a detective."

"Detective, I'll bet you can get into a lot of trouble detecting."

"I've calmed down since I last saw you Fred."

"I'll bet. I still have those pictures of you with our European female counterparts in the hot tub."

"I'd like to forget about that night Fred."

"It sure was a good time."

"Yeah, until that family came in to use the facilities and caught all of us naked and drunk."

"You didn't have to stand up and offer to help the guy's teenage daughter into the hot tub."

"I had had too much to drink and didn't give it a thought."

"The police that showed up didn't give it a thought either. If it wasn't for your badge, you would have spent some time in jail for endangerment or at least for corrupting the morals of a minor."

"Fred, the girl was seventeen and a pretty good looker as I remember. I'm sure I wasn't the first guy she got a good look at."

"Maybe so friend, but her mother was speechless when she saw you. Well maybe not speechless. I think she gasped."

"Do you think it was the shock of seeing naked drunk people in the same hot tub?"

"Nah, I think it was your equipment. She must have been fantasizing. She probably wished the husband and kids had just stayed in their room."

"Back to business Fred. What would you like me to do?"

"Can you make it to Rio sometime in the next week for the initial security meeting? Most of the big countries will have their representatives there and I'd like for you to join me."

"I'm sure I can do it. Where do you plan on staying?"

"We'll stay at one of the posh hotels down in Ipanema. You'll like the scenery. I'll have my secretary make reservations for you. She'll take care of everything."

"Do you mind if I bring someone?"

"Got a steady woman now?"

"Kind of. She's a real looker. You'll like her."

"No problem. The committee allows each of us to bring a guest along on all trips."

"Great. Then I'll wait for your secretary's call and I'll see you in two weeks."

"See you then Frank."

Hanging up the phone, Jenkins picked up a report from his in-basket about the cougar attacks. In the report, Officer Trudy had summarized the different attacks for the DA. At the end of the report, she had been asked to provide her opinion about the evidence.

Trudy's report read as follows: "DNA evidence from Mr. Tom Bowman was confirmed by the laboratory in the Sage and Kent cases. No DNA was present in the Benard case. Semen in the Fletcher cases didn't come from Mr. Bowman but the hairs found on her underwear did belong to Bowman."

Jenkins read further but didn't find what he was looking for. He called Officer Trudy.

"Pam, it's Frank. I was just reading your report to the DA regarding the cougar cases. I didn't see anything in it about the attack on you."

"That's because I don't consider myself one of the cougars."

"I didn't mean to imply you are."

"Plus, there wasn't any DNA evidence left during the attack at my house that could be used in those cases."

"That's only because you are so stubborn and wouldn't go to the hospital to be tested."

"Frank, a woman knows when she has had sex. I wasn't sexually assaulted."

"It doesn't have to be intercourse to be a sexual attack."

"That's true. I didn't get hurt. So I didn't want to pursue it any further."

"We'll have to use what we have so you can tie Bowman to the other victims."

"He admitted to being at Chapin Beach when Ms. Benard was attacked but says he wasn't involved in the Kent, Fletcher or Sage cases. If he wasn't, then someone else was."

"Well, we can continue with the cases where we have solid evidence and keep looking at the others."

"That's what the DA said. The DA thinks both Ms. Sterns and Mr. Bowman should be tried together."

"I'm not sure about Ms. Sterns. From what I gather, the cougars aren't going to cooperate in prosecuting Ms. Sterns."

"The pack's sticking together?"

"Something like that."

"Well, let's see how things unfold."

"Ok."

As the day wound down, Jenkins stopped by Captain Tomlinson's office.

"Captain, I'm all set with the USOC. I talked to Fred Travis on the phone earlier. I'm going to meet with him in Rio along with the security teams from other countries for an initial planning meeting sometime in the next few weeks."

"What kind of commitment do you think they will require?"

"Travis indicated a few meetings will be needed to get things organized and then most of the work can be done from here until the event gets closer."

"Will you need anything from the department?"

"No. Travis indicated everything is covered by the USOC including reimbursement for my time and expenses."

"Keep me informed as things progress. I'll send information up the ladder as you make it available and I'll get you off the duty roster as soon as you know the date of your trip."

"Sure thing Captain."

"How are the cougar attack cases proceeding?"

"Trudy is working with the DA. Her latest report indicated the evidence against Bowman is very strong in all but two of the cases. The DA is only pursuing those at this time."

"What about the Sterns woman?"

"Both Trudy and the DA admit all the evidence regarding Ms. Sterns is circumstantial. The DA wants to see how things progress."

"Captain, I know Ms. Sterns had the DNA from Bowman and other men frozen in her freezer. She provided some of the DNA to the scenes of the attacks. We haven't been able to prove it, but I saw the bags in her freezer on two different occasions. The last time I looked, there was one labeled Tomlinson."

"So you know. I didn't want to say anything."

"That's alright Captain. She had one labeled Jenkins as well. She knows about you and Ms. Fletcher and she has your DNA. I think she might be compelled to use these things against us if she's prosecuted."

"Jenkins, some things should remain secret. I'm not proud of what I did, but I don't want to throw my whole life away because I made a few bad decisions."

"I know what you mean Captain. After all, how would it look if it was discovered that the investigating detective had slept with the accused?"

"She had her reasons and the cougars aren't going to cooperate in prosecuting Ms. Sterns. I think she has suffered enough. Prosecuting Bowman will allow us to bring this matter to an acceptable close."

"I agree."

"Plus, with your relationship with her, you'll be able to keep an eye on her activities from now on."

"I understand."

"That will be all Jenkins. Let me know if you need any further assistance with this matter."

"Ok Captain."

When Jenkins left Tomlinson's office, Captain Tomlinson called his secretary on the intercom.

"Jenny, can you come in for a minute?"

Jenny Harper knocked on the Captains door and entered.

"I'd like you to go to records and pull the files for the cougar cases and the file on Ms. Sterns. Bring them to my office."

"Sure Captain."

Fifteen minutes later, Jenny knocked and walked in again with a stack of files under her arm. "This is all of them Captain."

"Thanks Jenny. I want to look at a few things and then you can put them back."

When Jenny had left the office, Tomlinson went through the files and removed any information he felt would be harmful to Katherine Sterns in a trial. Then he went into her file and did the same thing. When he was done, any damaging evidence that might have hurt Katherine Sterns had been removed from the official police files. He put the stack of files neatly into his out-basket and called Jenny back in.

"I'm all set with these files Jenny. I couldn't find what I was looking for. Please return them to records."

"Will do." She left the office with the stack of folders under her arm and Captain Tomlinson scribbling notes on his notepad.

Chapter 4

Jenkins went back to his office. He understood exactly what Captain Tomlinson was inferring. Tomlinson didn't want Katherine pursued lest he end up being exposed.

Jenkins moved the mouse on his computer and it came to life. He selected the electronic file for Tom Bowman and began reading. The information on file covered the accident where Mr. Sterns died as well as the current cases. He recalled Katherine being upset about something Bowman had said to her at the burial of her husband and about something Bowman indicated Sam Sterns had left for his wife. As he read further, he found what he was looking for. Mr. Bowman had told Ms. Sterns he did it for her. When she pressed him further, she said her husband had died and now he, Tom Bowman, could be with her. Could Bowman have killed Sam Sterns?

The notes in the file indicated Mr. Bowman had moved from Cape Cod to Virginia and sometime later, back to Cape Cod. When he moved back, he moved by himself. His wife had divorced him. Ms. Sterns had indicated Mr. Bowman contacted her upon his return to Cape Cod in an attempt to get together with her. During interrogation, she said she did meet with Mr. Bowman a number of times, even getting sexually involved with him on more than one occasion. When she was asked about her role in the cougar attacks, she merely said she had introduced Mr. Bowman to some of the women who were attacked and had told him where they lived when he had asked her. She denied any direct role in the actual attacks but made it perfectly clear she wanted to see Mr. Bowman pay for his crimes.

Jenkins closed the file and pondered his next step.

At three o'clock, he decided to take a ride to Sundancers and see if Mr. Bowman was there. Entering the bar, he asked Margarita Ortiz if she had seen Mr. Bowman that day. "Yes detective, in fact, Mr. Bowman is outside sitting on the deck. Can I get you something?"

"No thank you."

Jenkins walked past the bar and out to the deck. Bowman was sitting off in the corner looking over the Bass River.

"Mr. Bowman, can I speak with you?"

"Detective Jenkins, haven't seen you in a while. What can I do for you?"

"While I was reviewing your file a few questions came to mind."

"What can I help you with?"

"First, when Mr. Sterns died, you told Ms. Sterns that you did it for her. What was it that you did for her?"

"I had to mutilate her husbands body in order to write a distress message on the ice-floe we were stranded on and I knew she would be seeing the body. I didn't want her to think I had to do the things I did to Sam's body for nothing."

"But why did you say you did it for her?"

"I don't know. Sam asked me to look after her and to give her the anniversary gift he had gotten her. I think that's why I said what I did."

"She thinks there might be more to it than that."

"Like what?"

"I'd rather not say."

"Is she accusing me of something other than what actually happened?"

"You have to remember Mr. Bowman, she lost her husband. And you did make advances."

"Yes I had sex with her one time when Sam was alive, but I didn't pursue her any further."

"What about after your rescue. You went to her house and tried to touch her."

"I was only consoling her."

"So you weren't trying to get her into bed again?"

"No. I gave her the gift and left."

Jenkins took out his note pad and opened it. He flipped through a few pages. "What about when you came back to Cape Cod after having moved to Virginia?"

"My wife ended up divorcing me. I came back here a single man. I saw Katherine at a bar one night and talked to her. She seemed ok with me calling on her, so I did."

"Now this is important. Did she approach you or did you approach her?"

"You mean when I returned from Virginia?"

"Yes."

"I guess I approached her. She was sitting at the bar at Sundancers and I approached her. We talked a little and then went to her place."

"Then what happened?"

"I spent the night."

"Did you sleep with her?"

"Yes."

"Did you have sex?"

"Yes."

"Did you use a condom?"

"I don't understand where you are going with these questions."

"You'll see where I'm going. Just answer my question."

"What does all this have to do with my relationship with her?"

"Well? Did you use a condom or not?"

"I didn't have one. Then she got one out of her nightstand and put it on me."

"Do you know what happened to the condom after sex?"

"I threw it in the trash basket."

"Do you know where it went from there?"

"I assume it want out with the garbage? Why are you so interested in a condom?"

"Have you ever looked in her freezer?"

"For what?"

"Oh, you'd be surprised at what she has in there."

"No I haven't."

"Ok, talk to me about the cougar attacks. How did you identify who you attacked and when?"

"The first time I saw Katherine when I came back from Virginia, I was having a drink at Chapin's. She was there with another woman. I overheard the two talking about their plans for the night. Katherine had said she was going to Sundancers. The other woman, Ms. Benard, said she was going to take a walk on Chapin beach which is just up the road from the restaurant."

"So you followed Ms. Benard?"

"I left just before Ms. Benard did. I went up to Chapin Beach and waited for her. At first, "I was just going to try to talk to her but I startled her at the beach. She fell and hit her head on a rock. I just reacted."

"Did you intend to hurt her?"

"Absolutely not."

26

"Why didn't you stay and help her?"

"I don't know."

"So you just left her there?"

"Yes."

"How did you decide to go after the other women?"

"Well, I met up with Katherine a few days later after the incident with Ms. Benard and we talked about it a little."

"What did she say?"

"She said she wouldn't mind if some of the cougars were taken out of commission for a while."

"How did you interpret that?"

"I just thought if I helped her out, she would look favorably on me."

"You mean have more sex with you?"

"Well yes."

"And did she?"

"I told her I had tried to meet with Ms. Benard the night I saw them at Chapin's. I told her about surprising Ann at the beach and how Ann fell and hit her head. Katherine was mad at first but then her tone changed and I think she was grateful."

"How do you mean?"

"Well, we talked a little more and then she led me to her bedroom. We had great sex."

"What about Ms. Fletcher?"

"I saw Katherine at Sundancers again a few days later and she asked me over again. After we had sex, she said she wished something would happen to Ms. Fletcher like what happened to Ms. Benard. I didn't say anything to her at that time, but I got the message."

"So you followed Ms. Fletcher home one night and attacked her?"

"That's right. But I didn't sexually assault her. I have no idea how my hair got on her underwear."

"Let's go back to the night where you went home with Ms. Sterns and she made the comments about Ms. Fletcher. Did she have you use a condom that time?"

"Yes."

"What did you do with the condom?"

"Again, I threw it in the trash. Wait a minute. Are you saying Katherine took the condoms out of the trash and used them to spread my DNA around?"

"Now you're getting the picture."

"How could she do such a thing?"

"Actually pretty easily. All she had to do was collect the condom after having sex and put it in a zip-lock bag. Then freeze it. Whenever she wanted to spread your DNA around, all she had to do was defrost the semen in the condom and squeeze it around as evidence."

"You're kidding?"

"Actually I'm not."

"Why did you hit the women in the head?"

"I didn't hit Ms. Benard. When I pushed her, she fell and hit her head on a rock. She was knocked out."

"What about Ms. Sage?"

"I had been at Sundancers where I had a drink with Ms. Sage. At one point, she had to use the ladies room. I put some of the sleeping pills I got from Katherine's into Linda's drink when she was in the ladies room. When she returned to the bar, another guy came over and talked to her about going to the beach. I didn't want to go with another guy being there so I backed out."

"So you are saying you didn't go to Ms. Sage's house?"

"No I didn't."

"Then how do you think your DNA got on Ms. Sage?"

"I don't know."

"Your hairs were found on her."

"I think I see what you meant by the condoms but how could my hair been found at some of the scenes?"

"Did Ms. Sterns ever say anything about wanting Ms. Sage out of the picture?"

"Not specifically, but I remembered what she told me the first time when I had picked her up at the bar."

"You just took it on your own to go after Ms. Sage?"

"No, no, I told you I didn't attack Ms. Sage."

"Then Katherine must have been the one to put your hair and Kenny Brown's DNA there."

"How could she have put my hair there?"

"When you stayed at her house, did you use her bathroom?"

"Yes, and now that you mention it, she suggested we take a shower when we were done. After getting out of the shower, I used her brush on the vanity. Could she have gotten hair from there?"

"Maybe she collects hair samples as well. I think Katherine is a very cunning cougar. Anything is possible. The DNA tests from Ms. Sage showed DNA from the same person on the inside and outside of the condom. The Lab also identified your hairs."

"Could the condom have leaked?"

"No, so what the test showed was someone spread Mr. Brown's DNA around before Mr. Brown had sex with Ms. Sage. Then when Mr. Brown used his condom, it ended up showing his DNA on both the inside and outside.

"If only Mr. Brown's DNA was present, where did my hair come from?"

"If she spread Mr. Brown's DNA from the zip-lock, she probably took hairs from the brush you used at her house and put them on the condom in the zip-lock bag she had from

Kenny. Otherwise, you would not have been a suspect in that case. My guess is she used the wrong semen from her collection especially if she was trying to implicate you. Is there anything else you want to say?"

"That's it for Ms. Sage, but Katherine said she wouldn't mind if something happened to Ms. Kent to take her out of the picture for a few days."

"Did you interpret that to mean she wanted you to do something to Ms. Kent?"

"I just figured she would be happy if something happened."

"So you took it upon yourself to go after Ms. Kent."

"No, I went by her house but decided not to go in."

"Did you see anyone else there?"

"You mean like Katherine? No, I didn't."

"DNA was found there as well."

"Katherine must have been following me and when I didn't stop she must have, and then spread DNA around."

"Now you're getting the picture."

"Oh, I see. But why would Katherine be coming after me?"

"Think about it Mr. Bowman. She holds you responsible for the death of her husband. She probably holds you responsible for the loss of her baby and who knows what else she has against you. If you think about it, she had a pretty good plan to implicate you in the cougar attacks."

"Maybe so, but I didn't sexually attack any of those women."

"You're going to have a tough time in court with your DNA and hair being all over the place."

"You're probably right. What can I do about it?"

"It will be your word against hers. I don't have any more questions for you right now Mr. Bowman, but I would be careful around Ms. Sterns if I were you."

"Oh don't worry Detective, I'll be careful."

"Mr. Bowman, I'll probably want to discuss these attacks again if you don't mind. Think about the details again if you would and let me know everything and anything you can the next time we talk. Even the smallest detail might be important."

"I'll do my best Detective."

Chapter 5

When Katherine Sterns, then Katherine Miller, was in College, she had earned a reputation as a party girl. One night she had been invited to a frat party. It was for a fraternity member who was about to get married, a Michael Benson. Katherine dressed in a tight body fitting blouse, no bra, shorts and black flats, and arrived at the house around 7 pm. Ben Sloan, the designated doorman of the night, greeted her.

"Hi Katherine, come on in."

"Hi Ben, expecting a big crowd tonight?"

"Sure are. We're having a bachelor party for Mike after the regular party. Hang around if you want."

"I might just do that."

Katherine had been at the frat house a number of times. She knew a few of the members from classes and from some of the parties on campus. She knew who Mike Benson was, but had never really met him. As she entered the house, there were people everywhere. Drinks were flowing. In the center of the main room, there were a group of guys playing a game of beer pong. She recognized one of the players, Zack Thomas.

The objective of the game is to bounce the ping-pong ball into one of the cups of beer on the other side of the table. When this happens, the other team had to drink. Zack's team looked to be on the losing end of the game. While Katherine was watching, Zack had to drink four times within the span of ten minutes. When the game was over, Zack came over to Katherine.

"Kat, glad you could make it," said Zack in a slurred voice.

"Looks like you lost at beer pong, Zack."

"Those guys brought in a ringer. They found some guy who must be collegiate champ or something. He couldn't miss."

"That or you're already impaired."

"I can hold my own."

"So you think Zack. Was Mike Benson your playing partner?"

"Yeah, Mike's pretty toasted already. He's getting married."

"I heard. Ben told me about the after party."

"You interested?"

"In coming?"

"Yeah. We tried to get a stripper for him, but it didn't work out."

"Based on looking at Mike, I'm not sure even a stripper could bring him around."

The two looked over at Mike and he was guzzling down a beer surrounded by a few guys who were toasting him. Zack turned to Katherine, "Yeah, you're probably right. Mike wouldn't even know it if the most beautiful woman in the world was standing in front of him naked."

"Well, if you need someone to encourage him at the end of the night, let me know. I'm game."

"Sure thing Kat."

"So what was the guy's name who beat you at beer pong?"

"Sam Sterns.   He belongs to one of the other fraternities on campus.   They challenged us to a beer pong game.   I guess they got the best of us."

"Sure did.   Can you introduce me to Sam?"

"Ok, now where did he go?"

Zack left Kat to see if he could find Sam Sterns.   A few minutes later, he came back into the main room with Sam in tow.

"Sam Sterns, this is Katherine Miller."

"Hi Katherine."

"Hi Sam."

"Nice game of beer pong.   You and your partner kicked ass on Zack and Mike."

"Mike was an easy target.   He'd already been drinking when the game started.   Accuracy counts in this game, ya know?"

"What about Zack."

"Zack had the misfortune of being Mike's partner.   We focused on Mike during the game and he missed most of his shots.   Zack just ended up having to drink due to his partner's inability to land a ball."

"So you actually had a strategy?"

"Always."

Zack excused himself.   He could see Katherine was interested in talking with Sam and Zack had to make sure Mike didn't pass out before the after party.

Sam said to Katherine, "You want to go out on the porch and talk?"

"Sure, can you get me a beer while I'm using the bathroom?   I'll meet you on the porch."

Sam went and retrieved two beers. Then he went out on the porch and found two seats off in a corner. In a few minutes Katherine appeared. She looked around and found Sam. Sam thought she was beautiful and was pleased it was him she was looking for.

"Thanks for getting the beers."

"You're welcome. So Katherine, what're you majoring in?"

"Some might say parties."

"No, really."

"I'm taking classes in communications and public relations."

"What do you want to do when you graduate?"

"Find a rich man and marry him."

"Really?"

"Really. How about you Sam?"

"I'm an accounting major. I hope to start my own practice when I graduate and build it into a huge corporation."

"Doesn't that take a long time?"

"Usually, but my friend Andrew Dunn and I have an idea of how to help other businesses. If our ideas work out, we could build a thriving practice in a very short period of time."

"How would you do that?"

"We would specialize in technology accounting. There aren't many technology advanced accountants in the world and we plan on making technology the centerpiece of our business."

"Sounds good."

The two continued to talk for two hours. The party started to wrap up nearing midnight. Sam said to Katherine, "Would you be interested in going out?"

"Sure. Give me a call sometime."

She reached into her purse and wrote her number down on a piece of paper and handed it to Sam. Sam took the number and put it in his wallet. The two said their goodbyes and Sam promised to call her. Sam's playing partner found him and said he would meet him outside the frat house in a few minutes. They had other pong challenges to win on campus. The pot gets bigger the later it gets. Sam extended his hand to Katherine. She reached in and gave him a kiss on the cheek.

"Call me."

The regular party was breaking up, and a few of the frat members had already started to clean up the place. Katherine saw Zack in the kitchen. "So Zack, are you still having something for Mike?"

Zack pointed to a guy on the couch who looked like he was asleep. "Mike looks like his night's over."

Just then, Mike stood up. "No it isn't. I heard you Zack."

"Mike, you up for a bachelor party?"

"Sure am. Where we going?"

"Up stairs."

"What's up there?"

"You'll see."

Zack turned back to Katherine, "You game?"

"Yeah, this could be fun."

Zack and two other members grabbed a couple of beers and led the way upstairs. Mike followed them. Katherine followed Mike. When they got to the top of the stairs, they all went into another common room, which was surrounded by bedrooms. Zack put a chair in the middle of the room and said to Mike, "You sit here Mike."

Mike sat in the chair and then all of the lights were turned out. A blindfold was slipped over his eyes. The guys around the perimeter, about a half dozen in number, shouted Mike's name.

"What are you guys doing?" Mike asked.

36

Then, one light in the corner was turned on. Katherine came out of Mike's bedroom. She stood in the doorway as the three guys who had brought Mike upstairs looked at her. Mike pulled the blindfold down and followed their stare. Zack turned on the CD player. A sexy jazz number started to play, its saxophone a perfect background.

Katherine reached down to the bottom of her blouse and pulled it up and over her head. Mike's jaw dropped at the sight of her breasts. The other guys clapped. Katherine did a slow dance over to Mike's chair. When she got there, she took his beer out of his hands and placed the red cup between her breasts. She moved the cup up and down and then put the cup to Mike's lips. Slowly she tipped it allowing him to take a drink. Next, she set the cup down on a table and she came back to Mike and unbuttoned his shirt.

Mike was clearly inebriated. As she put her hands on his chest, he reciprocated. She gently kissed him on the side of his head, allowing her long hair to dangle across his face. Mike couldn't take his hands off her breasts. Then, Katherine stepped back and unbuttoned her shorts. The guys whooped from the sidelines. Mike reached out to help her, but she stepped back out of his reach.

Slowly, she unzipped her shorts and moved them down her long legs. All the guys went wild as she moved back into Mike and undid his belt. She unhooked his pants and unzipped them. Mike tried to get up but Katherine pushed him back. Then Mike put his hands on both sides of her underwear and started to pull them down. Katherine stood back and pulled them back up. She smiled and encouraged him to stand up. When he did, she dropped his pants to the floor. Mike stood there in the middle of the room in just his underwear. A bulge in the front indicated Mike wasn't totally inebriated. Katherine took his hand and led him to his bedroom. The other guys cheered and booed as Katherine closed the door behind her.

She led Mike to the bed. Slowly, she took his underwear off him. She told him to lie back on the bed. As he did, she removed her underwear and straddled Mike. She lowered herself and took control. After a few minutes of heavy breathing, they both reached climax. Katherine went to the bathroom and upon returning found Mike sound asleep. She got under the covers and cuddled up to him.

When the phone rang the next morning a clearly startled and hung over Michael answered it. It was his fiancé. He turned the other way and saw Katherine curled up under the covers. He picked up the covers and saw Katherine had nothing on. Michael told his fiancé he would see her later in the afternoon. When he hung the phone up, he turned the other way to face Katherine. He took note that he too was naked. He put his arms around Katherine and coaxed her to join him. She reached down and felt him ready. She said, "I like morning sex."

"Then come here." He got on top of her and had sex with Katherine again.

After that night, Katherine only saw Michael around campus a few times and they said hello or waived. Michael was married at the end of the fall semester of his senior year. By chance, in one of the senior year spring classes, Michael and Katherine sat next to each other. About half way through the semester, Katherine asked Michael how married life was going.

"Fine although the sex was nothing like I had with you."

She asked him if he would like to come over to her place one night and she would refresh his memory. He did. He felt bad about cheating on his new wife, but not enough to keep him from getting into bed with Katherine.

That time was back in college. Katherine thought Michael Benson had added a few pounds and aged a little, but he was definitely the same Michael Benson she knew from her college days.

Katherine had to talk to her friend, Dottie Masters, to see what she thought of Michael Benson.

"Dottie, it's Kat."

"Hello Kat." Dottie said in a whimper tone.

Katherine detected depression in Dottie's voice, "What's the matter Dottie?"

"I got some bad news from my doctor today."

"What? Tell me," said Katherine in a suddenly concerned voice.

"I have cancer."

"You're kidding me?"

"No, my doctor told me today the tests came back positive."

"I didn't know you were being tested!"

"I didn't want to tell anyone until it was confirmed and now it has been."

"Dottie, I feel so bad for you. I'm coming to see you tomorrow."

"You don't have to Katherine. I'll be fine."

"No Dottie, you need your friends at this time."

"Ok, do you want me to pick you up at the airport?"

"No. I'll catch a cab. I'll be there by noon."

"See you then."

Katherine forgot to say anything to Dottie about Michael Benson. Dottie's news took her mind off everything. She hung up and called Frank Jenkins.

"Frank, it's Katherine."

"Hi Kat, what's up?"

"I'm going to Washington in the morning to visit with my friend Dottie Masters. I just got off the phone with her and she told me she has cancer."

"That's too bad."

"Sure is. She's only in her mid-forties."

"Did she say what kind it is?"

"No, I didn't want to talk about it over the phone. I'm going to visit with her for a few days. I'll talk to her while I'm there."

"Anything you want me to do for you while you're gone?"

"No, but if anything comes up about my court case that I should know about, will you call me on my cell?"

"Sure Kat."

"You're a good friend Frank. I'll see you in a few days when I get back."

Katherine hung up the phone and then went to her computer to make travel arrangements for the trip. After scheduling her flights and printing her boarding pass, she hastily packed a bag for a few days. She called her attorney and told her where she would be and how to reach her. Then she got ready for bed.

Chapter 6

A few days after Sam met Katherine at the frat party, he called her.

"Hi Katherine, it's Sam."

"Sam, I was hoping you would call."

"Sure was a good party at Zack's, wasn't it?"

"Sure was. You playing any more beer pong?"

"Nah, the night went downhill from there."

"So you don't do those things all the time?"

"No. As I had said to you, I have a game plan for after college and I spend most of my free time working on writing software for my business when I graduate."

"How much more do you have to do?"

"Most of the software is written and we're testing it now. I think everything will be ready for next fall after we graduate."

"So you and your friend Andrew will be starting your business then?"

"That's the plan."

"I hope it'll all work out for you."

"Me too. Say Katherine, are you interested in going to dinner with me on Saturday night?"

"Sure, what did you have in mind?"

"Oh, I thought we could have dinner at Marcel's and then hang out in the lounge to hear the band that starts at nine."

"Sounds good. What time do you want to pick me up?"

"How about seven."

"Seven it is."

She gave him her address and started thinking what kind of outfit this software writer would like.

Katherine Miller had excelled throughout school. She was a B+ student in most everything she took. Early on in high school, her body developed into a woman's body. She was tall, had long legs and nice figure. These features in addition to being a cute blond made her a target of the upper class boys and even some teachers and professors. It didn't take long and Katherine found herself involved with someone. The first boyfriend pressured her into bed. She quickly learned her way around and before too long, she had developed a reputation. She continued her ways in college and by her junior year, she guessed she had already slept with over twenty-five different guys. She liked sex.

Sam Sterns arrived at Katherine's on-campus apartment just before seven. He dressed in casual neat clothing, clean jeans, and open button down white shirt over a purple graphic tee of some band. When he knocked at the door, Katherine opened it and Sam's jaw dropped. She wore a tight low-cut blouse with a pair of rather tight fitting slacks that may have been black, but Sam wasn't sure he remembered that part accurately. She had on a pair of stilettos raising her height to six feet. She looked great and challenging.

"Wow," were his first words.

"Do you like it?" she said as she turned around for him to get a 360 degree look.

"What's not to like?"

"Then let's get going and Sam, stop looking at my chest."

"I'm sorry but you're dazzling."

"When's the last time you got cozy with a woman Sam?"

"I don't know and that probably says it all."

"Well, stop looking and if you're good, you'll get to see more when we get back."

The comment brought a smile to Sam's face. Up until this point in time, he had only gotten to first base with a couple of girls in high school but had never gone all the way. Sam was excited thinking Katherine would be his first. He wondered if she had any idea he was a virgin.

The two went to Marcels for dinner. Katherine ordered a martini, Sam a beer. Sam was the perfect gentleman. He opened doors for her, held her seat, stood when she would excuse herself to the ladies room and spoke to her with respect. Katherine liked Sam. She thought he would make some woman a good husband.

After dinner, the two went into the adjacent lounge. They had more drinks and listened to the band. When the band started their second set, Sam asked Katherine to dance. The band played a slow song, unchained melody, always a girl's favorite. Katherine got as close to Sam as she could. Being the perfect gentleman, Sam was careful where he placed his hands. At one point, Katherine said, "Sam, I won't break. You can hold me tighter."

"I'm just not used to being with such a beautiful woman."

When the music stopped, the two walked back to the table where they had been sitting. A lady walking through the bar had been selling roses when Sam went over to her and purchased all the roses she had left. He brought them back to Katherine and gave them to her. She was impressed. Then she leaned over to Sam and kissed him passionately for the first time.

"Why don't we go back to my place?" said Katherine to Sam who was now all consumed by her.

Arriving back at Katherine's apartment, she asked Sam to put the flowers in a vase, which could be found in a cabinet in the kitchen. While Sam was in the kitchen, she went into the bedroom and changed. Sam finished arranging the flowers and carried them into the living room. He stopped in his tracks and stared.

"Put those flowers over on the table Sam and come here."

He did as instructed. As he sat on the couch next to Katherine, she unbuttoned his shirt and ran her hands over his chest. Sam couldn't stop looking at her. Here she sat in a satin camisole accompanied by just her underwear. Sam had never been with a woman and to look at Katherine, he didn't know what to do next.

Katherine did. She kissed him slowly at first and then kissed him with her tongue. It didn't take much to get Sam aroused, he knew what to do and what she wanted him to do. Katherine touched his pants. "Let's see what we have here?" She undid his belt and pants. Sam was overcome with excitement.

"Let's take this to the bedroom."

On the way, they both shed their clothing with the help of the other. In bed, they kissed and touched each other. Very soon, they were making love. Sam reached climax first followed by Katherine. When they were done, they lay in bed embracing and kissing for a long time. Sam was hooked.

"Can I see you again?" Sam asked as he held her in his arms.

"I don't see why not."

"Great."

"Sam, you said you and your friend Andrew are going to start your own business when you finish school. Where do you plan on living?"

"We're thinking of setting up business either on Cape Cod or the South Shore area. Why do you ask?"

"I'm planning on moving back to Cape Cod when I graduate. It would be nice to see you when we move back home."

"So you're from Cape Cod?"

"My folks moved there when they retired a few years ago so it is now."

"I went to high school there and I'd like to start my family there."

"So you're thinking about a family also?"

"Yes and I think I've found the person I'd like to start it with."

"Sam, are you proposing? This was just our first date."

"I think I know what I'm doing."

"Sam, have you ever been with another woman?"

"What do you mean?"

"Is this the first time you've had sex?"

"Why?"

"If it is, you might want to be with a few other women before making a life long commitment?"

"Why? I know what I want."

"You might think you do now, but what happens in a few years?"

"Don't you believe in love at first sight?"

"Not really."

"I do. I wouldn't have sex with you unless I knew you were the one."

"Sam, what am I to do with you?"

That's how it all started. After that night, the two dated many times. Katherine dated other men but Sam didn't know about it. Sam adored her and gave her everything. He treated her like a princess. At the end of their senior year, he asked her to marry him, and she accepted.

As planned, Sam and Andrew Dunn started their business right out of college. It didn't take long and the two had a number of clients and a fledgling business. Katherine and Sam decided to buy a home in West Dennis. Andrew had a bachelor pad in Hyannis. On a few occasions when the three were out to dinner, Katherine would flirt with Andrew although nothing ever came of it. Andrew respected his partner and didn't want anything to come between them.

Once during a summer company picnic, Katherine and Andrew found themselves inside the Sterns' residence alone while everyone else was outside. Sam had asked Andrew to get something out of the basement and when he went in to get the item, Katherine followed him. She had closed the door to the basement behind her and descended the stairs. Andrew was reaching up to a high shelf when Katherine approached from behind. She wrapped her arms around him allowing her hands to settle just below his belt.

"Let me help you," she said gently.

"I think I can get it," Andrew stiffly said as he reached for the bag on the top shelf.

As he brought the bag down with the football in it, he turned and was confronted face-to-face, body-to-body by Katherine in her bikini.

"I found it," Andrew declared.

She put her arms around him and held him tight.

"What are you doing?"

"What do you think I'm doing?"

"Kat, we can't do this."

"Yes we can," she reached around her back and unclipped her top. It fell to the floor. She stepped back a step or two allowing Andrew to see her. He reached up and stopped as his hand was along her side.

"I can't do this to Sam."

She took the bag out of his hand and let it drop to the floor. Then she took his hand and placed it on her breast.

He didn't resist.

She reached down, "You want me and I want you."

"That may be, but we can't."

Just then, Sam opened the door at the top of the stairs and yelled, "Andrew, did you find it?"

Katherine quickly picked up her top and stood around the corner from the stairs so Sam wouldn't see her.

"I found it," replied Andrew. He picked up the football and went up the stairs looking back at Katherine as he went. When the door closed, Katherine put her top back on, waited a minute or two and then went back upstairs. She went out into the yard to find the guys all playing a game of football in the back yard. After the game, she brought three beers over to Sam and Andrew, "Nothing like a good game."

Sam said, "We need to do more of this."

Katherine said, "If you like getting sweaty and physical contact."

Andrew just looked at her but didn't say anything.

The incident was the last time Andrew allowed himself to be caught alone with Katherine. It wasn't that Andrew didn't like women. He did. It was just that he didn't want to jeopardize his relationship with Sam. Then one night,

47

Katherine called Andrew to tell him something had happened to Sam. She asked him to come over. Not thinking, Andrew rushed to her side. It didn't take much and she manipulated him into bed. But where was Sam?

Chapter 7

While Katherine Sterns had numerous indiscretions during her life, the cougar animal instinct in her didn't begin to manifest itself until the untimely death of her husband. Sam and Katherine had a good life. He had worked hard and built up a respectable accounting business serving numerous clients in the Cape Cod area. Unfortunately, his life took a dramatic turn one day during the winter when he and his best friend Tom Bowman ventured out onto the ice floe in Cape Cod bay for a day of fishing.

During one afternoon at the Bridge Bar, Tom Bowman had talked with a group of fellow fishermen who told a tale about having gone ice fishing on Cape Cod bay. The fishermen had boasted about having caught some pretty big codfish through the ice on the recent outing. Tom Bowman spoke with the group and they provided him with details of their excursion. Later on, Tom retold the story to his fishing partner Sam Sterns. The two made preparations for an ice fishing outing by retracing the details Tom had learned from the group at the bar.

The following Saturday morning, Sam and Tom gathered their gear and ventured out for a day of ice fishing. At the outset, the weather cooperated, providing a sunny, mild temperature. The two picked up lunches and bait and then went to Paines Creek in Brewster. They loaded all of their gear onto sleds and went out on the ice following what looked to them as the same path the storytellers had indicated. After drilling holes in the ice and settling down to fishing, the two started to catch fish.

The action was exhilarating. Both men caught fish. The day progressed past noontime and well into the day. At one point, Tom Bowman looked around and noted the weather starting to change. The action was beyond expectations and the two didn't pay much attention to the changing conditions. Then later in the afternoon, Bowman looked around and was surprised at what he saw. His sight followed the tracks the two had made when venturing out on the ice but to his dismay, their vehicle was not to be found at the end of their tracks.

Scanning the surroundings, Bowman told his friend with some alarm of his discovery. The ice floe had broken away from land and was adrift on Cape Cod Bay.

The two quickly packed up their gear and made haste attempting to get off the ice floe. They were unsuccessful in their attempts. As nightfall came, the two did all they could to prepare for what was about to come.

The ordeal began with the two making attempts to draw attention to their plight. They tried making a fire, tried using the one cell phone they had and even shouting at the top of their lungs. Unfortunately, all of their efforts went undetected. The ice floe they were on quickly traveled on the outgoing tide towards Provincetown. From there, the two found themselves traveling south along the outer Cape Cod coast into the Atlantic Ocean. From time to time, they could just make out landmarks, which Tom Bowman would speculate as to each landmark's identity. All during the ordeal, the two were unable to attract any attention.

Over the next few days, the two men did everything they could to try to survive. While they were not prepared to spend days on an ice floe, they utilized their outdoorsmen skills to position the fishing shelter they had with them to withstand the elements of the open ocean. They used their skills to melt snow for water and rationed what food they had. Throughout the ordeal, they would try to use the cell phone they had to communicate with someone, anyone. Unfortunately, the cell phone battery had been low and signal strength varied from minimum to non-existent as the ice floe traveled.

When the two men had gone missing, their families and authorities tried to find them. The men had not been forthcoming with their spouses about their plans for the day, which delayed the authorities in locating them. Both Mrs. Sterns and Mrs. Bowman provided information to authorities in an attempt to help locate the missing men. However, the information they were providing served only to mislead the authorities in directions other than where the men actually went that day. When Tom Bowman's vehicle was eventually found, the ice floe had already broken away from shore and traveled beyond the vision of shore. It was only by chance the authorities discovered the mystery of the traveling ice floe from Cape Cod bay.

As the ordeal went on, Katherine Sterns summoned her husband Sam's business partner Andrew Dunn to her home to alleviate the loneliness. During his visit, he succumbed to her advances ending up in bed with her. Over the next few days, the same scenario played out a few times. He was there to comfort her.

Unfortunately, after being on the ice for a few days, Sam Sterns fell through the ice floe while attempting to drill a hole for fishing. Tom Bowman was able to get his friend back onto the ice floe but the damage had been done. Sam's clothing became totally saturated when he broke through the ice. As soon as Tom Bowman got Sam out of the water, he took his wet snowmobile suit off and put his own on his friend. Sam had been in the water for only minutes, but when the water temperature is hovering around freezing, it only takes minutes for hypothermia to set in. In the early morning hours, Sam lapsed into a coma and died.

Bowman, in desperation tried everything he could to get rescued. He remembered his friend telling him to use his blood to write a message on the ice in hopes of having someone spot the distress message from the air. Bowman extracted the blood from his dead fishing partner and wrote the word "HELP" on the ice floe.

Finally, after having been adrift for a number of days, a passing fishing trawler spotted Tom Bowman on the ice floe. Coincidentally at the same time, a passenger on a commercial jetliner approaching Logan Airport spotted the distress message Bowman had written on the ice floe. Authorities successfully mounted a rescue just as the ice floe the two had been on broke up.

Arriving at Air Station Cape Cod, the wives were ushered into different rooms and told of the ordeal. Mrs. Sterns was devastated. Mrs. Bowman, who had become close to Mrs. Sterns, felt bad for her friend. Upon getting her husband home to see his children and recuperate, Mrs. Bowman tried to convince her husband to wait a few days before going to see Mrs. Sterns. Bowman had to see her right away and went to the Sterns residence the same day. While trying to comfort her, Mrs. Sterns thought Tom Bowman was trying to seduce her. She became angry and confrontational and asked him to leave. When Andrew Dunn arrived she asked him to keep Tom Bowman away from her. At the burial when Tom Bowman approached Mrs. Sterns, she rebuked him and let out that she had slept with Tom Bowman prior to her husband's death.

Lisa Bowman was completely embarrassed in hearing about her husband's infidelity. She showed her displeasure with him as they left. In an attempt to save their marriage, she convinced her husband Tom to move to another state. The two, along with their children, did move.

Then one night, Tom Bowman, while talking in his sleep, fantasized about his liaison with Katherine Sterns. According to his wife Lisa, he babbled on about the night he had with Mrs. Sterns at the Route 28 motel. On another intimate occasion, Bowman accidentally called Lisa by the name Katherine. Lisa Bowman could not ignore her husband's obsession any further. She told him to get out and then filed for divorce.

Now he was back on Cape Cod.

Chapter 8

One never knows whom one might meet at a funeral. After the death of Sam, Katherine met Charles Chamberlin at Sam's wake. Mr. Chamberlin introduced himself to Katherine and told her he had done some consulting work for the deceased. At a gathering after Sam's burial, Mr. Chamberlin again approached Ms. Sterns telling her he would like to turn the information he had gathered for Sam over to her at some point in time. While talking to him, Andrew Dunn approached her and indicated he needed to get some information from Sam's home office and computer. Katherine said there was something wrong with the computer. Mr. Chamberlin said he knew things about computers and would be happy to assist if she would like. Mr. Dunn and Mr. Chamberlin went into Sam's office where Mr. Chamberlin took a look at the computer.

"I see what's wrong. The computer has been infected with a virus."

"Can it be fixed?" Andrew Dunn asked.

"Sure, this will only take a few minutes. I'll download a virus scanner and then run it to isolate the problem."

"I'm going to get a drink while you're fixing the problem. Do you want me to get you anything?"

"Sure, I'll have a beer," said Chamberlin.

When Andrew Dunn left the room, Chamberlin took a CD out of his pocked and installed PCTrackR. He quickly set the program to monitor the activities on the computer and to send him a file containing the keystrokes periodically. When Mr. Dunn came back into the room, Chamberlin was just finishing running the virus scan.

"That should do it," said Chamberlin as he stood.

Andrew Dunn took a seat at the computer. He found the files he was seeking and printed them out. Walking out the door, he said to Chamberlin, "Thanks Mr. Chamberlin. I need these files."

"You're welcome. I'm glad I could help, and call me Charles."

The two met Katherine and told her everything was set with her computer. Mr. Dunn had a few files and printouts in his hands and indicated he had found what he was looking for.

Chamberlin had used this technique once before on the woman who had hurt him in an automobile accident. He had developed a dislike for wealthy widows. With his success at installing the monitor software on an unsuspecting widow, Mr. Chamberlin would read the Cape Cod Times every day scouring the obituaries for potential targets. Some of the obituaries provided viable targets some did not. Mr. Chamberlin's plan was to identify half dozen or so targets and to then take them for significant sums of money.

Over the next few weeks, Mr. Chamberlin identified and successfully met four other widows who met his criteria. He utilized the same technique of attending the wake to gather information and meet the widows. As his routine became more polished, he found himself becoming more involved than he had anticipated with a few of the widows.

In one case, Charles Chamberlin became involved with one of the widows, a Ms. Carol Tindle. He took her on a trip to Key West where the two relaxed and enjoyed each other's company. Mr. Chamberlin began to fall for Carol Tindle and had second thoughts about his pending crimes. By then, he had installed his monitor software on four widows' computers and was receiving information regularly. When a keystrokes file would come to him attached to an e-mail, Chamberlin would carefully analyze the data extracting any bits of information he felt important to his cause.

He had gathered the URL's identifying the institutions the widows had used for investments along with ID's and passwords for their accounts. Chamberlin was able to access the widows' accounts without the widows' knowledge. His plan was to track the widows' assets and then position himself to take some of those funds when the timing was right.

Along the way in gathering information, Chamberlin found himself obtaining legitimate clients for his financial consulting practice. In fact, his business success had never been better. One client, Rhonda Ronaldi, had requested Chamberlin to represent her in selling her dead husband's business interests. Chamberlin had agreed. In a fairly quick transaction, he netted a very nice commission. For a while, he thought about abandoning his plans against the widows and continuing his successful practice. If it were not for the constant pain he felt resulting from the initial car accident, which caused him to go after widows in the first place,

Chamberlin probably would have dropped his plans against the widows. But it was a daily reminder of his anger.

Chamberlin had set up an offshore account in the Cayman Islands and another Swiss account. Since both countries have non-disclosure policies regarding account information, all he had to do was transfer funds from the widows' accounts to his offshore accounts.

Just as Chamberlin was executing his crimes, authorities became suspicious of his activities and were getting close. A few by-chance events tipped Chamberlin off to just how close the authorities were getting. He put his plan in motion and within a few days he successfully transferred large sums of money from his widow targets to his offshore account in the Cayman Islands. From there, he moved the funds to his Swiss account ensuring the funds would never be traced.

From time to time Chamberlin would throw a red herring across the trail of the authorities attempting to misguide them. These actions eventually proved valuable in providing him with the necessary distractions enabling him to escape with a significant sum of money. From there, Chamberlin left the country under an assumed name. He hadn't been seen or heard from since.

When Sam Sterns had died, Katherine became Andrew's partner in Sterns and Dunn. Since she didn't know much about business, she left the day-to-day decisions to Andrew Dunn. The only problem for Andrew was that Katherine wanted to keep tabs on things by being intimately involved with Andrew Dunn on a regular basis. That just didn't work for Andrew. She cramped his style. She was just too needy. Then along came Chamberlin. Andrew liked Chamberlin because he took Katherine off his hands. Plus,

Chamberlin was able to help Andrew Dunn out with a few other situations.

Katherine Sterns had been attracted to Charles Chamberlin. Once she put her mind to it, she was going to have whatever was on her mind and this time she wanted Charles. It didn't take much and Chamberlin found himself in bed with her. She was good, and good-looking. Chamberlin thought he could get used to his newfound status. The two had a relationship up to the point where Chamberlin discovered she was pregnant. When she disclosed the child was not his, he sought to distance himself from her.

As the authorities became involved investigating the widow crimes, Frank Jenkins, now a Detective with the Dennis Police department became re-acquainted with Katherine Sterns. After Katherine returned from a trip to Washington, she had Frank over to cheer her up. They ended up sleeping together and Jenkins began spending more and more time with Katherine Sterns to the point where other people at the station became aware of the relationship.

Chapter 9

Not too long after the widow caper, Detective Jenkins found himself in the middle of another investigation this time involving some of the cougars on Cape Cod. A number of middle aged women who frequented the bar scene in the mid-Cape area found themselves the target of attacks that looked to be sexual in nature. Over a period of a few weeks, five different women had been attacked. Each of the cases had similarities but were different enough to make them look almost random. In a few of the cases, authorities were able to secure DNA evidence intended to leave no doubt as to the parties involved. Unfortunately, in the cougar cases, it became difficult determining if the DNA evidence resulted from an attack or from other activities.

Jenkins was able to establish a timetable where the attacks began. The timetable coincided with Tom Bowman's return to the Cape Cod area. Tom Bowman had moved back from Virginia. Jenkins had some concern regarding Bowman's recollection of the case where Sam Sterns died. He didn't like Bowman but didn't realize Katherine had devised a scheme to get back at Tom. She had told him she was sure Tom killed Sam. Jenkins didn't know it, but Katherine had provided Bowman with information about the cougars, where they lived and what they would be doing. She intimated to Bowman she would like harm to come to them but was careful not to specifically ask for his help. She had devised a plan whereby she planted Bowman's DNA as evidence at some of the attack scenes via semen or hair.

When Jenkins fell for Katherine, he would talk with her about the attacks, thus providing her with insider information. He told her things about the attacks that helped her in providing even more information to Bowman. In the end, Jenkins put it together and thought she had joined forces with Bowman to commit the crimes. When Bowman was arrested, he confessed to a few of the attacks but not all of them. He denied having sex with any of the cougars and indicated he only attacked the women to stay in Katherine's good graces.

Detective Jenkins met with Tom Bowman again to talk about each of the attacks. He hoped Bowman would be able to add new details to what he had previously discussed. Detective Jenkins asked Captain Tomlinson to sit in on one such discussion.

"Mr. Bowman, let's review each of the cougar attacks again."

"I don't know what else I can tell you Detective."

"Start from the beginning so Captain Tomlinson can hear what you can remember."

Captain Tomlinson added, "Sometimes having someone different hear the same story, something might jog your memory."

"Ok."

Captain Tomlinson sat back and listened. Detective Jenkins opened his notepad and said, "First, Ms. Ann Benard was attacked up at Chapin Beach. What do you know about it?"

"I was there but I was only trying to talk to her. I overheard Ann talking with Katherine at Chapin's. I thought I might be able to get Ann to influence Katherine on my behalf but when she showed up at the beach, things didn't work out and I panicked."

"What did you do to Ms. Benard?"

"I didn't do anything to her."

"Why did you just leave her there like that?"

"I don't know. I just panicked."

"What about the others?"

"Well, a few days later, I did get to talk with Katherine. She invited me over one night and said there were too many cougars working the bars. When I asked her what she meant, she told me the competition for guys was too much and something needed to be done about it."

"Did she specifically ask you to go after anyone?"

"As I told you, no. After she said what she said, I asked her who the cougars were and she rattled off the names Ann Benard, Tina Fletcher, Sue Kent and Linda Sage."

"So you took it upon yourself to go after these women?"

"Yes. It all started out in a harmless way. I just happened to be at Chapin's the night Ann and Katherine were there. I went to Chapin's to see what was going on. Then, after they showed up and had a number of drinks with those guys I heard Ann talking about taking a walk on the beach. I saw that as an opportunity to talk to Ann."

"What guys are you talking about?"

"Bobby, Kenny and Ed."

"What did they do?"

"Oh, nothing other than have drinks with the women. Then Bobby got into a disagreement with Ann after the others left. I saw it as an opportunity and I acted on it. I had heard Ann say she was going to take a walk at Chapin Beach so I went there and waited for her."

"Where did you wait?"

"I had been there fishing before so I knew the off-road path. I drove down it a short distance and parked by one of the dunes. Then I went back and waited behind the parking lot sign. Sure enough, after about fifteen minutes, Ann Benard showed up. She got out of her car and walked right towards the beach. When she got to the sign, she leaned on it and took off her shoes. She didn't even see me. Then as she started to walk to down to the beach, I approached her."

"Did you hit her with something?"

"No, but I think I startled her and she fell down, she hit her head on a rock. She was knocked out. I panicked. I ran to my car and left right away."

"So you didn't try to help her?"

"No. I checked her and she was breathing so I figured she would eventually come to."

"Ok, what about Tina Fletcher?"

"I followed Ms. Fletcher to her home up by Mayflower Beach. I parked down the street from the beach in one of the driveways where it looked like no one was home. Then I walked over to Ms. Fletcher's house. When I walked around the house, the light on her back porch suddenly came on and I had to jump in the bushes to avoid being seen. She came out on her porch with a glass of wine in her hand, then she went down to the beach."

"So you followed her?"

"I stayed off the beach as far as I could. Then I saw these large rocks on the beach and knew it would present a good place to jump her."

"So you hid right there?"

"I did. She must have walked up the beach for another twenty minutes or so and I thought about dropping my plans altogether when suddenly there she was."

"She didn't see you?"

"No, she had taken her shoes off and was walking in the small stream of water coming out from under the rocks. When I jumped her, she fell backwards and hit her head on one of the big rocks."

"So you didn't hit her?"

"No."

"What about sexually attacking her?"

"I didn't sexually attack her either."

"So you have no idea how your DNA came to be found on her either?"

"No I don't."

"Did you take her underwear off?"

"No."

"What about Linda Sage?"

"I had drinks with Ms. Sage at Sundancers one night. At one point in the evening, she had to use the ladies room. When she left, I took the opportunity to slip one of the pills I got from Katherine Sterns into her drink. I already explained that to Detective Jenkins."

"So Ms. Sterns gave you pills to put into Ms. Sage's drink?"

"No. On one of the times when I had been over to Ms. Sterns house, I saw a bottle of sleeping pills in her nightstand. I remembered from the prior time that she kept condoms in her nightstand and when I went to get one, I discovered the bottle of pills. When Katherine went into the bathroom, I took some of the pills."

"Did she know you took them?"

"I don't think so. The bottle must have been half full and I only took a few."

"So you stole the pills from Ms. Sterns and used them to drug Ms. Sage?"

"That's right. Then some other guy came over and talked to her about going to the beach. That was when I backed out."

"Well, how did your DNA end up on her and her clothing?"

"I don't know, but when I left Ms. Sage and called Katherine's house, I didn't get an answer. She wasn't home."

"Do you think she might have followed Ms. Sage home?"

"I guess she could have. I didn't have sex with Ms. Sage."

"What about Sue Kent?"

"I didn't do anything to Ms. Kent. I don't know anything about her attack."

"So you say you didn't have anything to do with her attack?"

"That's right."

"Well, Ms. Kent was knocked out at her home by someone and when Officer Trudy go there, she scared the intruder away."

"It wasn't me."

"Trudy got the description and license plate of a vehicle parked down the street and it was your Jeep."

"What night did the attack occur on Ms. Kent?"

Jenkins looked at his notepad and gave Tom Bowman the date.

"I remember the night. You came to Katherine's house that night and I answered the door."

"That's right."

"Katherine had taken my car to go do something. You came by while she was out. Then she returned after you had left."

"Do you remember what she was wearing when she went out?"

"Yes, she borrowed my dark blue hooded sweatshirt when she went out. She had black jeans on and black sneakers."

"So she would have been hard to see in the dark?"

"Now that you mention it, yes."

"What about Pam Trudy?"

"I didn't have anything to do with any attack on Officer Trudy."

"Did Ms. Sterns ever say anything to you about her?"

"Not really. Although I know she saw Officer Trudy and you at Sundancers one night and she was pissed."

"Did she say anything?"

"She said some day Officer Trudy would get hers. That's about all I remember."

"Do you think Ms. Sterns could have attacked Officer Trudy?"

"I don't know."

"What about Ruby Crane?"

"Was she the woman who was attacked the night of the comedy show?"

"Yes. Do you know anything about her attack?"

"You might want to talk with some of the guys at the Bridge Bar. If I recall correctly, Ms. Crane left the bar with one of the young guys just before the show got started. About half way through the show the two came back into the bar and the comedian made a joke about it. I think the guy she had been with was a little put off by the remarks. Ms. Crane kind of blew him off after the comedian's comments."

"Ms. Crane said she had left with Paul Bremer. Do you think he could have attacked her?"

"Either he did or someone else did who saw the interaction between Ms. Crane and Bremer when they came back into the bar. His reaction made him an ideal target for someone who might be after Ms. Crane."

"And you stayed for the entire show?"

"Yes I did, and if you ask the bartenders at the Bridge Bar, I'm sure they will back up my story."

"Oh, we'll verify your story."

"Listen Detective, I have cooperated with you in your investigations. I admit to playing a role in some of the attacks, but I never sexually assaulted anyone and I didn't physically hurt anyone. I was only trying to talk to or scare these women to put them on guard. I thought if I made them uneasy, things would be easier for Katherine and she would look favorably on me."

"You mean she would have sex with you more often?"

"Yes."

"I don't know how this will all turn out Mr. Bowman, but you broke a few laws and will have to be held accountable for your actions. I'll talk with the Prosecutor and if your information proves true, I'm sure you will be dealt with fairly."

"I guess I can't ask for anything else."

"Your case will be coming up soon. If you haven't already hired an attorney, I suggest you get one."

"I've been provided with a public defender."

"Like I said Mr. Bowman, if you haven't hired an attorney, go get one. That's all for now."

Tom Bowman got up and left. After he had gone, Jenkins said to Captain Tomlinson, "I don't know. He might be telling the truth."

"You have his hairs and semen from a few of the attacks. In my book that makes him guilty," said Tomlinson.

"Maybe so, but he's sticking to the same story he told me the last time I talked to him."

"Do you think Ms. Sterns could be that devious?"

"She's used to getting things her way."

"Well, if Bowman's story has any truth to it at all, we might all be in big trouble."

"Why?"

"I think she could make trouble for all of us. I just have a hunch about her."

"She's really a nice lady once you get to know her Captain."

"Oh, I know her type. Just hope Bowman's wrong."

"I'll keep digging Captain. If there's something there, I'll find it."

"Just be careful Frank."

"I hear you."

Chapter 10

A big Boston law firm had represented Katherine Sterns for all her legal needs and was now representing her in the case of the Cape Cod cougar attacks. The firm's senior partner, Steven Kennedy took a personal interest in Katherine whenever she called. Kennedy liked to handle high profile clients allowing him to be in the news regularly. He also had a weakness for beautiful women. Whenever Steven Kennedy walked into a courtroom, everyone knew they were in for a fight. He had the reputation of being very clever and very smart with detail. During their meeting in Boston, Katherine detailed everything she could remember about Michael Benson, now Judge Benson, Tom Bowman and the charges against her.

"Tell me Katherine, you say you know the judge in the case?"

"Yes. I knew a Michael Benson when I was in college."

"And you think the Judge and the person you knew in college are the same person?"

"I'm sure of it. He got his undergraduate from UMass didn't he? And his wife's name is Marci, isn't it?"

"Yes, but anyone could know those things."

"True, but my recollection is from his college days."

"Even so, why do you feel these things are important?"

"Let's just say I know the judge as well as Marci knows him."

"What do you mean?"

"That's all I want to say for now, but if more information is needed at a future point in time, I'll tell you more."

"If the judge has had a prior contact with an accused, the judge should probably withdraw him or herself from the case."

"Don't let that happen. I'm sure the Judge will be fair."

"Exactly what kind of contact did you have with the Judge?"

"We attended some of the same classes, that sort of thing."

"I don't think anything like that would present a problem for the Judge."

"Neither do I."

"Unless you're not telling me something."

"That's it for now, honest."

"All right, then tell me about Tom Bowman."

Katherine went on to talk about Tom Bowman and her husband Sam. She told about as much as she could recall. She included fishing trips, times when the two got drunk at the Bridge Bar and even about the time she slept with Bowman. At the end of her talk, she described how she felt when she found out Sam died and then how Tom tried to give her the gift he said Sam had gotten her for their anniversary.

Attorney Kennedy asked Katherine if she would mind being interviewed by a psychologist. He indicated she suffered immensely and the mental anguish of having her husband die had a profound effect on her perhaps even Post Traumatic Stress Syndrome. She agreed to the interview. Kennedy probed her about her relationships with men both before and after Sam's death. He was especially focused on the relationships after Sam's death, given her new wealth.

The last thing the attorney focused on was Katherine's relationship with the women who had been attacked. Katherine expressed her concern about the welfare of the other cougars and indicated she never wanted any lasting harm to come to them. When the meeting concluded, Kennedy indicated he had quite a bit of information he could use in her defense. He called his secretary and asked if the office psychologist was available to interview Katherine.

Katherine met with Dr. Henry Waxman. Waxman posed a series of questions to Ms. Sterns trying to determine what her fears were and to formulate a profile of her as a woman who had lost her husband. When done, Waxman met with Kennedy and told him that Katherine suffered from depression, lack of self-esteem and a deep hostility towards men trying to take advantage of her. Kennedy would use these things if necessary in her defense.

During the preliminary hearings preceding the trial, Katherine asked Kennedy to set up a meeting with Judge Benson. Kennedy didn't think a meeting was a good idea and tried to convince Katherine not to do it. Katherine being the persistent person she was, and wanting to have her way insisted. Finally, Kennedy relented and requested the meeting.

"This isn't a good idea Katherine."

"Steven, I know what I'm doing and besides, it's my neck on the line."

"We already have a solid defense. You don't have to do this."

"I don't want to be painted as a nut case. I'm sure the Judge will see things my way."

"You're paying the bills, but for the record, I'm against you doing this."

"It's my call."

"Ok, but I don't like it."

"Steven, I'm staying at the Copley Marriott. Take me to dinner tonight and I'll convince you that I'm the same Katherine you have known all these years."

"What time would you like me to pick you up?"

"Any time. We don't have to go anywhere. The hotel has a good restaurant. We can either order room service or eat in the lounge."

"How about eight?"

"Call from the front desk when you get there."

"See you around eight."

"I'll be ready."

At a few minutes before eight, the phone rang in her room. "Come on up Steven. I'm in suite 101."

A few days later, the two met at the courthouse. Kennedy indicated the two o'clock meeting would be held in Judge Benson's office. They waited for a few minutes in the Judge's waiting room when the Judge's secretary finally said, "The Judge will see you now."

As the two stood to go in, Katherine said, "Steven, you wait here. I'll call you in if it's necessary."

"I can't let you go in alone," he said in a concerned voice.

"Don't worry Steven, I have it all under control."

Katherine went into the Judge's office and closed the door.

"Ms. Sterns, isn't your attorney joining us?"

"Not right away your honor. I'd like to speak with you for a minute first if I may?"

"This is highly unusual."

"Please Judge, I only need a few minutes."

"Ok, then please take a seat."

"Judge Benson, you probably don't remember me, but I remember you."

"What do you mean?"

"We met in college. Do you remember the night of your bachelor party?"

"No, I don't."

"You had quite a bit to drink that night as I recall."

"I'm not sure I like where this is headed. I think we should stop this conversation."

"Not so fast Judge. First, you need to hear me out."

Michael Benson sat back down folding his arms across his black robe.

"Continue."

"When you woke the next morning, do you remember your fiancé calling you on the phone?"

"Yes, I remember." He stood and looked at her. "If you know that, then you must have been there. Were you the stripper?"

"That's right Mike. I used to go by the name of Katherine Miller. What do you think your wife would say if she knew about your little escapade before she married you?"

"That's blackmail."

"I didn't say I would do anything. I merely asked the question."

"It might be uncomfortable, but she would forgive me. It's been a lot of years Katherine. We're all older and wiser."

"Then what about that night the next semester when you came over to my apartment to get reacquainted?"

He sat down with a frown.

"As I recall, you said she wasn't really that good in bed and you wanted to be with me."

"It was the alcohol talking."

"But we didn't have any alcohol the second time."

Benson leaned back in his chair. "So what do you want from me Ms. Sterns?"

"Just be fair. The police have some questions about how my husband died. I want Mr. Bowman to pay for what he did."

Katherine stood and walked to the door. As she opened it, her attorney was standing there ready to come in. "Thank you your honor for taking the time to speak with me," she closed the door behind her.

"What happened in there?" Steven asked.

"We had a little talk. I think the Judge will see things our way."

"Can't you be more specific?"

"No, that's all that needs to be said."

"Look Katherine, I don't like being kept out of discussions pertaining to a client."

"It's all right Steven. Judge Benson remembered me from his college days. We just talked for a little while catching up on past times."

"This is highly unusual Katherine."

"Then again, I'm a highly unusual client, Steven."

The two left the courthouse.

"Do you want to come back to Copley before I head back to Cape Cod?"

"I've got a few things to handle back at the office. I should probably get back."

73

"Don't be silly Steven. Don't tell me you're going to put business ahead of pleasure?"

"You do have a point. I can go to the office later. Let's take my car."

The two left in his car.

Chapter 11

Getting back home, Katherine fixed herself a martini. She walked out on her back deck holding her cell phone in one hand and drink in the other.

"Hello Frank, what're you doing?"

"Katherine, I just finished speaking with Captain Tomlinson."

"What did the good Captain have to say?"

"You mean about your case?"

"Why else would I be interested?"

"Well, he decided, and I concur, that your case and Bowman's should be kept separate."

"Why do you think that?"

"Captain thinks Bowman acted on his own in attacking the women. He also thinks there are mitigating circumstances in your case."

"He doesn't know the half of it."

"What do you mean by that comment?"

"Oh nothing. I just think Tom Bowman needs to pay for what he did."

"Look Katherine. I know you think the death of Sam happened in some way other than what was described by Mr. Bowman. But we just don't have any evidence to support any other theories."

"Just look at what he tried to do after Sam died. He lied about the gifts and tried to sleep with me again. He even got divorced from his wife."

"Well, he did sleep with you again and you allowed it to happen."

"I was just doing what I had to do to gather evidence against him."

"But you didn't have to sleep with him so many times and you didn't have to plant his DNA at some of the attack crime scenes."

"I did what I had to do to make sure he pays for what he did."

"Katherine, you're a vicious woman. Your anger worries me. Captain Tomlinson is concerned also."

"Tomlinson doesn't have to worry. I'm not going to say anything about him."

"You don't have to say anything. I saw the zip-lock in your freezer with his name on it the last time I was over. I told him about it and he's afraid you'll show up in court with his DNA or his will show up at some other crime scene."

"I'd never do any such thing."

"Well just the same, you have things on people where they could be significantly hurt if they came out."

"Let's just say I have insurance policies."

"Like I said, Katherine. You're a vicious and dangerous woman."

"Thank you Frank, and you and Tomlinson don't have to worry. I've made sure my case will go my way."

"And just how did you do that?"

76

"Nothing you need to know about, but I had a meeting with the Judge a little while ago and I feel confident the Judge will see things my way."

"Did you sleep with the Judge?"

"Don't be silly Frank."

"Judge Benson has a reputation for being tough. He'll see right through your scheme Katherine."

"My scheme? I don't think Mike would do any such thing."

"I knew something was up when you smiled the first time you were brought in front of Judge Benson."

"If you need to know, I knew the Judge before he was a Judge. Now let's leave it at that."

"So you did sleep with the Judge. You must know something the Judge doesn't want known."

"I have my information."

"I'll bet you do."

"Listen Frank, another subject, do you have any plans for the evening?"

"Why do you ask?"

"I'm going to Washington tomorrow. I'll be gone for a few days and I wanted to see if we could get together."

"What did you have in mind?"

"I'm having a drink on my back deck right now and I thought we could have a quiet dinner and an evening together. We can talk more about Rio."

He thought about it for a minute and then figured it would be better to keep her happy for the time being.

"I can be there in an hour or so. Just let me finish up a few things."

"Great. I'll have drinks and dinner ready when you get here."

"See you in an hour."

Jenkins wrapped up his day at the office. He stopped by Ring Brothers market on the way home and picked up a few assorted desserts to bring to Katherine's. Then he went home took a quick shower and changed into a pair of jeans, sweatshirt and sneakers. An hour later, he arrived at Katherine's.

She greeted him at the front door with two martinis.

"What do we have here?" She said taking the box from him. It was neatly tied with a red and white string.

"I stopped at Ring Brothers and picked up dessert."

"That's good. I didn't make anything for dessert. I thought we would improvise."

"We can, after having what's in the box." Frank winked naughtily.

She opened the box and smiled. He had brought her pastries and tiramisu. These were two of her favorites.

"Frank, you shouldn't have."

"It's nothing."

"You're so thoughtful. Now, I'm going to have to be nice to you."

Chapter 12

Katherine took the eight o'clock flight to Washington. By nine thirty, she was in a cab headed to Dottie Masters house. She arrived and knocked on the door. Dottie answered. Katherine had a look of shock on her face. Dottie had a scarf over her head. Her face was very pale. Her eyes were sunken back into her skull.

"Dottie, you should have called me sooner."

"I didn't want anyone to know Kat. I thought it would go away."

"What have the doctors said?"

"I have a very aggressive form of cancer. My chances of survival are slim."

"How long?" Kat said putting her arm around her friend.

"The doctor said I have a ten percent chance of living another year."

"Oh Dottie," Katherine began to cry. Dottie cried as well.

"What happened?"

"I was having my regular doctor visit. One of my friends I had been sleeping with had mentioned to me he felt a lump in my right breast."

She moved her hand to the area where the lump had been found.

"My doctor checked it out and I did have a lump there. After x-rays, tests and a lot of probing, the doctor told me I had cancer."

"Did you have it removed?"

"I thought we had caught it early enough but the doctor said the cancer had already spread."

"How bad?"

"I have it in my lymph nodes and the cancer has recently shown up between a few ribs."

"Did you get chemo?"

"Yes. I did both chemo and radiation."

"Did it help?"

"Not really, I was really sick for a few weeks. When I had a MRI after the treatment, the doctor said she didn't see any tumors."

"Well, that's good news."

"I thought so as well but when I went back for a visit last week, she told me the cancer had returned."

"Can't they do more chemo or radiation?"

"No. The cancer reappeared between the ribs and has now invaded my liver."

"Dottie, what can I do?"

"Just being here is comforting."

"I'll stay as long as I can."

"Thanks Kat."

The two sat and talked for a few hours. It was getting late in the day. Dottie asked, "Have you had anything to eat?"

"I had breakfast at home and then came right here. I didn't have time to get anything on the way."

"Do you want to go out?"

"Are you up to it?"

"Hell Kat, I'm not going to get any better. I might as well get as much out of the time I have left as I can."

"That's a good perspective Dottie. Where do you want to go?"

"Let's go get dinner and then go bar hopping."

"Are you sure?"

"Kat, I need something to brighten my life and now you're here."

"Ok. Let me change and I'll be ready to go in a half hour."

Both ladies went and got ready. Dottie set Katherine up in her spare bedroom. Katherine dressed casually in slacks and a nice cashmere sweater. After a half hour, she walked out into the living room. Dottie was dressed in a pair of tight Capri's. She had a halter-top on giving the impression she had grown in the past half hour. Her scarf was pulled back with a barrette holding it in place. She had on enough make-up to look like she was ready for action.

"You look ready," remarked Katherine.

"I need some action," was Dottie's response.

The two left Dottie's. They took a cab to a nice restaurant Dottie had been to before. Walking in, a few heads turned to look at the two. Katherine just smiled.

They had a nice dinner. When done, Dottie said, "I know of a club near here where we can have a good time."

"I'm with you."

Dottie hailed a cab and they got in. When the cab stopped in front of a building on a busy street, they got out. There was a line of people waiting to get in. Kat looked up and read the sign, "The Cat House".

"Looks like an interesting place."

"If we can't hook up here and we can't get laid, then we're lost." Dottie said.

"Are you sure you're up for this?"

"Look Kat. I don't know how much time I have left, so I'm going out under my own terms."

"Ok."

They waited about fifteen minutes to get in. Then they were admitted and went inside. The building was like a circus. There were bars on three levels with a band playing on the main stage on the first floor. The center of the building was open all the way to the roof. Lights flashed all around as the music played loudly.

"Let's start over here," said Dottie leading Kat to a bar.

"Two martinis," ordered Kat.

"And a shot of Petron," added Dottie.

"Can you drink like this with the meds you're taking Dottie?"

"So I've stopped taking the meds, they made me sick. I'm not going to worry about it Kat. I'm here to have a good time."

The two danced and drank for a few hours. Dottie had become rather inebriated and was putting her hands all over a young guy at the bar. Katherine had a few drinks but didn't allow herself to get drunk.

"Dottie, I think we should get going."

"Kat, this is Jimmy. He's coming home with us."

"Hi Jimmy. My friend has had a little too much to drink."

"Yeah, me too. So what's your name?"

"Katherine."

"Jimmy, you ever been with two women at the same time?" Asked Dottie.

"No, but I'd like to," he said smiling.

"Dottie, I don't think we should," Kat said calmly.

"Come on Kat, have some fun with me?"

"Ok. Then let's get out of here."

"Lead the way," Dottie said slurring her words.

"Coming Jimmy?" Kat said looking back at him as they started to walk away.

"I'm right behind you."

The three went outside. Jimmy went to the curb and waved for a cab. They all got in. Dottie told the driver where she lived. A few minutes later, the three were getting out of the cab at Dottie's.

Kat and Jimmy had to carry Dottie into the house. When the got inside, they took Dottie to her bedroom. Katherine put Dottie to bed and told Jimmy she would be out in a few minutes.

She came out of Dottie's room and closed the door. She sat on the couch next to Jimmy, "She's asleep or rather passed out. I don't think we will hear from her again until tomorrow."

"Too bad, I was looking forward to both of you."

"Well it isn't going to happen."

"How about just us then?"

"I don't know Jimmy. I'm here to be with my friend. I don't want to upset her if she wakes up."

"If she wakes up, she can join us."

"I don't know."

Jimmy stood up and took off his shirt. He had a well-built body. Katherine took one look at it and found herself wondering if the rest of his body offered as much. She stood not having decided what to do next when Jimmy put his arms around her. He kissed her softly. She returned the kiss. He worked his tongue into her mouth slowly sending a tingling feeling down her body. He slowly lifted the sweater over her shoulders. Then he undid her bra allowing it to drop to the floor.

Katherine reached down and undid his belt and pants. They dropped to the floor. He returned the favor. The two of them were standing in the living room in their underwear as Katherine noticed a sizeable bulge in Jimmy's underwear. She reached in. Jimmy put his hands on her underwear and slowly lowered them. She pushed his down as well.

He lowered her to the floor. She received him. The two kissed and moved in a single motion. Their breathing became very heavy. Jimmy stiffened and exploded inside her. She climaxed as well. He continued for some time until she became dry and had to force him to stop. She got up to go to the bathroom and when she returned, Jimmy was sound asleep naked on the floor.

Katherine went to her bedroom and went to bed. She would deal with Jimmy and Dottie in the morning. She woke to someone knocking at her bedroom door. She could see the sun shining in the room around the edges of the shades. It was Dottie. She had a portable phone in her hand.

"It's for you."

"Who is it?"

"Your attorney."

"Oh. I had given him your number when I came down."

Katherine took the phone.

"Hi Steven. The day after tomorrow? Ok. I'll be there."

The call was so short, Dottie hadn't even had the time to leave the room.

"What was that all about?"

"I have to be back on Cape Cod the day after tomorrow for a court appearance."

"What's that all about?"

"Some of my friends were attacked by Tom Bowman. I have to testify in the case."

"Tom Bowman. Wasn't he with Sam when Sam died?"

"Yes. And now I'm out to make sure he gets what's coming to him."

"Oh Katherine. You should be careful."

"I am, don't worry."

Jimmy had gotten up hearing the two women talking in the bedroom. He walked in, naked.

"Who are you?" asked Dottie.

"You don't remember?" asked Katherine.

"No."

"You had Jimmy come home with us from the club last night."

"Really?"

"Really."

Dottie looked at Jimmy standing there, naked, out of sorts with a limp appendage.

"I've got to be going," Jimmy said.

"Don't forget to get dressed," Kat said and the two laughed.

Jimmy went into the other room and dressed. They heard the door close and both laughed again.

"What happened? Did I sleep with him?"

"No, you passed out and left that duty to me."

"You're kidding?"

"Dottie, you know me. I don't kid about sex."

"Was he good?"

"I'd say."

"I'll have to look for him the next time I go there."

"That's good that you're looking forward to a next time Dot."

"Oh Kat. I know this cancer is going to get me but I'm not going to give up."

"That's the spirit. You go girl."

"So did your attorney have anything else to say?"

"No, but the court date means I have to go home tomorrow."

"Then we had better get going. If I only have another day of fun with you, I want to make the most of it."

Katherine used Dottie's computer to change her return flight plans. The two got dressed. They went shopping, had lunch out and were out again that night for dinner. The night was calmer than the previous night as Katherine said she didn't want to fly after having too much to drink. They stayed up until three in the morning talking about the past, occasionally crying about what the future might bring.

In the morning, Katherine said her goodbyes and flew back to Cape Cod. As the plane left the tarmac, she wondered when she'd be back, and if Dottie would still be alive.

Chapter 13

Katherine took the early shuttle from Reagan Airport in D.C. to Logan. She arrived in Boston around 9:15 am. Waiting for a shuttle to take her to her car, she called Frank.

"Frank, I'm back."

"How did it go?"

"Not good. Dottie said her doctor told her that her condition would probably deteriorate pretty quickly."

"That's too bad. I feel bad for you."

"I just hope she doesn't suffer too much."

"Do you want me to come over?"

"I'm not home yet. I'm still at Logan. I should be back on the Cape late morning. Can we get together for lunch and talk?"

"Sure. I'll meet you at Sundancers around noon."

"I'll see you there."

Katherine ended the call just as the shuttle arrived. She got on for the short trip short-term parking. She got into her car and by ten she was on Route 3 heading back to Cape Cod. At the end of Route 3, traffic came to a crawl.

"What now," she said as traffic crawled along. After about fifteen minutes, she could finally see the top of the bridge. Rounding the last curve before the bridge, she saw construction cones narrowing the two lanes down to one. She knew what that meant. Major repairs were being made to the Sagamore Bridge, which happens from time to time, backing up traffic for miles. At 11:40 am, she pulled into Sundancers parking lot. Dee waived to Katherine as she walked through the door. Katherine took up a stool near the door.

"What will it be, Katherine?"

"Give me a martini, Dee, if you would."

"Sure. How are things going?"

"I just came back from visiting a friend in D.C. She has cancer."

"That's too bad. I'm sorry to hear that."

"Me too."

"How far along is it?"

"She has breast cancer. Her doctor says it has spread to her ribs."

"No Shit. Your world shrinks rapidly when something like that happens."

"You're right."

"How's your friend taking it?"

"She isn't letting it slow her down. She's determined to make the best of the time she has left."

"How so?"

"She took me to a bar down there where we drank too much. She even picked up a young guy."

"A real cougar, huh?"

Then Dee realized what she had said. "I'm sorry Katherine, that was really insensitive of me."

"It's all right Dee. No offense taken."

"Are you going down to see your friend again?"

Just then, the door to Sundancers opened and Frank walked in. He took up the stool next to Katherine and ordered a diet coke.

"Starting early?"

"The trip was difficult on me Frank. I need something to relax me."

"I can understand your grief. Having a close friend confront something like that can be hard."

"It sure is. I go back a long way with Dottie. We went to college together. If something happens to her, I'm going to miss her."

"I feel for you."

"So Frank, where are we?"

"I spoke with your attorney at court yesterday and he said you have to be in court tomorrow. I think everything will work out for you."

"I sure hope so."

The two ordered lunch and talked more about Dottie. Eventually the conversation got back around to the legal situation. Katherine probed Frank for anything and everything she could get out of him. She wanted to find out if anything new had been uncovered. After lunch Frank said, "So what do you have planned for the afternoon?"

"I have to talk with my attorney. Then I have to get things straightened up at my place, do laundry and get ready for tomorrow."

"I'll call you later on this afternoon when I'm done at work."

"Ok. Maybe we can do something tonight?"

"Talk to you later."

The two left Sundancers. Jenkins went back to work. Katherine went home.

Katherine had played her relationship with Detective Jenkins in such a manner as to allow her to give inside information regarding the attacks on the cougars. While she didn't specifically use the information she had to gain favorable treatment from the police department, both Captain Tomlinson and Detective Jenkins knew she was in possession of career ending information should she elect to abuse it.

Captain Tomlinson had taken the unusual steps in removing any damaging facts from all of Katherine Sterns' files ensuring an acquittal for lack of evidence. His actions also bought her silence for his indiscretions. Both Tomlinson and Jenkins felt they had a good case against Tom Bowman and figured his role in the death of Sam Sterns probably contributed significantly influencing Katherine Sterns' actions. They agreed she had suffered enough already and decided to only pursue Bowman.

Late in the afternoon, Captain Tomlinson called Detective Jenkins into his office.

"Frank, the next time you talk with Ms. Sterns, let her know I heard from the DA and all charges against her are going to be dismissed. I'm sure she'll be pleased."

"I know she will."

"The woman has suffered enough. Plus, even though we have our suspicions regarding the events surrounding her husband's death, we are not going to make much headway pursuing Bowman in the matter."

"I agree. We should've gathered more information when the two were picked up off the ice floe."

"That may be, but the ice was breaking up. Bowman's story will hold up unless he discloses something else."

"I don't think he's going to change his story."

"Especially now that he's being charged in the cougar attacks."

"He'll serve time for those attacks. The DA says they'll ask for a minimum of eight years."

"If he gets eight, then he'll be out of commission for a long time."

"When do you think you'll see her again, Frank?"

"I'll call her later today."

"Good. Just remind her how we helped her situation."

"She's pretty smart Captain. I'm sure she'll be appreciative."

"Then let me know if it doesn't go as you think."

"Will do."

At the end of the day, Frank called Katherine.

"Katherine, I have some news for you."

He could detect her sniffling. "Is something wrong?"

"Yes, I just got off the phone with my friend Dottie. She's discontinuing all her treatments. The doctors have told her there is nothing else they can do. She had very little time left."

"That's too bad. I'm sorry to hear it."

"Do you think you can come over tonight? I don't want to be alone."

"Sure, I can be there in an hour."

"What was it you wanted to tell me?"

"It can wait. I'll see you in an hour."

"Ok."

Detective Jenkins hung up the phone. He wanted to tell her about the conversation he and Tomlinson had but the timing just wasn't right. On his way home, he stopped at the liquor store and purchased a bottle of wine, Katherine's favorite merlot. Then he went home and changed into casual clothes. About an hour after leaving work, he arrived at Katherine's home.

"Hi Frank." The two embraced as she opened the door.

"Hey Katherine, how are you doing?"

He could see her eyes were all red and swollen. As he entered the living room, there was a box of tissues on the coffee table and a pile of used tissues in the trash can next to the couch.

"Frank, she only has a few months to live."

"That's terrible. I thought they told her she had another year maybe more?"

"She's only forty-six."

"Isn't there any other treatment she can get?"

"No, the results of tests indicated the cancer has already spread to other organs. I feel so bad for her."

"Is there anything I can do for you?" He said as he held her close.

"Can you stay with me tonight? I don't want to be alone."

"Sure."

"I could use a glass of that wine you brought with you."

"Let me open it."

Frank took the bottle to the kitchen and opened it. He poured two glasses and brought them into the living room. Katherine was sitting at the end of the couch all curled up. He sat next to her and handed her the glass. She accepted it and after one sip, finished the whole glass.

"Can I get you another?"

"Please."

He went to the kitchen and refilled her glass. When he returned, she had finished his glass.

"You might want to take it easy."

"I don't want to feel anything."

92

"Maybe so, but you have to go to court tomorrow. You don't want a hangover. It shows and doesn't reflect well on you."

"You're probably right. What was it you wanted to tell me when you called?"

"Nothing it can wait."

"No, tell me. I want to know."

"Well, Captain Tomlinson spoke with the DA and they both agree all charges against you will be dropped."

"I'm glad to hear it. What about Tom Bowman?"

"We will continue to press forward with the case against him. From all the information gathered, he did attack a number of women on his own even if it was to get into your good graces."

"Graces, he only wanted to get into my pants."

"Sex is a powerful motivator and Bowman figured his actions would get him into bed with you. I don't think he realized your revenge would get him what he wanted without him having to attack those women."

"I know he made up the story about how Sam died. A woman knows when things are other than what they seem. It's a sense we women have."

"I've been told that before."

"What do you think will happen to him?"

"The Captain thinks the DA will recommend three eight year sentences with a minimum of five years."

"That sentence isn't enough for what he did to Sam."

"You might feel that way, but he is going away for a long time. We don't have sufficient evidence on him regarding Sam's death to pursue the case any further. We'll have to take what we can. He'll be off the streets for a long time."

"I appreciate what you and Captain Tomlinson did for me. How can I repay you?"

"You have already suffered enough. We thought the circumstances surrounding your losses more than covered your actions."

"Plus, it buys my silence. Does it not?"

"Katherine, we're not looking at it that way."

"But it does."

"If you say so."

"I do."

She picked up her glass of wine and made a toast. "To Tom Bowman getting all he deserves."

Frank clicked her glass with his. Then she put her glass down on the table and stood. She held her hand out for him, "Let me repay you properly."

She led him to her bedroom.

Chapter 14

Day one of Tom Bowman's trial began with posturing by Bowman's attorney trying again to have Katherine Sterns tried at the same time. Judge Benson would have no part of a joint trial and ruled against the request.

The prosecutor summarized the case against Tom Bowman. Charges of assault, restraint and sex crimes were all described in great detail. Prosecutor Ann Levine made the final opening statement.

"Mr. Bowman in his obsession to have a relationship with Ms. Sterns took advantage of information he coerced from Ms. Sterns and then committed these crimes. It is our intention to prove Mr. Bowman's guilty of these crimes and we ask you find as such."

Then Mr. Bowman's court appointed attorney, Harold White, made his opening statement.

"My client, Mr. Bowman is innocent of these charges. We intend to show that Ms. Sterns used sex as an incentive to convince my client to participate in certain acts against persons identified in the prosecutor's charge but only to the extent of scaring these people. My client insists he did not commit any physical assault in any of the incidents already mentioned and most certainly didn't commit any sexual crimes."

Attorney Levine called her first witness, Dee Crowe.

"Ms. Crowe, please tell us where you work."
"Sure. I work at Sundancers as a bartender."
"Do you know the accused?"
"Yes. Mr. Bowman has come into the bar on a number of occasions."
"Have you ever seen Mr. Bowman with Ms. Sterns?"
"A few times."
"How would you describe their relationship?"
"Pretty much the same as the other people at the bar. They talk, have a few drinks."
"Have you ever noticed anything out of the ordinary between the two?"
"No. Ms. Sterns usually ends up with someone else at the bar."
"Who might that be Ms. Crowe?"
"Lately, she's been with Detective Jenkins."
"What do you mean with Detective Jenkins?"
"You know, they meet at the bar and then leave together."
"Are you saying Detective Jenkins is romantically involved with Ms. Sterns?"
"I don't know about romantically, but the two have been seen at the bar together on a number of occasions recently."
"Have you ever observed Mr. Bowman talking with Detective Jenkins?"
"Not really. But I'm usually pretty busy."

"Is there anything else that you want to add to what you've already told us Ms. Crowe?"

"No."

Darlene Crowe was dismissed without having to answer any questions from Tom Bowman's Attorney Harold White.

Next, Ron Jessup was called.

"Mr. Jessup, can you tell the court how you know the defendant?"

"I really don't know the defendant. I work as a bartender at Sundancers along with Ms. Crowe. We hear things from time to time at the bar. Sometimes what we hear is the liquor talking, sometimes it's gossip."

"Have you ever seen Ms. Sterns with Mr. Bowman?"

"Sure, they have a drink from time to time."

"Did you ever hear the two talking about any of the attacks?"

"I can't say I have. Everyone at the bar was talking about the attacks when they happened. But I can't say specifically about anyone or any conversation."

"Have you ever seen Ms. Sterns with Detective Jenkins?"

"Yes."

"When was that?"

"I remember one night because Dee, that's Darlene Crowe, and I had a bet about which cougar would hook up first. She won the bet."

"For the court, what is a cougar?"

"A middle aged woman looking for a younger man."

"And what do you mean hook up?"

"You know, what cougar would leave the bar with a man first."

"And who left first?"

"Ms. Sterns. She left with Detective Jenkins shortly after we made the bet."

"What was the bet, Mr. Jessup?"

"Loser makes breakfast."

"Oh, do you live with Ms. Crowe?"

"No."

"Then, I don't understand the bet."

"Think about it. If I win or lose, what else do you think I get?"

"I think I see what you're getting at Mr. Jessup."

Ron looked around the courtroom and saw Dee sitting in the back with her head down just shaking it as to say "no."

"Sorry Dee. I didn't mean to get you into trouble."

"Please stick to the questions Mr. Jessup."

"Sure."

"Did Mr. Bowman ever show any anger towards any of the victims that you are aware of?"

"Not that I am aware of."

"Is there anything that you can recall from your knowledge of Mr. Bowman?"

"Nah, I think I already said all I know."

Attorney Levine didn't have any further questions but Attorney White asked, "Mr. Jessup, do you know a Mr. Kenny Brown?"

"Yes I do."

"How do you know him?"

"He comes into the bar regularly."

"Have you ever observed Mr. Brown talking with any of the victims of the attacks?"

"All the time."

"Did you ever see Mr. Brown get angry at any of the women?"

"Well, yes."

"Please, tell us what you know."

"One time, Kenny had a little too much to drink and he got into an argument with Sue Kent. He hit her."

"So Mr. Brown has a temper?"

"Sometimes, usually when he drinks too much."

"And how often does that happen?"

"Every now and then."

"Were there any other times when Mr. Brown had an altercation with any of the victims or any other women?"

"Yes, I recall another time when Kenny and Tommy Anderson got into a fight over something Kenny said to Tina Fletcher."

"What did he say?"

"He said Tina was only sleeping with a certain police captain in order to keep herself out of jail."

"Had she done something wrong?"

"I'm not sure. I didn't hear that part of the conversation."

"But you remember the two fighting over something Mr. Brown said to Mr. Anderson about Ms. Fletcher?"

"That's right."

"I have no further questions, Mr. Jessup."

Judge Benson looked at his watch. He noticed it was nearing four o'clock. He informed the attorneys that court would be continued the next day.

Tom Bowman spoke with his attorney for a few minutes and then walked out of the courtroom. There were a number of people standing in the foyer all looking rather mad.

Kenny Brown said, "I wouldn't show my face at Sundancers if I were you Bowman."

"If I were you, I'd leave Cape Cod," came a shout from Tommy Anderson.

"You're scum," said Sue Kent.

Tom walked past the crowd but didn't stop. As he approached the door, Katherine was turning away from

Detective Jenkins about to leave when she said, "You're going to get yours Tom."

Detective Jenkins was at Katherine's side when he added, "Captain Tomlinson is going to be pissed when he hears about today's testimony."

"All because of Tom Bowman," Katherine said as the two walked out past Bowman."

"Katherine, I didn't do anything wrong," Tom tried to say to her as she walked by him.

"Keep your distance Bowman," Jenkins told him extending his arm to keep Bowman back.

"This has all been a setup," Bowman came back with as he stepped back.

"You'll get your say on the stand," Jenkins replied.

Chapter 15

After leaving the courthouse, Tom Bowman went to Sundancers to have a drink. He took up a stool at the end of the bar. Margarita Ortiz was bartending and approached him.

"What'll it be Mr. Bowman?"

"Can I have a Bud draft?"

"Anything else?"

"No, that'll be all."

Margarita went and poured the beer. Ed Phillips had been seated at the other end of the bar when Tom came in. He didn't wave or say anything to Tom. After Tom got his beer, Tom picked it up and walked to where Ed was seated.

"How you doing Ed?"

"Tom, I'm surprised you're in here given all that's happened?"

"Just stopping in for a beer."

"Look Tom, you've done some pretty bad things to the women we know. I think you should consider not coming back."

"This is a public place Ed. I'm as entitled to be here as the next guy. I thought we were friends Ed."

"I don't think you should call anyone in here a friend Tom. How could you do what you did to these people?"

"You don't understand Ed. I didn't intend for anyone to get hurt. I only wanted to please Katherine."

Just then, Katherine walked into the bar with Frank Jenkins.

"Well here she is now Tom. Why don't you go try to please her?"

Tom picked up his beer and walked back to where he had been seated. Katherine and Frank just walked past him and sat at a table in the dining room. Tom kept looking over the divider at the end of the bar to see what the two were doing. The plants were just high enough to block some of his view of their table.

"I can't believe he's in here," said Katherine in a surprised voice.

"Do you want me to ask him to leave?" Frank asked looking back towards the bar.

Katherine pointed to Harry Adams coming out of the kitchen and approaching Tom Bowman, "I don't think you need to say anything. I think Harry's going to throw him out."

Harry approached Tom and reached over to pick up the glass of beer, "You're not welcome here Mr. Bowman. I would appreciate it if you would leave and not come back. I'll pay your tab."

Tom got up to protest but noticed Tommy Anderson, Paul Bremmer and Kenny Brown standing behind Harry Adams.

"You should be kicking her out of here and not me," said Tom as he pointed to the dining room where Katherine was seated.

"She set this all up. She's the one who collected your semen." He pointed to Kenny. "And then spread it around on some of the victims. She got me as well."

"You're shit Bowman. You attacked my friends and now I intend to kick your ass," Kenny said in a harsh voice. "In fact, let's go outside right now and get this over with."

Kenny was quite a bit bigger than Tom and probably outweighed him by fifty pounds and was at least six inches taller. Plus Kenny was pretty muscular.

"I'm not looking for a fight Kenny. I just think you need to consider all the facts," Tom said as he stood and started for the door.

"I know all I need to know. I told the girls I would take care of whoever attacked them and that's just what I'm about to do." Kenny started to follow Tom to the door.

Harry stepped in and grabbed Kenny's arm.

"Kenny, let it go. I don't need the police here tonight. This guy has already hurt my business enough. He'll get what's coming to him."

"He sure will."

"Are you threatening me Kenny?" Tom asked as he reached the door.

"I'm just telling you like it is."

Harry turned his back to Tom and said to the group of men, "Drinks are on me now let's let this bum go."

They all turned to the bar where Margarita had already started to set up everyone's favorite drink. Katherine having observed the confrontation got up from her table and came to the bar.

"Thank you Harry for getting him out of here."

"No problem. What was it he was saying about you screwing around with the crime scenes?"

"I'm not sure what he was getting at. I think he's trying to put the blame off on someone else."

Frank had come up to the bar when Katherine left the table but he sat at the far end of the bar near Ed Phillips. Margarita came over to him and asked if he wanted another beer. When she gave it to him, Katherine had just been talking with Harry. Jenkins said to Margarita, "I've seen the semen she keeps in her freezer you know. Bowman's right about that part."

No one else other than Ed could hear Margarita and Frank's voices. Margarita said, "How could she get the DNA from the guys?"

"She would have them use a condom and then she put the condoms in zip-lock bags, labeled and froze them."

"Could she do that?"

"Sure. DNA doesn't evaporate and the lab can capture and analyze it from a crime scene if it were to be present."

"So she could have misled the police into accusing innocent people of a sexual attack?"

"Sure looks like it."

Ed didn't say anything. He just sat there and sipped on his drink listening to the conversation between Margarita and Frank. Finally, Katherine left the group of guys at the other end of the bar and approached Frank and Ed.

"Ed how are you doing today?"

Ed looked at her with a nasty look on his face. "So what did you do with the condom I used when we were up at the beach?"

"Ed, what are you talking about?"

"You told me you wanted to keep the environment clean. I believed you. Did you spread my DNA around at any of the crime scenes?"

"I don't know what you're talking about Ed?"

"Yes you do Katherine. We had sex up on the beach by the bay and then again at your house. You had me use a condom and then you said you would take care of it. I bet you did."

Frank sat back and just listened. He knew Katherine had been with other men but he hadn't seen any of them this angry at her. He turned to Ed, "Mr. Phillips, I think this has gone far enough. You should apologize to her."

"Apologize? I should ring her neck," Ed said as he stood and looked like he was going to come at her.

Frank stood and got in between the two. "I think you should leave," he said to Ed.

"I'm on my way out of here. You'll get what's coming to you Katherine," he said as he brushed past her.

"What was that all about?" Frank said smiling as the two sat back down at the bar.

"I don't know. He must be losing it." Katherine seemed uncharacteristically nervous.

Margarita observed Ed's outburst and called Harry over when Ed stood up.

"What the hell's going on in here tonight?" Harry asked Margarita in disbelief.

"Ed's usually a pretty quiet guy but whatever Katherine said or did, really pissed him off."

"To the point where he wanted to attack her?" asked Harry.

"Ed said he wanted to ring her neck," Margarita said, holding her hands up to the ceiling as if to say "beats me."

"I've watched Katherine work her magic from my office up front a few times. There might be some truth to Bowman's claims about her."

"If there is any truth to it, the cougars aren't buying it," Margarita said as she pointed to a group of women approaching Katherine.

The whole group of women, Ann, Tina, Linda and Sue all came up to Katherine and Frank.

"What was that all about Kat?" asked Ann.

"Ed must be losing it. He thinks I set him up. I always thought he was too quiet. He must be guilty of something."

"Look Kat," said Tina. "We all know what you've been through. Don't listen to what those guys are saying. We're with you."

Margarita leaned over to Harry. "They might change their tune if they heard what the Detective told me when Katherine was over talking with you and the guys."

"What did he say?"

"He said she has condoms in zip-lock bags in her freezer with the names of most of the guys in here. He said he's seen them. I'm sure Ed overheard our conversation and that's what got him so mad."

"Nothing surprises me. Don't say anything about what you heard tonight Margarita. I don't want to start a riot."

"Ok Harry but someone needs to tell the other cougars that Katherine just isn't telling all she knows."

"It will all come out in time."

Margarita went back to bartending and Harry went into the kitchen. The women talked to Katherine for a few more minutes and then disbanded.

Frank said, "Why don't we get out of here?"

"Sure."

He paid the tab and then they got up and left. Getting into his car, he noticed Ed Phillips sitting in his pick-up with the engine running. As Frank and Katherine left Sundancers parking lot, Ed followed them.

Chapter 16

Court continued the next morning. Ann Benard was the first witness called by Attorney Levine.

"Ms. Benard, do you know Tom Bowman?"

"Yes I know who he is although I don't know him personally."

"How do you know him?"

"I've seen him around town and a few of my friends know him."

"Which friends know him?"

"I know Katherine knows him."

"How do you know she knows him?"

"We had talked about her husband's death a few times and Tom's name came up a few times."

"What did Ms. Sterns say?"

"She said Tom had been with her husband when he died. One time, she said she thought Sam, that was her husband's name, might have died differently than the way Tom told it."

"Did she say anything else about him?"

"One night when we were at Chapin's restaurant she said she thought one of the men across the bar looked like Tom Bowman."

"Anything else?"

"Not that I can remember."

"Was there any other interaction between you and Mr. Bowman when you were at Chapin's?"

"No."

"I have no further questions for Ms. Benard," said Levine.

Attorney White approached, "Ms. Benard, did you see Mr. Bowman when you went for your walk at Chapin Beach?"

"No."

"Did Mr. Bowman follow you after you left Chapin's Restaurant headed towards Chapin beach?"

"I don't know. I wasn't looking for anyone following me."

"Do you know when Mr. Bowman left Chapin's Restaurant?"

"No."

"So you have no knowledge of Mr. Bowman participating in the attack on you in any way, do you Ms. Benard?" Attorney White said as he turned and walked back to the defense table.

"No, I don't."

"No further questions of Ms. Benard."

Ann Benard was excused.

Levine next called Tina Fletcher.

"Ms. Fletcher, can you briefly tell us what happened to you?"

"I had gone home after a night out. When I got home I had a glass of wine outside and decided to take a walk on the beach. I walked for a while up to Mayflower Beach and then started back. The next thing I knew a young couple was helping me up. I had been knocked out and they helped me to my feet."

"Did anyone follow you home?"

"I didn't see anyone."

"Did anyone know you were going for a walk on the beach?"

"No one could have. I only decided to take a walk on the spur of the moment."

"Did you see Mr. Bowman when you were at Sundancers before the attack took place?"

"Yes."

"Did you see Mr. Bowman leave Sundancers?"

"No I didn't."

"So he couldn't have followed you home?"

"Not that I knew of unless he was waiting somewhere near the bar in his vehicle."

"Did you know if he was waiting somewhere for you?"

"No."

"Who else did you see at the bar that night?"

"Let me see, I saw Ann leave with Bobby Jones and Katherine Sterns was there with Frank Jenkins."

"Was Ed Phillips there?"

"Yes. I remember him being there because Sue and Linda were talking about him and I think he didn't like what they were saying about him."

"Why?"

"Well it wasn't much later and he paid his tab and left rather quickly. He bumped into a guy on the way out and had a few harsh words with the guy. That was so not like Ed."

"Does Ed have a temper?"

"I don't know. I just know he was a little upset that night."

"Do you know if he followed you home?"

"I don't think so because I saw his car leave the parking lot headed the other way."

"Ms. Fletcher, let me ask you a few more questions about when you got home. Did you notice anything unusual when you got to your house?"

"No. Everything seemed normal."

"Did you see any vehicles that didn't belong in your neighborhood?"

"No."

"One more question. Did Ms. Sterns leave the bar before you did?"

"Yes. She and Frank left together in their respective vehicles."

"Do you know where they went?"

"No. I assume they went to Katherine's house. She likes the home field advantage."

"Both of them?"

"Yes, everyone knows the Frank and Katherine have a thing going."

"I have no further questions for Ms. Fletcher." Attorney Levine sat down.

Attorney White stood and approached Ms. Fletcher.

"Ms. Fletcher, do you have any reason to believe that my client attacked you?"

"I don't know how his hair got on me."

"What do you know about his hair?"

"The police found my underwear near where I was attacked and they sent them to the lab to have them analyzed. The report came back with hairs from Mr. Bowman. I have never slept with Mr. Bowman so I have no idea how his hair got on my underwear."

"Could someone have put his hair there?"

"How could that happen?"

"Didn't the lab indicate DNA from two different men on the underwear in addition to hairs from Mr. Bowman?"

"Yes."

"Would you please tell the court whose DNA the lab found on your underwear?"

"Kenny and Lou."

"Kenny?"

"Yes, Kenny Brown."

"And Lou?"

"I'd rather not reveal his last name."

"Your honor, please instruct the witness to answer the question."

Judge Benson turned to Ms. Fletcher, "Answer the question Ms. Fletcher."

"Lou Tomlinson."

"Do you mean Captain Lou Tomlinson of the Dennis Police Department?"

"Yes."

"Are you having an affair with Captain Tomlinson?"

"We see each other from time to time," she said as she scanned the room looking for Captain Tomlinson or his wife. When her eyes found him in the back of the room, she could see the sad expression on his face.

"Could Captain Tomlinson or Kenny Brown have attacked you?"

"Why would they?"

"Did you see Tom Bowman at any time on the night of your attack?"

"No."

"No more questions of this witness."

Attorney Levine next called Sue Kent to take the stand.

"Ms. Kent, do you know Tom Bowman?"

"Yes, I've talked to him at Sundancers a few times."

"Did he ever threaten you?"

"No."

"How did your attack take place?"

"I came home from a night out. When I got into my house, I straightened up a few things and then went to the bedroom. I thought I heard a noise outside in the garage. I looked out the window but didn't see anything. I was about to go take a look when someone struck me from behind as I came out of my bedroom. I don't remember anything else until Officer Trudy came to my assistance."

"Do you know how long it was from the time you were knocked unconscious until the time Officer Trudy arrived?"

"I don't think it was very long but I really don't know."

"Who do you think did this to you?"

"I don't know but a condom Officer Trudy found at my house had Bowman's DNA and the swabs Officer Trudy took at the scene had Bowman's DNA."

"So Tom Bowman sexually attacked you?"

"It looks that way but why would he attack me? I don't really know him."

"Did you ever have sex with Ed Phillips?"

"Yes, the night before I was attacked."

"So you admit having sex with him before the night of the attack?"

"Yes."

"Did you two ever have a fight?"

"I wouldn't call it a fight but one night I was talking to some of the other girls over at Sundancers. I was telling them about Ed and we were laughing. Ed thought we were making fun of him and he got upset."

"Did he threaten you?"

"No, he just left the bar."

"What were you talking about with the other girls?"

"About Ed's size."

"What do you mean size?"

"You know, size matters."

"Ok, I think I know what you are referring to."

"If you had been with Ed, you would know what I'm referring to," said Linda as her eyes found Ed seated in the third row in the courtroom.

"Didn't Officer Trudy tell you she observed someone standing over you in your bedroom when she looked through your bedroom window?"

"Yes and she said that was when she tripped over the downspout and scared the intruder off."

"Did she say she knows who the attacker was?"

"No, she didn't get a look at the intruder's face."

"Objection," came from Attorney White. "Your Honor, this is all hearsay. If the Prosecutor wants to bring Officer Trudy's testimony into this case, let her call Officer Trudy to the stand."

"Sustained."

"Nothing more for this witness."

Attorney White approached Ms. Kent.

"So Ms. Kent. If I understand your testimony, you were attacked at your house and the attacker was frightened away by Officer Trudy. Then Officer Trudy found a condom and had it tested for DNA, which revealed DNA from Tom Bowman. Is that true?"

"Yes."

"So that is the only reason you suspect my client played any role in your attack?"

"Yes."

"Do you have any idea why a condom having my client's DNA in it would be found at your home?"

"No."

"I have no further questions for this witness."

"You're excused Ms. Kent," said Judge Benson.

The last witness called for the day was Linda Sage.

"Ms. Sage, do you know Tom Bowman?"

"Yes."

"How do you know him?"

114

"I met him at Sundancers."

"Did he ever threaten you?"

"No."

"On the night of your attack, did you speak with Mr. Bowman?"

"Yes, we were having drinks at Sundancers, Tom, Kenny and me."

"Kenny?"

"Kenny Brown."

"Then what happened?"

"We were talking about going for a swim up in Cape Cod Bay. Tom didn't want to join Kenny and me. I told Kenny I would meet him up at Corporation Beach in a little while and then went home to get a few things. I never got to leave my house."

"Do you know where Mr. Bowman went when he left Sundancers?"

"No. He just said he wasn't going with us to the beach."

"Do you know when he left the bar?"

"No."

"Did he follow you home?"

"I don't know."

"After the attack on you, did the police find a used condom in your bedroom?"

"No."

"So you had sex with Kenny twice, once with a condom and once without?"

"No, we only had sex once and he used a condom."

"Are you sure he didn't have sex with you when you were knocked out?"

"I don't think so, but you'll have to ask him that question."

"Did you have sex with anyone else that day?"

"No, but the lab did say they found hairs and DNA belonging to Tom Bowman on the condom."

"How could that have happened?"

"I have no idea."

"No further questions," said Attorney Levine.

Attorney White jumped up and approached Ms. Sage.

"So you admit to talking with my client the night the attack took place?"

"Yes."

"And you admit you had agreed to meet with Kenny Brown on that night for a swim?"

"Yes."

"And you say you had sex with Mr. Brown after the attack in question?"

"Yes."

"Is it possible that Mr. Bowman's hairs somehow got onto your clothing when you had drinks with him at Sundancers?"

"I don't see how that could have happened."

"How close did you sit to Tom Bowman when you were at Sundancers?"

"Right next to each other. We were sitting on bar stools."

"Could your bodies or clothing have come in contact with each other?"

"I guess. Or he might have followed me from the bar and attacked me at my house."

"Objection your honor, the witness is speculating."

"Sustained, please just answer the questions Ms. Sage."

"Yes your Honor."

"Ms. Sage, you have no reason to believe that my client attacked you do you?"

"Other than the hairs being found, I don't."

"Nothing more for this witness."

Linda was excused.

Judge Benson had heard enough for the day and the afternoon was getting late. "Court will adjourn for the day and resume at nine tomorrow."

As everyone stood to leave the courtroom, Tom Bowman walked past Kenny Brown.
"I'm coming for you Bowman," Kenny said angrily.
Katherine overheard the threat and smiled.

Chapter 17

After court, everyone convened at Sundancers except Tom Bowman. Tom decided to go to the Bridge Bar. Linda, Tina and Sue were seated at a table in the bar area. Kenny, Bobby, Ed and Tommy were seated around the bar. Katherine was sitting by herself at the end of the bar by the waitress station where she could just hear what the other women were saying.

"So Linda, what do you make of today's testimony?" Sue asked.

"I'm not sure Katherine is as innocent as we had thought. What if she did sleep with the guys and collect their DNA just to implicate them or throw the authorities off?" Tina said as she looked over her shoulder at Katherine sitting by herself.

"I think Tom Bowman might be under some spell from her. Just listen to the guy, he's totally into her," commented Sue.

"Yeah, I got that impression also," added Linda.

"That still doesn't mean Tom is innocent," said Tina.

"Maybe so, but you know how guys are. If they think doing something for one of us gets them in bed with us, they will do anything we ask them to do or they might even make something up," said Sue.

Ann Benard walked into the bar and went over to where the other women were seated.

"Well, what did you think Ann?" Tina asked.

"I don't know. I do know Kat's been through quite a bit over the past year or so. How would each of you react if the same kind of things happened to you?" Ann asked as she looked at each of them.

"You make a good point Ann," commented Sue. "I'd have cut his balls off if it was me. I just don't understand why she went to all the trouble when all she had to do was ask Kenny to take care of it."

"I'm sure the other guys want some revenge as well. We haven't heard the last from them yet," said Tina as she looked to the bar.

Kenny had heard what the women had been talking about. He went over to Tommy Anderson, "You know Tommy, we should take care of Bowman. When did we ever let a guy take advantage of our situation?"

"Paul was saying the same thing," responded Tommy.

"Paul? You have got to be kidding me."

"He's pissed."

"I always thought he was gay."

"Not Paulie. Remember the night at the Bridge Bar when they put on the comedy show?"

"Yeah."

"Paulie hooked up with Ruby Crane. She showed him a real good time. Later on that night, I told him all the cougars were like her and he should get to know them better."

"How did he respond?"

"He's working at it. He ended up being questioned about the attack on Ruby and thought he was a suspect at first.

119

But then the DNA tests exonerated him. He thinks someone set him up. When I asked him, he thought it might be Bowman."

"Why would he name him?"

"I don't know other than Bowman has been charged in the other cases."

"But Bowman hasn't been charged in the attack on Ruby Crane."

"Not yet. Keep in mind the attack on Ruby took place in another town so her case will end up being handled separately."

"Good point."

"Paulie said he was going to get Bowman."

"You think he has it in him?"

"He's a real bear when he gets mad and right now he's really pissed."

"That's good to know," said Kenny pondering what he and Tommy had talked about. Kenny picked up his beer and walked to the end of the bar where Katherine was seated.

"Kat, what do you make of all this court stuff?" Kenny asked her.

"I think Tom Bowman should pay for what he's done."

"You speaking for yourself or for them as well?" Kenny was pointing to the group of women seated at a table.

"Mostly for myself, but he should pay for what he did to my friends as well."

"Kat let me ask you another question. What do you think of Paul Bremmer?"

"What do you mean?"

"You know. I thought he might be a little light."

"Not Paulie. He's as interested in women as much as the rest of you."

"I don't know."

"Trust me, I know."

"Bowman's attorney has done a good job suggesting his client didn't do the attacks alone. Know anything about that?"

"I know what your are getting at Kenny. But I didn't attack anyone."

"Maybe not, but you might have played a role in these cases by spreading around DNA from some of the guys you have slept with."

"Look Kenny, I want Bowman to pay for what he did to Sam and to me. He needs to pay."

"Oh, he'll pay all right."

"What are you going to do Kenny, beat him up?"

"I'm not making any threats Kat. I'm just saying anyone involved in these attacks is going to pay."

Kenny picked up his beer and walked back to the other end of the bar. Tommy asked him, "What did she have to say?"

"She's guilty as sin," said Kenny. "She wants revenge so bad against Bowman, she'll do anything."

"Anything?" Tommy asked.

"Tommy, you going to try to hook up with her?"

"Already have," was his response.

"Why Tommy, you devil. I knew you were working on some of the cats, but I didn't know you hooked up with Kat."

"I did and when I did, that Detective Jenkins showed up at her house."

"Did he catch you in the act?"

"Nah, we had already finished. Kat was cleaning up."

"Did you use a condom?"

"Yeah. Now that you mention it, she was in the kitchen throwing it away when Jenkins showed up."

"Throwing it away huh?"

"Or maybe saving it for a future use?"

"You think?"

"I think she's capable of anything."

"She can't be planning on getting me implicated in anything can she?"

"Don't be surprised Tommy."

"I'll see about that," Tommy said as he picked up his beer and walked to where Katherine was seated.

"Kat, how you doing?" Tommy asked.

"Tommy, young Tommy. What do you want?"

"Kat, I just had a little talk with Kenny. I was wondering, that afternoon when you and I hooked up, what did you do with the condom?"

"What?"

"What did you do with the condom I used?"

"I threw it away."

"You sure?"

"I'm sure."

"Rumor has it you have been collecting used condoms from the guys you sleep with."

"Now why would I do that?"

"I'm not really sure."

"Listen Tommy, if I wanted to bring attention to a guy, there are a lot of things I could do that would put him in a world of hurt."

"Like what?"

"Any women can seduce a guy into a sticky situation and then claim rape. A few bruises, a little semen and a sympathetic doctor and the guy goes to jail for a long time."

"Would you do that?"

"I'm just saying we women have our ways if we put out mind to it."

"That's scary."

"So you shouldn't come down here accusing me of anything. If I wanted to, I could make you or any other guy's life miserable."

"I guess. Maybe Bowman is as guilty as Kenny said he is."

"Kenny said that did he?"

"He sure did and he said Bowman's going to pay."

"Yeah, I heard him say that as well."

"It's sure good that Bowman didn't show up here. Everyone's kind of wired up."

"I don't think he'll show here for a while."

"Where do you think he is now?"

"I don't know. When Sam was alive, he and Tom used to hang out at the Bridge Bar quite a bit."

"You think he is there right now?"

"Could be."

Tommy picked up his beer and went back to the other end of the bar. Katherine paid her tab and got up to leave. As she was walking out Dee said, "Calling it an early night Kat?"

"I've got things to do. See you tomorrow."

"Have a good night."

"Kenny, Kat said Bowman used to hang out at the Bridge Bar when her husband was still alive. Want to take a ride over there and see if he's there?"

"That might not be a bad idea. Let's go see if he's there."

"Ed, we're going to the Bridge Bar to see if Bowman's there, care to join us?"

"Yeah. I'd like to get even with that creep if he's there."

"Ed, just don't go ballistic on us," Kenny said laughing.

The three paid their tabs and went outside. They got into Kenny's van and headed to the Bridge Bar.

Walking into the Bridge Bar, they saw Tom Bowman seated at the far side of the bar by himself. Kenny took the stool on Bowman's left. Tommy and Ed took up stools on his right.

"To what do I owe this pleasure guys?" Tom asked.

"Look Bowman, you attacked our women. You lied about everything," accused Kenny.

"What are you talking about?" Tom replied.

"Did you plan to implicate us in your crimes?" said Ed in a shaky voice.

"You know, you guys need to think about what you're saying. Just how would I implicate you? What do you think, I sift through Kat's garbage every week looking for used condoms?"

"You could get them from her freezer," declared Tommy.

"Oh, I know she collects them. All you have to do is look in her freezer. You'll see her whole collection," said Tom.

"Why would she collect used condoms?" Ed asked.

"For the exact reason you're asking me. To implicate others in criminal acts," Tom said as he sipped his beer. He was surprisingly calm, considering the accusations.

"You mean she's been collecting the used condoms after having sex with us and then saving them in her freezer?"

"Now you're getting the picture," replied Tom.

"And then she defrosts the condoms and takes them to crime scenes and spreads the contents around?" questioned Ed surprisingly.

"Bingo," said Tom giving a thumbs-up signal.

"Why would she go to all the trouble?" Tommy asked.

"You'll have to ask her," replied Tom. "If this was about getting me in trouble, I'd say she failed. If not....." His voice trailed off.

"Look Bowman, you still attacked the women," accused Kenny.

"I wasn't attacking them. I only wanted to scare them."

"For what reason?" asked Kenny.

"Kat had told me someone needed to make the other women less likely to want to hookup with some of the guys at the bar. She thought if the woman became fearful they might think twice about hooking up so easily."

"Why would she be concerned about them?" Tommy asked.

"I don't know but women do strange things when they don't think they are the center of attention," said Tom.

"I don't buy it Bowman. You're just trying to put the blame off on her."

"Why would I do that?"

"To save your own ass," said Kenny.

"From what? I might have committed a misdemeanor or something, but I don't think these charges are as serious as the prosecutor thinks they are."

"We'll see about that," said Kenny. Then he said to Ed and Tommy, "Let's get out of here."

The three left the Bridge Bar without having a drink or a fight.

Chapter 18

Court resumed at nine the next morning. Attorney Levine called her first witness, Bobby Jones.

"Mr. Jones, do you know Mr. Bowman?"

"I've seen him around although I don't know him personally."

"Have you seen Mr. Bowman with Ms. Sterns at Sundancers from time to time?"

"Yes I have."

"Do you remember the dates?"

"I'm not good at things like that. No I don't specifically remember the dates."

"Did you ever see Mr. Bowman leave the bar with Ms. Sterns?"

"I may have, I'm not sure."

"Mr. Jones, didn't you tell the police you thought Mr. Bowman was the person attacking the women from the bar?"

"I don't remember telling anyone anything like that. You must be thinking of someone else."

"Mr. Jones, I have a report here from the police indicating you made a statement about Mr. Bowman when you were interviewed one day at Sundancers."

"I don't remember making any statement. If someone talked to me at the bar, then I might have been drunk. If that were the case, I might have said anything."

It was evident Attorney Levine was unhappy with the testimony of Mr. Jones. Attorney Levine must have thought Mr. Jones testimony would be a smoking gun against Tom Bowman but Mr. Jones' inability to recall the events under oath detracted from the accusations.

Disgustedly, Attorney Levine said, "I have no further questions for this witness."

Attorney White took over and walked to the witness box.

"Mr. Jones, do you know if Mr. Bowman was at Chapins Restaurant the night Ms. Benard was attacked?"

"I don't know, he could have been there."

"Do you know if Mr. Bowman was at Sundancers the night Ms. Fletcher was attacked?"

"I can't say specifically."

"Do you know if you were at Sundancers the night Ms. Kent was attacked?"

"Yeah, I was there."

"Did you see Mr. Bowman there also?"

"Can't say I did."

"So Mr. Jones, you really have no idea as to the whereabouts of Mr. Bowman at any time, do you?"

"No I guess I don't."

"One last question Mr. Jones. Do you recall making any statements to the police about any of the cases in question?"

"No I don't."

"Thank you Mr. Jones. That will be all."

Bobby Jones stepped down. Attorney Levine called her next witness Kenny Brown.

"Mr. Brown, do you know Mr. Bowman?"

"Yes."

"Can you explain how you know him?"

"I met him at Sundancers."

"Did someone introduce you to him?"

"Yes, Linda Sage."

"Do you remember the date?"

"Well not specifically the date, but I met him the same night Linda was attacked."

"Are you sure about that Mr. Brown?"

"Yes. Linda was sitting at the bar talking to Mr. Bowman. When I approached, she introduced me to him. Linda wanted to go skinny dipping up in the bay and asked Bowman and me to join her."

"Did you?"

"I was supposed to but she never showed up."

"Did Mr. Bowman?"

"No, he backed out. I don't think he wanted any part of what Linda was planning."

"Did you see Linda leave the bar?"

"No, I had already left to go gather a few things. Then I went up to Corporation Beach to wait for her. When she didn't show up, I went over to her house."

"And what did you find?"

"The door wasn't locked so I let myself in. The lights were on so I called out to Linda. When she didn't answer, I looked around and found her out cold on her bed."

"What did you do then?"

"I woke her up."

"Did she indicate anything had happened to her?"

"No, but she didn't understand how she had passed out and was even more confused as to why she was lying on her bed naked."

"Did she look like she had been harmed in any way?"

"No."

"What did you do then?"

"Well, Linda told me to shed my clothes and turn the lights off."

"So did you?"

"Yes. We had planned on going swimming in the bay and then going back to her house afterwards. So I just figured we cut the beach out."

"Then what happened?"

"We fooled around and then fell asleep."

"When you had sex with Ms. Sage, did you use a condom?"

"I always use a condom."

"Did you notice anything unusual after that?"

"Linda said the condom must have broken because she had liquid on her legs. I later found out the condom had my DNA inside and outside but didn't leak. Since I only had sex with Linda once that night, I have no idea how that could happen."

"Could someone have planted your DNA on Ms. Sage while she was out cold?"

"I guess so, but who would do something like that?"

"Did you know Mr. Bowman's hairs were found on the condom?"

"How could that be if I opened it when I was at Linda's?"

"Ah ha Mr. Brown, then someone would have had to put the hairs on Ms. Sage before you had sex with her?"

"Yeah, that or after."

"What did you do with the condom when you were finished with it?"

"I threw it in Linda's trash can in her bedroom."

"And that was the last you saw of it?"

"Yes."

"I have no further questions of Mr. Brown."

Attorney White was quick to jump up.

"Mr. Brown, could someone have put Mr. Bowman's hairs on the condom after you had sex with Ms. Sage?"

"I guess so."

"Could Mr. Bowman's hairs somehow been in Ms. Sage's trash can?"

"I don't see how that could have happened unless he was in her bedroom."

"If he were there, do you think that could have happened?"

Attorney Levine objected. Judge Benson responded, "I'll allow the question."

"I guess."

"Mr. Brown, do you have any knowledge whatsoever as to Mr. Bowman's role in any of the attacks in question?"

"Not really."

"Thank you Mr. Brown, that will be all."

After another day of testimony, Judge Benson adjourned the court indicating the trial would resume at nine the next day.

Dee Crowe and Ron Jessup were standing behind the bar at Sundancers talking. There were only a few patrons in the bar at that time so the two were not very busy.

"Ron, how do you think the case is going?" Dee asked.

"From what I gather, all the evidence is pointing to Bowman. His DNA showing up kind of seals the deal."

"But what if the DNA was being planted?" Dee looked at Ron with her eyebrows raised. "Don't you think it's possible?"

"I don't know. Someone would have to have really planned this whole thing out. Just think about it."

Harry Adams came out of the kitchen with chef Antonio. The two sat at the bar and ordered a drink.

"Harry, what's up with the bar being so empty?" Antonio asked.

"Everyone's at the courthouse. It's a real drama."

"Even so, we should be doing a booming business by now."

"Don't worry, everything will pick up once this mess goes away."

"How will that happen?" Antonio asked.

"I have a feeling something dramatic is about to happen."

"Like what?"

"I don't know, just a feeling."

The two looked out the door and noticed a line of cars entering the parking lot.

"Looks like court is out for the day," said Dee.

"That's good news for us," replied Antonio as he finished his drink, got up and went back into the kitchen.

"Looks like our slow time is over," Ron said to Dee.

"Looks like it."

"Anything else boss?" Dee said looking at Harry.

"Yeah, let me know if either Ms. Sterns or Mr. Bowman show up would you?"

"Will do. Will you be in the office?"

"Yeah."

Harry Adams got up and left through the kitchen. The door to the bar opened. Linda, Sue, Tina, Bobby, Kenny, Ed, Tommy and Ann all came in at the same time.

Kenny started talking to Bobby about Kenny's testimony.

"Kenny, the attorney made a good point about Bowman's hair."

"Like what?"

"Like how did Bowman's hairs get on the condom?"

"As I said in court, I don't know how it could have happened if I opened a new condom when I was there."

"That's the point. Either Bowman was there before you or after you."

"Or someone put those hairs on the condom."

"Who would be that smart?"

Kenny looking out the door saw Katherine getting out of her car and he pointed at her, "She would."

"Kenny, you've been with Kat. Why would you say something like that?"

"Whenever I had sex with her, she always wanted to clean things up. She always took the condom I used and did something with it. Maybe there's something to what Bowman was saying."

When Dee saw Katherine enter the bar, she called Harry.

"She's here."

"Thanks Dee. Let me know if you see any trouble starting."

"Sure Harry."

Margarita Ortiz who had just come on duty at the bar and was putting her bag under the bar near where Kenny and Bobby were seated overheard the conversation the two were having. She stood up, "I overheard Detective Jenkins talking

132

about Katherine having zip-lock bags in her freezer containing used condoms. Does that mean anything to either of you?"

"Where did you hear that?"

"Right here at the bar the other day. The Detective was sitting down there at the end of the bar when I heard him say it to Tom Bowman."

She looked to her right and saw Ed Phillips sitting there, "Ed, you were here the other day when Detective Jenkins was talking to Tom Bowman about the condoms in Katherine's freezer. You heard him didn't you?"

"Yeah, I was here. I heard something like that. But I still don't believe it."

"See Bobby, she's a conniving one," said Kenny.

"I'm going to ask her about it," said Bobby as Katherine took up a stool on the other side of the bar. Bobby picked up his drink and walked around to where Katherine was seated.

"Kat, some of the guys were talking about you saving used condoms in your freezer. What do you say about that?"

"Who says I do?"

"Your Detective friend for one."

"How do you know that?"

"Let's just say I know."

"Even if I do, it isn't any of your business."

"It is if one of them has the name Bobby Jones on it."

"Well, you don't have to worry about it."

"So you're saying you don't have one with my name on it."

"I'm just saying you don't have to worry. Now if you don't mind Bobby, I'd rather be alone."

Bobby got up and went back around to Kenny.

"She's up to something Kenny," said Bobby. "When I asked about the condoms, she didn't deny it. She just said I didn't have to worry."

"Bobby, I think any of us who slept with her has to worry as long as she has those used condoms in her freezer."

"You have a point."

"Someone has to do something," said Kenny downing the last of his beer.

Katherine had finished her one drink and got up to leave. When she did, Ed got up and followed her out.

Chapter 19

Attorney White had met with Tom Bowman before court began the next morning.

"Tom, when it's our turn to present witnesses, I only plan on calling you to the stand. The prosecution hasn't really presented much of a case up to this point and I think you can clear up much of the confusion for the judge and jury."

"Do you think it's a good idea?" Tom asked with a tone of uncertainty in his voice.

"I do. Ms. Sterns set you up. Then she planted evidence ensuring you would be tied to the attacks. After your testimony, there are going to be quite a few people who will change their minds as to exactly who should be held accountable for these attacks. It'll be enough reasonable doubt for sure."

"You're the attorney. I'll trust your judgment."

"That's what I'm here for."

"Do you think I should hire my own attorney?"

"I might be a court appointed attorney Tom but I'm still bound to provide you with the best defense. I know I can beat these charges. Just stick with me."

"Ok," Tom said although the tone of his voice sounded uncertain.

As court began for the day, Attorney Levine called Tommy Anderson to the stand.

"Mr. Anderson, do you know Mr. Bowman?"

"Yes. I met him a few weeks ago at Sundancers."

"Is there anything you can recall about Mr. Bowman you feel might be pertinent to this case?"

"Well, one night when I was at Sundancers, Mr. Bowman came in and sat next to us."

"Who's us?"

"I was talking with Linda Sage and Paul Bremmer at the bar when Bowman came in. He took up the stool on the opposite side of Linda."

"Then what happened?"

"Paul had to leave so I went outside to talk with him for a few minutes. When I came back in, Bowman had put the moves on Linda."

"What do you mean moves?"

"They were sitting kind of close together, touching each other."

"Then what did you do?"

"Nothing. I had lost my opportunity for the night with her so I moved on."

"Moved on?"

"Yeah. I went looking for another woman."

"What happened to Bowman and Ms. Sage?"

"From what I remember, Kenny came in and sat next to them. The three talked for a while and then Kenny left. Linda left a little later and Bowman left a little after her."

"So Tom Bowman left shortly after Ms. Sage?"

"That's what I remember."

"Do you know if he was going to meet her?"

"Couldn't tell you. All I know is he left right after her."

"Thank you Mr. Anderson. Your witness."

Attorney White approached Tommy Anderson.

"Mr. Anderson, do you know Ms. Katherine Sterns?"

"Sure, who doesn't?"

"In what capacity do you know her?"

"I'm not sure what you're asking?"

"Let me ask another way. Have you ever slept with Ms. Sterns?"

"Yes I've been with her a few times."

"Do you remember the last time you were with her?"

"Yes. She had me over one afternoon. We had sex and were then interrupted by Detective Jenkins."

"What do you mean interrupted?"

"We had just finished when he knocked on her front door. She went down and answered it. I heard them talking and I came out of the bedroom."

"What happened then?"

"Let me see. Katherine was in the kitchen. I thought she was throwing the used condom into the garbage. The Detective was standing in the front doorway."

"Did the Detective say anything to you?"

"Not really. I just grabbed my clothes and left."

"So the Detective stayed?"

"No, he left right after I did."

"Do you know what she did with the condom you used?"

"I thought she threw it away, but after hearing others testify, she could have done something else with it."

"Do you have any proof she did anything else with the condom?"

"No, but look what happened to those other guys?"

"I object your Honor. Mr. White is leading the witness. Plus, the witness is speculating."

"Sustained. Mr. Anderson, please just answer the questions," said Judge Benson.

"Sure."

"Mr. Anderson, is there anything else you wish to add," asked Attorney White.

"I overheard someone talking about condoms being frozen in Ms. Sterns freezer."

"I object," said Attorney Levine. "This is hearsay."

"Mr. Anderson. Please refrain from any speculation."

"I'm not speculating your Honor. I think this stuff is real."

"Mr. Anderson, if you are not a first hand witness, what you just said is speculation," said Judge Benson. "Your Honor, I have no other questions for this witness," said Attorney White.

Attorney Levine called Ed Phillips next.

"Mr. Phillips, do you know Mr. Bowman?"

"Yes."

"How do you know him?"

"I know him from around town and we've gone fishing together on a few occasions."

"So your acquaintance is more than in passing?"

"I guess you would say we were friends."

"Has Mr. Bowman ever said anything to you that might be important to this case?"

"One night when we were fishing up at Cape Cod Bay, he told me about his relationship with Ms. Sterns."

"He said he had a relationship with Ms. Sterns?"

"He said he had slept with her once before her husband had died and again recently."

"What do you mean recently?"

138

"He said he had met with her upon returning to Cape Cod after a short stay in Virginia. One thing lead to another and the two began a romantic relationship."

"Did he say anything else?"

"Only that he would do anything she wanted just to have her."

"How did you interpret his remarks?"

"Oh, he was rather specific. He told me he would do anything she wanted even if it were illegal."

"So he said he would do illegal things?"

"That's what he told me."

"Do you know if he ever followed through on any illegal activities?"

"He never specifically told me he did anything, but I know how taken he was with Ms. Sterns."

"Did he ever say Ms. Sterns asked him to attack any of the victims in this case?"

"No he didn't."

"Do you think he attacked these women?"

"I object your Honor. The question calls for speculation."

"Sustained. Please move on Ms. Levine."

"Ok your Honor."

"Mr. Phillips, have you ever been romantically involved with any of the victims in this case?"

"Let's see. I dated Linda Sage and I've been with Katherine Sterns."

"Ms. Sterns isn't one of the victims in this case."

"Oh, I thought you were asking which of the women I've been with."

"So you have only been with two women?"

"You didn't let me finish. I also know Carrie Morgan, Ruby Crane and a few others."

"So you know Ms. Crane as well?"

"Yes."

"She isn't part of this case but I understand she was attacked in another town and a case is proceeding in her town."

"That's my understanding as well."

"Did you have anything to do with her case?"

"No. I did follow her home one night but only to try to hook up with her. It didn't work out. I didn't have the nerve."

"Do you know if Mr. Bowman had anything to do with any of the attacks in this case?"

"Not really."

"Thank you Mr. Phillips."

Attorney White picked up his pad and walked to the witness box.

"Mr. Phillips, do you know Ms. Katherine Sterns?"

"Yes."

"And you had sex with her?"

"Yes."

"Can you tell the court when and where?"

"Sure. One night when I was going to watch the sunset up off Chapin Beach, she joined me. We had a few beers out on the beach watching the sun go down. At one point, she said it would be nice to make love right there with the sun setting. So we did."

"Did you use a condom?"

"Yes."

"What happened to the condom when you were done?"

"Ms. Sterns put it in a zip-lock bag and took it home."

"Do you know why she took it home?"

"I thought to throw away. She said she didn't want to litter the beach."

"Do you know if she threw it away?"

"No I don't."

"Did you have sex with her on any other occasion?"

"Later that same night, we went to her house so I could fix her computer. After I did, she asked me to stay the night. So I did."

"And you had sex again?"

"Yes."

"Did you use a condom that time?"

"Yes."

"Did she discard the condom?"

"Yes she did."

"Are you sure she threw them away?"

"No I'm not. Thinking about how DNA has showed up at some of the attacks, she could have used one of the condoms I used."

"Objection your Honor," said Attorney Levine jumping to her feet.

"Sustained. Please disregard the witness's last statement," ordered Judge Benson to the jury.

"Mr. Phillips, do you have any knowledge of Ms. Sterns spreading DNA from any used condom at any time?"

"No."

"Thank you Mr. Phillips. No more questions."

Chapter 20

After court, most of the attendees went to Sundancers. Tina, Sue, Ann, Linda, Bobby, Kenny and Ed were the first to arrive. They all took up stools on the window side of the bar. They all ordered their personal favorite drinks from Margarita and Ron. There seemed to be a moment of silence and in unison, the group took their first drink.

"Ed, you devil," said Bobby. "Here I thought you were this quiet reserved guy."

"I am. What are you saying?"

"I heard your testimony. You've probably slept with more women in here than I have."

"I don't think that's possible Bobby. You seem to hook up with someone different every night," Ed said taking another drink of his beer with a pretty proud smile on his face.

"Yeah Bobby, you're the poster boy for Viagra," added Kenny.

"Look who's talking," Bobby came back. "And I don't need Viagra."

"I do all right Bobby, but I'm not as active as you are," Kenny said.

"I'm just saying, Ed's been a real busy boy," Bobby said raising his glass as to toast Ed.

Tina saw Bobby raising his glass. She approached him, "So what are you celebrating Bobby?"

"Not me, Ed. You heard his testimony."

"What, are you getting a little jealous Bobby?" Tina asked.

"Not really, I just always thought Ed wasn't your type," Bobby said to Tina.

"So what makes you think you're my type Bobby?"

"I'm not complaining Tina, I was only stating my perception of Ed."

"Well, I think you have Ed all wrong. He may be quiet, but he does all right in my book."

"That's a pretty strong statement Tina. Do any of the other's feel the same way?"

Tina looked down the bar to Sue and Ann. She said, "Sue, come here for a minute."

Sue got up and approached Bobby and Tina.

"What's up?" Sue asked.

"Bobby was telling me his thoughts on Ed's testimony today. What do you think of Ed?"

"Ed's a hidden gem. He'd make any women in here real happy."

Bobby looked at Sue, "Like I do?"

"Bobby, you're not even a close second to Ed," Sue said with a cocky smile on her face.

"Then why do you hook up with me all the time instead of Ed?"

"Because I know with you it's one and done. I don't have to invest any time to get off. With Ed, I want to take my time and take it all in."

143

"You make it sound like he's the best you've ever had."

"Now you're getting the picture," Sue said as she started to walk away towards Ed. When she got to Ed, she put her arms around him, "Don't let Bobby get to you Ed, I like you just the way you are."

Ed turned to Sue, "Thanks Sue."

"You can thank me later if you want," Sue said as she brushed up against his arm.

Tommy Anderson, Linda Sage and Ann Benard were all seated at the far end of the bar talking by the windows.

Tommy said, "Ann, what do you make of all this DNA evidence stuff? Do you think Katherine put Bowman up to it?"

"I don't know Tommy. After hearing all the testimony, it sure looks like she had the opportunity to plant evidence."

Linda added, "I still don't understand why Katherine would go to such lengths. With her money, she could have gotten her revenge without all the hassle."

"Maybe she wanted to see him suffer," Tommy said as he picked up his drink.

"Some suffering," said Linda. "He got to have sex with Katherine."

"Yeah, but think about it. If you felt like you were wronged by someone who was obsessed with having sex with you and you wanted to get the person back, wouldn't you think that taking what the person most wants away would provide a great deal of personal satisfaction?" Tommy asked.

"Tommy, that's a lot of deep anger for someone to go that far," said Ann.

"Maybe so, but have you ever known Katherine to take any shortcuts and have you ever seen her when she puts her mind to something?" Tommy said.

"You're right Tommy," said Ann. "Katherine's like a pit bull when she gets her mind set on something."

"Even still, I just think we're making way more of this thing than we should be. The whole thing might be as simple as Tom Bowman being obsessed with sex and attacking us women just to get it," Linda said.

"You might be right Linda. We'll have to see if Bowman takes the stand and see what he says."

"Bowman's DNA was found in the attack on Sue, and me" said Linda. "So there's no way he can deny those attacks."

"Unless Katherine put it there," said Tommy.

Bobby had seen the three having their discussion. He walked over to where they were at the end of the bar and just stood behind Ann listening. After Tommy's comment about Katherine, Bobby said, "I wonder if she has any of my DNA in her freezer."

Tommy turned around, "What did you say Bobby?"

"I said I wonder if she has any of my DNA in her freezer. I overheard Margarita saying she heard Detective Jenkins saying Katherine has used condoms stored in zip-lock bags in her freezer and I was wondering if one of them has the name Bobby Jones on it."

"Hey, when I had sex with her, she insisted I use a condom. When we were done, she took it to her kitchen with her when Detective Jenkins had knocked on her door. I thought she was throwing it in the trash. Now I'm wondering if she has one in her freezer labeled Tommy Anderson?"

"Now won't you be surprised if your DNA shows up on someone you know you didn't have sex with, Tommy?" Linda asked.

"You bet I would," said Tommy in a mad voice. "Someone needs to check it out and see if she has our DNA Bobby."

"What are you going to do Tommy? You going to go break in to her house when she's not there?"

"Don't go doing something stupid Tommy," exclaimed Ann.

"Yeah, you don't have to break in Tommy. She keeps a spare key to the front door in her garage over the side door."

Bobby reached over his head as if reaching for the key.

"If you get caught Tommy, it isn't going to look good." Linda said as she turned to Bobby giving him a frown for telling Tommy where the key was kept.

"But if she still has the condoms, she could still get some of us into real trouble."

"I'm just saying Bobby, you don't want to take the law into your own hands. Why not wait and see where the trial goes?"

"Ok, Ok. I'll wait and see," Tommy said. "Margarita, get us all another drink if you would? On me."

"Sure Tommy."

Tommy picked up his beer and went over and sat next to Ed.

"I don't know Ed."

"I heard some of what you were saying to Ann and Linda. Makes ya wonder."

"Ed, someone needs to find out if Katherine still has those used condoms in her freezer."

"I can't believe she would do those things to us just to get back at Bowman," Ed said shaking his head.

"Ed, I may be young, but I'm not naive. I've learned that there is nothing more vicious in this world than a woman with an ax to grind. And Katherine seems to have it in big time for Bowman."

"I agree with you, someone needs to do something. Maybe Kenny will take care of everything."

146

"Maybe."

"It's been a long day. I'm going home," said Ed.

He paid his tab, got up and left the bar. The others sat there and talked for a little while longer and then they too left.

"Margarita, what do you make of all this?" Ron asked.

"I think the cougars are on guard and I think the guys want to know if Katherine is behind all of this mess."

"Do you think any of them will try to find out for themselves?"

"I know the guys are nervous that she may have condoms they used in her freezer. One of them might try to find out for themselves."

"Maybe Kenny, but I can't see any of the other guys doing anything like that."

"Maybe not, but you never know when something like this happens."

"Good point," said Ron. "Why don't we start getting things straightened up for the night? If no one else comes in, Harry said we should close at midnight."

"Sounds good to me."

"If we get out early, got any plans?" Ron asked with a smile on his face.

"No."

"What time did you tell your husband you would be home?"

"Around two."

"Then that gives you an extra two hours."

"What do you have in mind?"

"Oh, I was just thinking out loud."

"I might be interested."

"You might?" Ron said smiling at Margarita.

"Yeah. If we get done by midnight, we could go to your place for a little while."

"We'll be done by eleven thirty."

"Now you're sounding anxious Ron."

"Not anxious Margarita, excited. We've worked together all this time and this is the first time."

"What? You think I don't get horney?"

"That and that," he said pointing to the ring on her finger. She took the ring off and put it in her handbag.

"Does that make it better?" Margarita said as she brushed up against Ron who was bending over to pick up a rack of dirty glasses.

He shook his butt rubbing it against her, "Yeah, that makes it better." He didn't pick up the rack but rather stood and turned to face her. He put his arms around her waist.

"Not here Ron, someone might see us."

"Everyone's left. It's just you and me and the dishwasher."

"He might come out and catch us."

"Ok. I'll wait."

"I'll make it worth your while Ron."

Then Margarita went about cleaning up the bar. Ron picked up the rack of glasses again and headed to the kitchen.

Chapter 21

Court resumed at 9 am. Attorney Levine called paramedic Tom Donovan as her first witness.

"Mr. Donovan, can you describe for the court what you saw when you first reached Ms. Benard at Chapin Beach?"

"My partner, Mike Jones and I arrived on the scene about the same time as Officer Trudy. Mr. Fields directed us to the location where Ms. Benard was located. She was laying on the ground just off the off-road path to the left of the parking lot."

"Did you see anyone else there?"

"Only Mr. and Mrs. Fields and Officer Trudy."

"Did you see any other vehicles?"

"No."

"Thank you Mr. Donovan. I have no further questions."

Attorney White stood by the defense table, "Mr. Donovan, did you see Mr. Bowman at the scene?"

"No."

"Did you pass any other vehicles on your way to the scene?"

"I'm sure we did."

"Let me rephrase the question. Did you pass any other vehicles after you left route 6A going to the beach?"

"I don't think so but I really don't remember."

"Thank you Mr. Donovan. No further questions."

"Mr. Donovan, you may be excused," said Judge Benson.

"I'd like to call Paramedic Mike Jones to the stand," requested Attorney Levine.

Mike Jones who had been seated next to Tom Donovan approached and was sworn in.

"Mr. Jones, do you have anything further to add to Mr. Donovan's testimony?"

"I do."

"Please go on."

"Well, one of the suspects in the case is my brother Bobby Jones. Shortly after the incident with Ms. Benard, my brother and I were talking and he told me about some of the problems he was having with the women in his life."

"What did he say?"

"He told me he had met with Ann Benard on the night of her attack at Chapin's Restaurant and that he had a disagreement with her."

"Did he say what the disagreement was about?"

"It was something to do with sex. With Bobby, it is always something about sex."

"So why are you telling us this information?"

"It was after the attack when he told me about his argument with Ann. Bobby was concerned he would be perceived as the attacker."

"Did he say he attacked her?"

"Quite the opposite. He said he felt bad about their argument at the bar and he tried to find her up at the beach to apologize."

"Did he say if he found her?"

"He specifically said he didn't."

"Did you believe him?"

"Absolutely. He's my brother. I don't think he would lie to me."

"Again, why are you bringing this to our attention?"

"I figured it might help insure he doesn't get blamed for the attack."

"Thank you Mr. Jones."

Attorney White stood at the defense table again, "Mr. Jones, do you know Tom Bowan?"

"No."

"Did you see Mr. Bowman at Chapin Beach the night in question?"

"No."

"Thank you Mr. Jones. No further questions for this witness."

"Mr. Jones, you're excused," said Judge Benson.

Attorney Levine next called the emergency room doctor, Dr. Thomas Warren.

"Doctor Warren, you treated Ms. Benard on the night in question, is that right?"

"Yes I did."

"Can you tell us the nature of her injuries?"

"Sure. Ms. Benard had a laceration on her head requiring stitches. She also had numerous scratches, bumps and bruises on her body."

"Did you check her for sexual assault?"

"Yes."

"What did you find?"

"From what I could tell, Ms. Benard had not been sexually assaulted. The scratches on her body looked like they were made from an animal."

"Why do you say an animal?"

"The pattern looked like it had been made from a claw or something with nails."

He made a motion with his hand having his fingers extended and spread out.

"So you think she had been scratched by an animal?"

"That I can't say, but the marks looked like they were made from a hand or paw."

"Doctor Warren, I believe you were the attending physician when Ms. Sage came to the emergency room after her attack as well. It that true?"

"Yes. At the urging of Detective Jenkins, Ms. Sage came to the emergency room to be checked out. The Detective had instructed me to take a blood sample and have it checked for possible drugging and to check Ms. Sage for a possible sexual assault."

"Were you able to complete those tests?"

"Yes. Ms. Sage cooperated and came in. I was able to obtain blood and fluid samples and forward them to the lab."

"Do you know if Ms. Sage had been sexually assaulted?"

"From a doctor's perspective, it looked like Ms. Sage had been sexually active."

"How could you tell?"

"The swab had substances on it similar to what one would find after one has had sexual intercourse."

"What did the blood test reveal doctor?"

"Traces of sleeping pills."

"Anything else?"

"No."

"Thank you Doctor for coming down to testify."

Attorney White remained seated at the defense table. Judge Benson asked, "Your witness Mr. White."

"Doctor, could you ascertain if Ms. Sage had consensual sex or not?"

"If you mean did I see any bruising in that regard? The answer is no."

"I have no other questions for this witness."

"Doctor Warren, you may step down."

"Ms. Levine, please call you next witness," said Judge Benson.

"I'd like to call Doctor Peter Stone."

Doctor Stone took the stand and was sworn in.

"Doctor Stone, please tell us where you work?"

"I am an emergency room doctor at Cape Cod Hospital."

"Did you attend to a Ms. Fletcher?"

"Yes."

"Can you tell us what you found."

"Sure, Ms. Fletcher had been brought in by the paramedics. She had a laceration on her head along with scratches, a few bumps and bruises. It looked like she had been in a fight."

"A fight. Did she say she had been in a fight?"

"No. But when you work in the ER long enough, you get to know when it looks like a fight."

"What did you do for Ms. Fletcher?"

"I sutured the cut on her head and applied a topical antibiotic to her scratches."

"Did you check her for a sexual attack?"

"No. Ms. Fletcher insisted I only look at her exterior injuries."

"Did she say why she didn't want to be checked for a sexual attack?"

"No. She just didn't want any additional attention beyond fixing the cut on her head. As a matter of fact, she wanted to get out of the hospital as soon as possible."

"Why do you think she wanted to get out?"

"I think the hospital made her nervous. Some people get that way."

"Is there anything else?"

"No."

"Your witness."

Attorney White seated at the defense table said, "Only one question Doctor Stone. Do you know if Ms. Fletcher had her underwear on when you attended to her?"

"I don't know."

"Thank you Doctor Stone. I have no further questions for this witness."

Attorney Levine called lab technician Vince Morgan to the stand.

"Mr. Morgan, please tell us what your job involves."

"Sure. I work for the regional lab attached to Cape Cod Hospital as a technician. We perform analysis there for the hospital and for the local police departments."

"Are you familiar with the evidence in this case?"

"Yes."

"Please tell us what you know."

"Over the period of a few weeks, I had been asked to examine clothing and fluid samples found at the scene of some of the attacks. The police had requested additional examination of fluids from certain suspects and victims and asked to have the evidence compared to the samples taken. I was able to identify samples provided in the Fletcher, Sage and Kent cases."

"Can you tell us whose DNA you found in each case?"

"In the Fletcher case, I found DNA from Kenny Brown, Lou Tomlinson and Tom Bowman. In the Linda Sage case, I found DNA from Kenny Brown and Tom Bowman. In the Sue Kent case, a zip-lock bag and condom were examined and DNA from Tom Bowman was identified."

"Anything else Mr. Morgan?"

"No."

"Your witness."

"Mr. Morgan, you have identified DNA from fluids from a number of men. Some DNA and hairs from my client were also identified. How do you explain your findings."

"I don't explain them. I only report what I find."

"Did you find any fluids matching my clients DNA on anything directly from any of the victims?"

"Mr. Bowman's semen was present on the items tested for Ms. Sage. Hairs belonging to Mr. Bowman were identified in the other cases."

"How did you come to identify Mr. Bowman as a match to the hairs submitted to the lab and as the person whose semen was on the condom in the Kent situation?"

"I was asked to examine another two condoms by Detective Jenkins. Those condoms proved to contain fluid from Mr. Bowman. The DNA from the condoms, the hairs collected and the fluid sample provided by Mr. Bowman all matched. They belonged to Tom Bowman."

"Do you know how the police obtained the condom with Mr. Bowman's DNA in them?"

"I don't know."

"Did either of those condoms identify any other person?"

"Yes. Both had DNA on the outside belonging to Katherine Sterns."

"Thank you Mr. Morgan. No further questions."

Judge Benson excused Mr. Morgan. "It is nearing noontime. We'll break for lunch and continue at one-thirty. Attorney Levine, you can call your next witness at that time."

"Thank you your Honor. I'd like to ask Detective Jenkins, Officer Trudy and Captain Tomlinson to be prepared to take the stand after the lunch break."

Judge Benson spoke to his assistant and instructed her to ask the witnesses to be ready when court resumed.

Chapter 22

Detective Jenkins and Katherine Sterns went to the Harborside Restaurant for lunch. They both ordered the fish and chips. Katherine had a martini, Jenkins a diet coke. There was a commotion by the main door. When Jenkins looked up, Kenny Brown and Tom Bowman were in a scuffle. Jenkins got up and went over.

"What's going on?" Jenkins asked.

"Bowman followed you here. I followed him from the courthouse. He waited in the parking lot for a while and then came in. That's when I confronted him. He made up a lame excuse that he was reading something in his car before he came in but I think he's after Kat."

Jenkins turned and looked back at the table where he had been seated. Katherine was eating her lunch pretty much ignoring the drama taking place.

"I don't know what this is all about, but I think you two should leave now," Jenkins said pointing to the door.

"I'll see you back at court Bowman." Kenny said as he threw up his arm to push Tom Bowman away and then he left.

"I only came here to get a take out order. I have no idea what's wrong with him. He's crazy."

The hostess came back to the podium with a bag in her hand. "Order for Mr. Bowman?"

Jenkins looked at the hostess and the bag. "You might be right about lunch takeout Mr. Bowman, but if I were you, I would avoid Mr. Brown."

"I'm not avoiding anyone Detective. You saw that crazy man. The next time he does something like that, I want him arrested."

"Bowman, if I were you, I'd just let it go."

"Well, you're not me and I'm getting a little tired of being blamed for everything."

Tom Bowman paid the hostess, picked up his order and left.

Detective Jenkins turned and walked back to the table. Katherine was just finishing her lunch. She said, "What was that all about?"

"Just a misunderstanding."

"It sure looked like Kenny was going to come down on Tom."

"I think Mr. Brown jumped to conclusions."

"Maybe, maybe not," was her response as she smiled and picked up her martini.

Jenkins sat and ate his lunch. After a few minutes, he looked at his watch. It was ten minutes after one. "We have to get going. I'm on the stand this afternoon and court reconvenes at one thirty."

"Can't we have one more?" Katherine asked as she finished her drink.

"No. I really have to get back."

"How about tonight then?"

"We'll see."

Jenkins paid the tab and the two went back to the courthouse. They arrived at the courtroom just as Attorney Levine called Detective Frank Jenkins to the stand.

Frank Jenkins took the stand and was sworn in. Attorney Levine had a document in her hand when she approached the witness stand.

"Detective Jenkins, can you tell the court what this document represents?" She handed the document to Jenkins.

Jenkins looked the document over, "Yes, this is a lab report. It shows the results of DNA tests performed on persons and materials I submitted to the lab."

"Are there more than one request contained in the report?"

"Yes. You can see here where I had requested tests on materials and fluids on the dates specified." Jenkins pointed to a column on the report under the heading of Date.

"Can you summarize the report for the court?"

"Sure. The first request is from the Fletcher case and was to have a pair of woman's underwear tested for possible DNA."

"Did the test reveal anything?"

"Yes. The lab was able to identify DNA from dried material on the underwear."

"To whom did the DNA belong?"

"Kenny Brown, Captain Tomlinson and Tom Bowman all matched."

"Captain Tomlinson. Are you saying the Captain had sex with Ms. Fletcher?"

"No, I only know what the report states."

"You said the report identified Tom Bowman. Is that true?"

"Yes, his hairs were found on the underwear."

"And how about the second entry?"

Jenkins read the report further. "In this instance, I had requested testing on a condom found at the scene of one of the attacks."

"Was the lab able to identify to whom the evidence belonged?"

"Yes. The DNA belonged to Mr. Tom Bowman."

"Was there any other DNA found on the condom?"

"Yes. On the outside of the condom, Ms. Stern's DNA was found."

"How do you explain Ms. Stern's DNA being found on a condom retrieved from the scene of Ms. Kent's attack?"

"Either Mr. Bowman had used the condom when he had sex with Ms. Sterns and was about to use it again or the condom was planted at the scene to confuse the police."

"Could Mr. Bowman have planted the condom at the scene?"

"I guess he could have but I can't imagine why he'd want to implicate himself."

"Detective, what about the next entry?"

"This entry shows the results performed on another condom. In this instance, the test confirmed DNA from Kenny Brown and hairs from Tom Bowman were present."

"So, Tom Bowman's hairs were found on the condom. Do you think this would indicate Mr. Bowman handled the evidence?"

"No."

"No? If he didn't, who did?"

"I don't know."

"Of all the information contained in this report, have the police arrived at any conclusions?"

"Based on what we found, Mr. Bowman was involved in the attacks."

"Is there anything else you have to support your findings?"

"Yes. Ms. Sterns provided me with a condom from a sexual encounter she had with Mr. Bowman. She asked me to have it tested. The condoms she provided were used by the lab to identify Mr. Bowman's hairs which up to that point in time had been unidentified."

"That's all Detective Jenkins. Your witness."

Attorney White stood and approached.

"Detective Jenkins, are you sure Mr. Bowman committed sexual attacks on some of the women identified in this case?"

"I don't know if he sexually attacked any of them or not. I just know what the evidence suggests."

"Ah, suggests. Didn't you have a conversation with Mr. Bowman regarding the attacks?"

"Yes."

"What did Mr. Bowman say?"

"He said he was only trying to scare the women but that he hadn't committed any sexual act on any of them."

"Did he say why he struck any of the women?"

"He specifically said he didn't hit any of them."

"Did he say why he scratched the women?"

"He said he didn't scratch any of them."

"So why are you so sure he is your man?"

"DNA doesn't lie."

"It might not lie, but it might not tell you everything."

"No further questions at this time your Honor but I'd like to reserve the right to recall this witness at a later time."

Frank Jenkins was excused.

Next Attorney Levine called Officer Trudy.

"Officer Trudy, you responded to a number of the cases, didn't you?"

"Yes."

"Can you tell the court about Ms. Sage's attack?"

161

"Sure. Detective Jenkins had formulated a theory about the attacks. There were a group of women who were friends and a few women who had not been attacked from the group yet and Detective Jenkins wanted us to follow the two he thought were the most likely to be attacked next."

"Who were you assigned to follow?"

"Detective Jenkins and I went undercover one night at Sundancers. I was assigned to follow Linda Sage and he followed Katherine Sterns."

"Did the Detective have a relationship with Ms. Sterns?"

"I don't know. I try not to speculate about anyone."

"When you followed Ms. Sage, what happened?"

"I followed her home and parked down the street. Ms. Sage went into her house. I could tell from the pattern of lights going on that she was going to a room at the back of the house. After about fifteen minutes, a vehicle came down the street with its lights off. It parked just past Ms. Sage's house. Someone got out of the car and went into the house. I got out of my car and worked my way around to the back of the house. From my vantage point, I could see into a bedroom. I observed a person in a hooded sweatshirt standing over a naked body on the bed. The person standing was squeezing something out of a bag onto the naked body. That's when I tripped on the downspout making a racket."

"Were you able to apprehend the attacker?"

"No. I fell over and by the time I got around to the front of the house, the person I had seen through the window was leaving the scene in the vehicle."

"Do you know what kind of vehicle the person was driving?"

"Yes, it was a Jeep."

"Did you get the license plate number?"

"Yes, but it wasn't a number."

"What do you mean?"

"It was a vanity plate."

"Did you write it down?"

"Yes."

"What did it say?"

"FishCC."

"Did you check with the station regarding the plate?"

"Yes."

"What did you find out?"

"FishCC is registered to a Tom Bowman."

"That's all I have for this witness."

Attorney White stood, "Officer Trudy, did you see my client driving the Jeep that night?"

"I saw someone in a hooded sweatshirt. I didn't see the person's face but I did see someone standing over the body holding something and I did see someone drive away in Mr. Bowman's vehicle."

"Did you find anything?"

"Yes, a condom. It was found on the front lawn."

"Did you have it tested?"

"Yes."

"What did the test reveal?"

"It showed DNA from Tom Bowman on the inside."

"What about the outside?"

"The lab technician indicated the condom looked like it had been cleaned up as the only thing on the outside contained traces of cleaning substances."

"So the condom didn't contain anything tying it to Ms. Sterns did it?"

"No."

"No further questions."

Attorney White started to walk back to the defense table when he stopped and turned back, "Just one more question Officer Trudy. Have you had sex with Detective Jenkins?"

"Why do you ask?"

"I was just wondering if there might be some reason why Detective Jenkins might want my client convicted."

"Do I have to answer the question?" She asked as she turned to face the Judge.

"Yes," Judge Benson responded.

"I had sex with Detective Jenkins recently."

There was a hush in the courtroom when she responded. Katherine could be heard in the back of the room saying, "That Bitch. I knew he slept with her."

"Order in the court," said Judge Benson. "I think we are done for the day. Court will reconvene at ten tomorrow.

Chapter 23

Court began at ten. Judge Benson spoke to his assistant for a few minutes then said, "Will counsel for both parties please approach the bench?"

Attorney Levine and Attorney White came forward.

"Ms. Levine, I understand you only have one more witness?"

"Yes your Honor."

"Mr. White, your witness list only shows Mr. Bowman and Ms. Sterns. Do you plan on calling anyone else?"

"I'm reserving the right to recall Detective Jenkins. Other than him, Mr. Bowman and Ms. Sterns will be my only witnesses."

"All right. If all goes well, I'd expect deliberations can begin this afternoon or possibly tomorrow."

"Thank you your Honor," said Attorney Levine.

"Then please step back and call your witness."

Attorney Levine called Captain Tomlinson.

"Mr. Tomlinson, please state your name and occupation?"

"Lou Tomlinson. I'm Chief of Police for the Town of Dennis."

"Captain, are you familiar with the specifics in this case?"

"Yes. Detective Jenkins and Officer Trudy report to me. I have reviewed information regarding this case regularly."

"Captain, are regular briefings held at the police department?"

"Yes, every shift."

"What kind of information is exchanged?"

"The duty officer reviews current issues and important events."

"Has this case been part of the daily briefings?"

"Yes. After each attack, the written report submitted by the investigating officer is made available to the duty Officer who reviews it at the shift change meeting."

"Can you tell us if Mr. Bowman's name ever came up during any of these shift meetings?"

"Yes. After the third attack, Detective Jenkins had a theory about the attacks. He had prepared a report, which was reviewed at the shift change meetings the next day. In his report, he requested any officer seeing Mr. Bowman or Mr. Bowman's vehicle, to take a note of the location, date and time and report it back to him."

"Do you know if he received any feedback on his request?"

"Yes. Officer Trudy had responded a few times. After her response, Detective Jenkins requested Officer Trudy be assigned to assist him with his investigation."

"Was she assigned to him?"

"On an as needed basis."

"What does that mean?"

"At any time during her shift, she could be redirected to assist Detective Jenkins whenever he requested her assistance."

"Is Officer Trudy a good officer?"

"Yes. Her performance reports have been stellar. She is a model officer."

"I object your honor. What does all this questioning about Officer Trudy have to do with Mr. Bowman?"

"Your Honor, Officer Trudy's testimony is paramount to the prosecution's case against Mr. Bowman. Her credibility and her first hand observations are very important in proving Mr. Bowman's guilt."

"I'll allow it counselor, but please move it along."

"Yes your Honor."

"Captain Tomlinson. Have you ever known DNA evidence to be wrong?"

"No. My understanding is DNA evidence is one hundred percent accurate. In most cases, when confronted with hard DNA evidence, the perpetrator usually confesses."

"What kind of evidence does your department have in this case?"

"As you've heard here in court, our investigators have found Mr. Bowman's DNA at the scene and even on the victims in this case. Given his DNA being found multiple times, I'd say he's the person committing these crimes."

"What do you say to the defense attorney's claim that someone else planted the evidence?"

"Unlikely. I've never heard of anyone preserving DNA matter and then placing it around multiple crime scenes."

"Thank you Captain."

Attorney White stood and walked to the witness stand.

"Captain, you say you never heard of anyone planting DNA materials around multiple crime scenes. Does your comment mean it might be possible?"

"Possible, maybe, but I never heard of anyone doing something like that."

"Use of the word *maybe* might indicate something less than one hundred percent now, wouldn't it?" Attorney White asked as he turned around to face Tom Bowman. "In fact, if someone were to have saved Mr. Bowman's used condoms, then such a person might have been able to give the illusion of Mr. Bowman's presence someplace where Mr. Bowman had not been, doing something Mr. Bowman did not do. Isn't it a possibility, Captain?"

"I guess."

"Captain Tomlinson, isn't it true that Detective Jenkins and Officer Trudy have had a relationship which goes beyond their police duties?"

"I'm not sure what you mean."

"Oh come now Captain. You know what I mean."

"I don't get involved in the officers' personal lives so long as they perform their official duties properly."

"Is that a yes or no?"

"I don't know."

"Do you know if Detective Jenkins has had a personal relationship with Ms. Sterns?"

"Yes. I have spoken with him about his relationship with Ms. Sterns a few times."

"What was the nature of those conversations?"

"I reminded him not to let his relationship with Ms. Sterns interfere with his job."

"How did he respond?"

"He said he understood."

"Did you ever see Detective Jenkins with Ms. Sterns or any of the victims in this case in any non-official capacity?"

Captain Tomlinson was starting to sweat. He took out his handkerchief and wiped his brow. "Yes."

"Can you tell us more?"

"On one occasion, I saw Detective Jenkins exiting the Route 28 motel. He had been there with Ms. Sage."

"Why were you at the motel?"

"I had a meeting with someone."

"A meeting at a motel. Come on Captain, why were you there?"

Captain Tomlinson was visibly sweating now. His hair was all wet and he constantly wiped his brow. Tomlinson looked around the courtroom. He saw Tina Fletcher seated in the second row. Behind her he could see Katherine Sterns and Detective Jenkins. At the back of the room, he saw a face, which he was very familiar with, his wife.

"I was meeting with Ms. Fletcher."

"Isn't she one of the victims in this case as well?"

"Yes."

"What kind of meetings is it that the police have at the Route 28 motel? Detective Jenkins was there with Linda Sage. You were there with Ms. Fletcher," Attorney White turned towards Tom Bowman, "And we are here trying Tom Bowman when all the while the Police Chief and his lead Detective are conducting so called interviews at the Route 28 Motel? What is one to think Captain?"

"Think what you want. We were investigating the attacks."

"Oh, everyone can see you were. Is it standard procedure to take witnesses to a motel to conduct interviews Captain?"

Attorney Levine stood and objected.

"Captain Tomlinson isn't on trial here your Honor, Mr. Bowman is."

"Sustained. Please move on Mr. White."

"I have no further questions for this witness."

169

"You're excused," said Judge Benson.

As Captain Tomlinson stood, they heard a door slam loudly. When Tomlinson looked to the back of the room, his wife had left.

Attorney Levine called Katherine Sterns to the stand. After swearing her in, she sat down.

"Ms. Sterns, please tell the court how you know Mr. Bowman."

"Mr. Bowman and my deceased husband had been friends for a long time. One day a little over a year ago, the two went out for a day of fishing. Sam didn't return. He died after spending a few days and nights on an ice floe."

"Do you blame Mr. Bowman for your husband's death?"

"I think he had a lot to do with Sam's death. Since the crime scene where Sam died disappeared when the ice broke up, there was little the police could do to gather evidence."

"So you think a crime was committed?"

"I don't know."

"Ms. Sterns, have you ever been romantically involved with Mr. Bowman?"

"By romantically involved do you mean have I ever had sex with him?"

"Yes, that's what I'm asking?"

"Yes. I had sex with Mr. Bowman once just before Sam died and again recently."

"So you admit to being with him recently?"

"Yes. I thought I was over my anger towards Tom now that a year has passed, but I guess I really wasn't."

"So you had sex with him. Interesting anger. Did you ever ask Mr. Bowman to attack any of the victims in this case?"

"No."

170

"Did you ever go to any of the crime scenes where the victims were attacked?"

"I don't know specifically. Since I know all the victims and have been to each of their places numerous times, I guess you could say I have been to the crime scenes."

"Have you ever been to any of the crime scenes which are not residences of the victims in this case?"

"Let me see. Ann Benard was attacked up at Chapin Beach. I have been there before. Tina was attacked at Mayflower Beach and I have been there before."

"Were you at any of the locations on any of the nights when any of the attacks took place?"

"I don't think so."

"So to your knowledge, Mr. Bowman acted on his own in committing these attacks?"

"I guess."

Attorney White stood. "I object your Honor. Counsel is leading the witness.

"Overruled."

Attorney Levine continued, "Ms. Sterns, have you ever collected used condoms from the men you've been with?"

"I'm a neat person who cleans up afterwards, I'd say yes."

"Do you have any of the used condoms in your possession?"

"On me?"

"Or at your residence?"

"There might be one or two at my home. It all depends on whether the trash has been put out or not."

"Thank you Ms. Sterns. No more questions."

Attorney White was quick to jump up.

"Ms. Sterns, if we were to look in your freezer right now what would we find?"

171

"Frozen stuff."

"Would we find any used condoms in there?"

Attorney Levine said, "I object your honor. Ms. Sterns isn't on trial here."

"Sustained."

Attorney White next asked, "Ms. Sterns, can you tell us the names of all of the men you've been with?"

Attorney Levine again said, "I object."

Judge Benson again said, "Sustained."

Attorney White then said, "Ms. Sterns, have you ever spoken with Detective Jenkins regarding any of the attacks addressed by this case?"

"Yes. Detective Jenkins and I talk about some of the things going on in town from time to time so I'm sure we have talked about the attacks but the information is all public knowledge."

"Ms. Sterns, do you want to see Mr. Bowman convicted in this case?"

Attorney Levine said, "I object. Mr. White is grandstanding."

Judge Benson said, "Sustained."

Attorney White said, "Ms. Sterns."

Before she could finish the sentence, Attorney Levine said, "I object."

Attorney White said, "I haven't asked a question yet your Honor."

"Attorney White is trying to get the court to find Ms. Sterns guilty instead of defending his own client your Honor."

"I agree. Sustained. Mr. White, do you have any other pertinent questions for this witness?"

"I guess not your Honor."

"In that case, you are excused Ms. Sterns."

"Ms. Levine, do you have any other witnesses?"

"The prosecution rests your Honor."

"Mr. White, it's getting late in the afternoon. Why don't you pick it up first thing in the morning."

"Yes your Honor."

"Court will convene at 9 am promptly tomorrow," said Judge Benson as he rose, leveled his gavel and left the bench.

Chapter 24

Dee Crowe looked out the window. She had been making a frozen margarita for a patron when she said, "Get ready Ron. It looks like court just got out."

Ron Jessup looked out into the parking lot and saw a group of people approaching the door. "Looks like it. I better call Margarita."

Ron picked up the phone and pressed Harry Adams extension. "Harry, is Margarita in with you?"

"Yeah."

"Will she be coming back into the bar soon?"

"We see them Ron. She'll be right in."

Margarita had been in Harry's office, which is located in the building in front of Sundancers. Harry had been having talks with all of the employees trying to see what could be done to improve the place.

"Margarita, you'd better get back. We can continue this talk at a later time."

"Sure. I'll think about what you've already asked. I'm sure I'll have some ideas."

"Thanks."

Margarita left Harry's office. As she walked across the parking lot Tom Bowman came around the corner after parking in the boat ramp lot. Margarita said, "Why are you parking there Tom? There are still spots left in our lot."

"Just being cautious."

"Do you think someone will do something to your car?"

"I don't know but there are some people in there who aren't real happy with me right now."

He looked across the parking lot and saw Katherine Sterns walking in with Detective Jenkins. "And there's one who wants to see something bad happen to me."

Margarita turned to look. "Katherine?"

"Haven't you been following the testimony?"

"I hear a little from time to time."

"Well, I think she made it perfectly clear today that she thinks I had something to do with her husband's death."

"Wasn't it your idea to go ice fishing on the trip where he died?"

"Yeah, but Sam and I were always trying new places."

"I don't know Tom."

"For some reason, she thinks there was more to it than what happened. It did happen exactly as I described."

"She is still hurting Tom and she holds you responsible."

"But why would she do all those things?"

"Like what?"

"Like sleeping with everyone just to get back at me."

"Oh, I don't think she sleeps with guys to get back at you. It's her nature."

"You think?"

"That's just my opinion Tom. You'll have to excuse me. I have to get to work. Ron said things are getting real busy inside."

Margarita went in through the kitchen door. Tom walked around to the main door and went in. As he entered the bar, everyone turned and looked at him. There was a hush over the whole bar. Finally, Ron looked at Tom, "Can I get you something?"

"A beer please."

Tom took up a stool nearest to the door. He paid cash for the beer and took a drink. Ron said, "Do you think it's a good idea for you to come in here Mr. Bowman?"

"I know Harry asked me not to come back in, but I think it's pretty clear from the testimony that I didn't do all the things I've been accused of."

"Maybe so Mr. Bowman, but Harry was pretty specific."

Just then, Harry came out of the kitchen and walked over to Tom Bowman.

"Bowman, I told you before, you're not welcome in my place."

"I know. I just wanted to stop in and apologize."

"Apologize? If I were you, I'd stay as far away from these people as possible."

"They were in court. They heard what was said. I think they know I didn't do all the things I've been accused of doing."

"Even if you're innocent Mr. Bowman, you're not welcome in here. I don't need any trouble."

As Harry was saying the words, Kenny Brown came up behind him, "You might not want trouble Harry but Bowman just found some," and he let go a punch to the side of Tom Bowman's head. Tom fell sideways off the stool and hit the floor. Kenny was on him before anyone could react. Harry made an unsuccessful attempt to put his arms around Kenny. Kenny let go a flurry of jabs leaving Bowman curled in a fetal position on the floor.

Detective Jenkins came running over from the side of the bar and ordered Kenny to stop. When he didn't, Jenkins grabbed his right arm right after Kenny threw another punch at Bowman and pulled it behind Kenny's back. Jenkins put a handcuff on it. Harry grabbed the other arm and pulled it around Kenny's back so Jenkins could handcuff that arm as well.

"Cool down Mr. Brown," said Detective Jenkins.

"He's guilty and needs to pay for what he did," said Kenny in a heated tone.

"You should be after her, not me," said Bowman as he got up nodding at Katherine who was standing over by the DJ booth.

Margarita came over from behind the bar with a towel and handed it to Detective Jenkins. Bowman had blood coming from his nose. Detective Jenkins applied the towel to Bowman's face.

"She's the reason all this is happening. She's the one who collected your DNA and spread it around the victims, not me."

Detective Jenkins said, "I think you should probably leave Mr. Bowman. Don't say anything else. You have already created an incident."

"What are you going to do, arrest me? I'll press charges against that goon."

"Just get out of here."

Tom Bowman turned and walked to the door. As he was leaving, Ed Phillips got up from where he was seated and followed Bowman out the door. When Bowman had left, Detective Jenkins took the cuffs off Kenny, "Mr. Brown, you need to control your temper and hope he doesn't follow through on his threat."

"I'll get him."

"Are you threatening him?"

Kenny turned and walked back to where he had been seated at the bar. As he walked past Katherine, she said, "Thanks Kenny for defending my honor."

"Don't mention it Kat. That guy needs a beating."

Ed quickened his pace as he left the bar. He rounded the corner of the building just in time to see Tom Bowman open the door to his car in the boat lot. "Hey Tom, wait a minute."

Tom Bowman stood with his door open looking at Ed.

"What Ed, you after me too?"

"Tom, I heard what you said. I think Jenkins is covering for Katherine. She isn't as innocent as they think."

"Thanks Ed but this is between Kat and me."

"Me too. She has my DNA and might spread it around. If she ever got me involved and word got out, my business would go to hell. I have to maintain a positive, clean reputation. Someone needs to hold her accountable for what she's done."

"Well, I don't need any help. Thanks again."

"I know some of the other guys have some concerns as well. Maybe we should all get together and talk about it sometime."

"Thanks Ed, but no thanks. I can't get involved in anything while this trial is hanging over my head."

"We're here Tom if you need our help, except Kenny of course. He's just a dumb hothead."

"Thanks Ed."

Tom closed the door to his car and started it. After he left, Ed went back into the bar. Ed took up the stool he had been seated at which was right next to Kenny Brown.

"Ed, did you get a swing in at Bowman?" Kenny asked.

"Kenny, you might have Tom all wrong. He has a point about Katherine. She isn't as innocent in all of this as you think."

"Look Ed. I know you've been friends with Bowman. I see you two fishing up in the bay from time to time. That guy just isn't any good."

"I think you might be wrong, Kenny, but I'm not going to try to change your mind."

As the two were talking, Sue Kent walked up behind Kenny and put her arms around him. "Our hero."

Kenny turned to see Sue. She had on a tight fitting halter-top revealing quite a bit.

"I just don't like that guy," said Kenny putting his arm around Sue. "Want a drink?"

"Sure Kenny. You have any plans tonight?"

"Now I do."

Kenny ordered a beer for himself and a drink for Sue. Margarita made the drink, grabbed the beer and put them on the bar in front of Kenny. Kenny got up, took their drinks off the bar, put his arm around Sue and walked out to the back deck.

Tina Fletcher came over to where Kenny had been seated. She sat at the bar and ordered a martini.

"Ed, are you and Kenny planning on getting back at Bowman?"

"Why would you think that?"

"I saw the two of you talking. It looked real animated."

"I was just telling Kenny he might not be seeing all the facts."

"What do you mean?"

179

"I told him some of what we heard in court is different than what we thought. There is more to the story than we all know about."

"Are you talking about the attacks or Kat's relationships?"

"Yes and yes."

"Do you know something the rest of us don't know?"

"I'm just saying there might be more to it."

"Kat's our friend. I think we understand what she's been through and how she's been affected by all of this."

"Really?"

"Yea. It's a woman thing."

"I guess I'll never understand it then."

"Guess not. Why don't you buy me a drink? We can talk some more and later we might even compare notes."

"Sure. Your place or mine?"

"Mine."

Jenkins had walked over to Katherine after taking the cuffs off Kenny.

"Why did you put the cuffs on Kenny? Tom's the one you should have cuffed."

"Mr. Brown was the one throwing the punches. I had to eliminate the aggressor."

"I guess. I could tell Harry wasn't happy with a fight breaking out."

"Especially during happy hour. It's one thing late at night when the young crowd's been here for a while, drinking and all. But something like this just isn't good business for him at family time."

"I heard him talking with Dee the other day and he was saying exactly that. He said business is off twenty five percent since the attacks."

"I think the case is about to wrap up. Business should be able to get back to normal once that happens."

"That will make Harry happy."

"Me too. This case is causing problems in a lot of ways."

Jenkins pointed to Captain Tomlinson seated in the dining area with his wife who were deep in conversation. "I hope Captain can get himself out of his predicament."

"I don't know, she looks pretty mad," said Kat looking at the Captain and his wife.

"Just the fact she's here with him talking is a good sign."

"Don't be too sure," Kat said pointing. Tomlinson's wife had just slapped him in the face and walked out.

"You're right. That doesn't look good."

Captain Tomlinson got up and went to the bar. Without sitting down, he asked Ron for a shot of whisky. He downed the shot and asked for another. Jenkins got up and went over to him. Kat followed.

"Captain, anything I can do?"

Tomlinson turned to see the two. "You two have already done enough."

Tomlinson threw a twenty on the bar, walked to the door and left.

Chapter 25

When court resumed at 9 am the next morning, Attorney White called Tom Bowman to the stand.

"Tell us in your own words Mr. Bowman what you can about these charges."

Tom Bowman looked around the courthouse and let his eyes finally settle on Katherine Sterns who was seated next to Detective Jenkins. After telling how he had come to know Ms. Sterns and her husband, he told the story again in detail about the unfortunate outing where Sam Sterns died. His eyes remained fixed on Katherine throughout. Finally, he reached the part of his explanation of Sam's funeral.

"When Sam died, he had asked me to look after Katherine. He told me he had bought her a gift for their anniversary and asked me to make sure she got it. When I tried to fulfill his wishes, she took it the wrong way and accused me of coming on to her. She was wrong. I was only following through with my best friend's wishes."

Tom looked up again at Katherine and then continued.

"Shortly after Sam's death, my family and I moved to Virginia. Things didn't work out there. My wife ended up divorcing me and then I moved back to Cape Cod. When I came back, I saw Katherine one night in a bar. Then I saw her again at another bar and we started to talk. Enough time had gone by and we were able to start a new relationship. I didn't realize she had such resentment for me and never suspected I was being set up."

Attorney Levine objected. Judge Benson agreed and instructed the jury to ignore Mr. Bowman's statements regarding Ms. Sterns. Bowman started to turn red. He continued, "Ms. Sterns had sex with me a number of times over a few weeks. She talked to me about some of the women who frequented the same bars she did and indicated she wished there wouldn't be so much competition. I knew what she was implying so I took it upon myself to put the women on edge by scaring them. I didn't assault them."

Attorney White said, "Go on."

"I didn't realize Ms. Sterns was saving the condoms I used and then would spread the contents of those condoms around implicating me in sexual attacks. I guess I was fooled by her."

"So why did you do those things?" Attorney White asked.

"I wanted her to look favorably on me, which she did."

"How?"

"We had a lot of sex, good sex."

"So you're saying you did what you did for her but that you didn't assault any of the victims previously mentioned."

"That's right."

"How do you explain the physical things that happened to the victims like being hit on the head and scratches?"

"Ann Benard fell and hit her head and so did Tina Fletcher. I don't know about Sue Kent. I didn't do anything to her. I put a pill I got from Ms. Sterns' into Linda Sage's drink, but didn't do anything else. I didn't even go into her home."

"So you're saying someone else sexually attacked those women?"

"It wasn't me. That's all I know," said Bowman looking at Katherine Sterns.

"Mr. Bowman, were you at Chapin beach the night of the attack on Ms. Benard?"

"Yes."

"Were you at Mayflower beach on the night of the attack against Ms. Fletcher?"

"Yes."

"Did you put sleeping pills into Ms. Sage's drink on the night she was attacked?"

"Yes."

"Was your vehicle the vehicle identified by Officer Trudy at Ms. Kent's house the night of the attack on Ms. Kent?"

"That's my understanding now, but I didn't know about it at the time."

"I have no more questions for Mr. Bowman."

Attorney Levine stood and walked past Attorney White as Attorney White returned to the defense table.

"Mr. Bowman, let's start from the first attack. You said you did not strike Ms. Benard. Is that correct?"

"That's correct."

"The police found a rock at the scene about the size of a softball with Ms. Benard's blood on it. You say she must have hit her head on it when she fell. Is that correct?"

"Yes."

"Where did you park your vehicle when you went to Chapin Beach to surprise Ms. Benard?"

"I parked down the off-road access past the parking lot behind one of the dunes."

"The police did find a pile of rocks similar in size to the one found at the place where Ms. Benard was attacked. The pile was found between the dunes just past the off-road access. The police also found a set of automobile tracks near the pile of rocks that looked like someone had recently parked there. Are you sure you didn't take a rock from that pile and use it to strike Ms. Benard?"

"Yes, I am sure. I didn't hit her with anything."

"Mr. Bowman, in the attack on Ms. Fletcher, you said you hid behind large boulders on the beach where you surprised Ms. Fletcher. You said she fell backwards and hit her head on one of the boulders. Is that true?"

"Yes, she fell back and hit her head."

"Didn't you push her?"

"Only slightly."

"But you did touch her, didn't you?"

"Yes."

"Mr. Bowman, do you own a Jeep?"

"Yes."

"What is the license plate number on your Jeep?"

"It isn't a number. It's a vanity plate."

"Can you tell us what it is?"

"FISHCC."

"Does that mean something?"

"I like to fish and requested it when I registered the Jeep. FISHCC stands for Fish Cape Cod."

"So you're a fisherman?"

"Yes, I like to fish."

"Have you fished at Chapin Beach before?"

"Yes."

"Have you fished at Mayflower Beach before?"

"Yes."

"So you're familiar with those areas, isn't that so?"

"Yes."

"Mr. Bowman, in the attack on Ms. Sage, you indicated you put a sleeping pill in Ms. Sage's drink when you were having a drink with her at Sundancers, didn't you?"

"Yes."

"Why did you put pills in her drink?"

"I thought she was going to take me home with her and I wanted to make her more receptive."

"Do sleeping pills make women more receptive?"

"I had heard that sleeping pills when taken with alcohol slow down one's reactions."

"Doesn't the person end up falling asleep?"

"Sometimes."

"So you were hoping to go home with her and have sex with her when the sleeping pills took effect?"

"Something like that."

"Did you have sex with Ms. Sage?"

"No. Another man, Kenny Brown, talked Ms. Sage into going to the beach to go skinny-dipping. Ms. Sage ended up leaving Sundancers to go meet him. I didn't join them. Three-ways aren't my thing."

"So you say you didn't go to Ms. Sage's home?"

"No I didn't."

"Did you touch Ms. Sage in any way when you were at Sundancers?"

"I don't remember but if I did it wasn't inappropriate. We were in public."

"Mr. Bowman, is it your testimony that you don't feel you did anything wrong in any of these attacks?"

"As I said, I was only trying to scare the women. I didn't attack them and I definitely didn't sexually assault them."

"I have no further questions for Mr. Bowman."

"Re-direct your Honor," said Attorney White.

"Mr. Bowman, some people might think your presence at some of the places at the time of the attacks would constitute assault and battery. How do you explain your conduct?"

"I didn't physically touch anyone. My presence was more in the form of a surprise conversation, kind of like what kids do at Halloween time. Someone jumping out from behind a bush on a dark night might scare a person and cause them to be cautious. That was the kind of effect I was hoping to instill in the women."

"Are you telling the court that your actions were more like a childish prank?"

"Yes, and I apologize to anyone who was harmed by my actions."

"Thank you Mr. Bowman for your honesty although I have to question whether drugging a woman so you can take advantage of her is causing no harm."

"No further questions."

Tom Bowman was excused. He returned to the defense table.

Judge Benson said, "Mr. White are you ready for summation?"

"Yes your Honor."

"Proceed."

Mr. White picked up a zip-lock bag off the evidence table and approached the jury.

"Ladies and gentlemen of the Jury, you have heard the case presented by the prosecution and the testimony by Mr. Bowman himself. He freely admitted to being present at the time when Ms. Benard and Ms. Fletcher were injured. Mr. Bowman said he was only trying to scare the women in order to gain favors from Ms. Sterns. Ms. Sterns on the other hand made it a point to collect used condoms such as the one in this bag from various men in an attempt to tie those men to crimes she instigated. Ms. Sterns unjustly holds Mr. Bowman responsible for the death of her husband and for her subsequent misfortunes. As a result, she had demonstrated a total disregard for the safety and well being of the victims in this case and for the law. Mr. Bowman may be guilty of poor judgment but that doesn't mean he's a sexual predator. We ask that you return a verdict of not guilty."

Mr. White walked back to the defense table and took his seat.

Judge Benson said, "Ms. Levine are you ready for your summation?"
"Yes your Honor."
"Please proceed."

Attorney Levine stood and faced the jury.

"Ladies and gentlemen, in this case, you have heard from witnesses and experts. Some of the testimony has been conflicting. However, one fact is not in dispute. Mr. Tom Bowman admitted his presence in the attack on Ms. Benard and Ms. Fletcher. His DNA has been identified in the attack on Ms. Sage. He admitted to putting a drug in Ms. Sage's drink and then going to her house. Officer Trudy positively identified his vehicle as being seen at Ms. Kent's house around the time of the attack on her and his DNA was found at her residence. All of these undisputed facts can only lead to one conclusion. Mr. Bowman is guilty."

Judge Benson instructed the jury as to how to proceed. Then, they left the courtroom for deliberations.

Finally, after an hour or so, the foreman of the jury informed the judge that the jury had reached agreement. Everyone reassembled in the courtroom. Judge Benson said, "Has the jury reached a verdict?"

The foreman, an older gentleman of around sixty-five years of age stood, "We have."

"Would you please read the verdict?" instructed Judge Benson.

"On the charge of battery against Ms. Benard, we find the defendant guilty."

"On the charge of battery against Ms. Fletcher, we find the defendant guilty."

"On the charge of battery against Ms. Kent, we find the defendant not guilty."

"On the charge of battery against Ms. Sage, we find the defendant guilty."

"On the charge of sexual assault against Ms. Benard, we find the defendant not guilty."

"On the charge of sexual assault against Ms. Fletcher, we find the defendant guilty."

"On the charge of sexual assault against Ms. Kent, we find the defendant guilty."

"On the charge of sexual assault against Ms. Sage, we find the defendant guilty."

Judge Benson looked at the jury and asked, "Ladies and gentlemen of the jury, is there anyone in the jury who disagrees with the verdicts?"

No one answered. The all shook their head in a *No* motion.

"Ladies and gentlemen of the jury, thank you for your service. You are excused."

Judge Benson looking at something on his desk said, "I'm scheduling a sentencing hearing for two weeks from today. Any objections?"

Neither attorney objected.

"Mr. Bowman, you remain free on bond until the sentencing hearing. Counsels please submit your sentencing brief by the end of next week. Court is adjourned."

As Tom walked down the aisle, he passed Katherine Sterns, "You'll get yours," and kept walking.

Frank Jenkins leaned over, "What did he say to you?"

"Oh, nothing. He's just upset."

"Well, I'm glad that's over."

"Me too. Let's go to Sundancers and get a drink."

"I could use one myself."

"Are you still on duty?"

"Even if I am, I need a drink."

The two left the courthouse and went to Sundancers. When they walked into the bar, Ed Phillips was seated at the end of the bar by the door. He turned to see Katherine come in and said, "Are you happy now?"

"Don't pay any attention to him," said Frank as he took her arm and guided her to the opposite side of the bar.

"Ed is friendly with Tom. He's probably upset because he's going to lose his fishing partner for a period of time. Speaking of time, how long do you think he'll get?"

"Let's see, I think the charges of battery can carry a sentence of one to two years each. The charges of sexual assault can carry a sentence of five to ten years each."

"That would put him away for a long period of time."

"Don't get your hopes up so soon Kat. This being his first conviction, the Judge will probably go easy. Another thing is the sentences may run concurrent."

"Then he would be out in a few years."

"It might even be less than that. If the Judge is lenient, Bowman might only serve a minimal amount of time with extended probation."

"How will the sentences be determined?"

"Remember the last thing the Judge said. That he wanted briefs by the end of next week?"

"Yea."

"The Judge will use the information submitted and apply his experience in determining an appropriate sentence."

"So the Judge can use his own discretion?"

"Yes. The law dictates the minimums and maximums, but precedent impacts the outcome, too."

"That's good to know."

Dee came over to the two and asked what they wanted. Katherine ordered a dirty martini. Frank ordered a scotch and soda.

"Ordering a stiff one Detective?" asked Dee.

"It's been a trying day."

When Dee walked away, Katherine leaned in to Frank, "I want a stiff one, too."

"I'll bet you do."

"When we're done here, I'm taking you to my place and wiping away all your frustrations."

"I think I like the thought of that," said Frank as he picked up his glass and clinked hers.

"Oh trust me, you'll sleep well, no frustrations whatsoever."

Chapter 26

The two left Sundancers and went to her house. She planned to deliver on her promise.

"Frank, make us a drink if you would. I'd like vodka and soda with a twist of lime. There are limes in the fridge bottom drawer. Use shaved ice instead of cubes. Press the third button from the left on the ice dispenser."

"Any particular kind of vodka?"

"Triple Olive."

"Got it."

Frank retrieved the vodka from Katherine's liquor cabinet and took out two tumblers. Then he took a lime out of the bottom drawer in the refrigerator, cut the lime up and put one wedge in each glass. Next he went to the icemaker on the freezer side of the refrigerator and pressed the shaved ice button. He filled both glasses with half a glass of ice then poured vodka in each glass until it reached the top of the shaved ice. He added club soda to each glass and then squeezed another lime wedge over each glass.

After he finished making the drinks, he opened the freezer. When he looked in, he saw the same box of zip-locks he had seen a few times before. When he checked the bags, he saw three with Kenny Brown's name on them, one with Lou's on it, one with Ed Phillips' name, two with Tommy Anderson's name, one with Tom Bowman's name and the last one didn't have a name on it. He wondered to whom that one belonged. The bag was a different type than the other zip-lock bags.

Frank closed the freezer. He picked up the glasses and walked into the living room. Katherine was standing at the end of the hallway leading to the bedroom with nothing on.

"Come with me Detective. Remember, I promised."

Frank kept walking right to her. He followed her down the hallway and into her bedroom. She took the drinks from his hands and put them on the bureau. Then she turned and unbuttoned his shirt. As she did, he leaned in and kissed her on the neck. She unbuckled his belt and undid his pants allowing them to drop to the floor. She looked down and could see he was primed and ready.

"What do we have here?"

"As if you didn't know."

"Let me see," and she took a hold of both sides of his underwear pulling them down. She pulled them all the way to the floor and then slowly rose along his thighs kissing them as she ascended. Half way up, she stopped and lingered for a few minutes. Her actions were driving him crazy. Finally, he reached down gently placing his hands on the outside of her breasts. He coaxed her on to the bed where they made love for the next half hour.

"Didn't I say I'd make it worth your while?"

"You did."

"Was it?"

"Kat, you always make it worth my while."

"I'm glad you feel that way."

"Me too. Say, remind me in the morning to show you something I have in my jacket pocket, will you?"

"Sure. Want to go again?"

"You're reading my mind," Frank said putting his arms around her.

"I don't have to read your mind Frank," she lowered her hand and squeezed him. "Your subconscious is way ahead of your mind."

Jenkins threw the sheet off and got on top. They kissed a little and then were at it again. After a few minutes, they climaxed at the same time. When done, they both fell back on their pillows finding their own dreams.

Katherine was the first to rise in the morning. She showered, dressed and went to the kitchen. She made coffee and English muffins and slipped them into a warm oven. Jenkins came into the kitchen about a half hour later dressed in just his underwear.

"Frank, last night, you asked me to remind you about something you have in your jacket pocket."

"Yeah, let me get it."

Jenkins went to his jacket in the foyer and took out a brochure. Coming back into the kitchen, he put it on the table. Katherine picked it up and looked at it.

"2016 Olympics, Rio de Janeiro," was the heading on the document.

"What is this?"

"Remember we talked about this when we were in Key West?"

"Something to do with security or something?"

"Yeah. I was part of the security detail assigned to our Olympic team in the past."

"I remember you telling me something about it."

"Well, as I had told you, the Summer Olympics in 2016 are being held in Rio and I was asked to participate again in the security detail."

"What about your job?"

"It's an honor to be asked to support the USOC. The department gets complete funding for anyone who participates plus, the town gets favorable rewards from Washington just for sending someone."

"So your boss will give you the time off?"

"Sure. He's all for it."

"How long will you be away?"

"It's only a meeting every now and then and possibly a few days at a time to make sure everything gets set up properly. Then, I have to be onsite a few days before the Olympics and be there for about two weeks."

"Sounds like it would be interesting?"

"I've done it before although I was younger."

"Do you want to do it again?"

"Yes. I have always wanted to see South America and this would give me a chance to see some of it."

"Then you should do it."

"I'm glad you feel that way Kat. I heard from Fred Travis the other day. He's heading up the security detail. He said he wants me to make a trip with him to Rio next week."

"Next week. What about my hearing?"

"I don't have to leave until the end of the week. Your hearing should be over by then if it starts on Monday."

"But what if it isn't?"

"Listen, I can bring someone with me, all expenses paid. Why don't you come along?"

"I don't know. I'm not sure about this hearing."

"Don't worry, Captain Tomlinson has told me you are all set. He said he thinks everything is going to be dropped."

"What about Tom Bowman?"

"That's a whole different matter. He's going to be sentenced the following week."

"I want to be here for his sentencing."

"I think the Judge has a prelim hearing next week and sentencing the week after. We should be back in a few days, Tuesday at the latest."

"Let's see, if my hearing is Monday and it gets resolved and we leave on Thursday returning the following Monday, I could be back in time."

"Don't worry Kat. It will all work out."

"I'm not as comfortable as you are but if my hearing is over on Monday, then I'll go with you."

"I'm going to make the arrangements. If you cancel, it's on the USOC anyway."

"Ok."

"Listen, I have to get going. I have some things at the station I have to do along with getting this trip put together. I'll call you later on today. Maybe we can get together tonight."

"Oh, tonight? I can't. I have a meeting with Andrew Dunn tonight. I need to see him about some financial matters."

"Weren't you and Andrew close at one time?"

"Yes. When Sam died, Andrew was there for me."

Frank knew what she meant.

"I'm meeting him at Alberto's. I expect the meeting to go through dinner and maybe a little later."

"Then how about I call you later on in the evening?"

"Well, if I'm not home, leave me a message."

"Will do. See you later."

Frank picked up his jacket and left. He went to the station and the first thing he did was send Fred Travis an e-mail telling him he was bringing along a companion and asked Fred to have his secretary take care of the arrangements.

Katherine spent the day working around her place. At two o'clock, she took a shower and dressed for her meeting. She left home around three thirty and drove to Hyannis. Alberto's was not very busy at four o'clock so it was easy to find Andrew seated at the bar having a cocktail.

"Katherine, you look as beautiful as ever," he said as he kissed her on the cheek.

"How are you Andrew?"

"Couldn't be better. The business is doing great."

"I'm glad to hear it. Sterns and Dunn's success is very important to me."

"Business later, what will you have to drink?"

"A dirty martini please."

Andrew ordered her drink. After the bartender delivered it, he made a toast, "To a beautiful woman."

They touched glasses and took sips of their drinks.

"I'm happy to hear things are going well Andrew. That's why I wanted to see you. I want to cash out my 401k with Sterns and Dunn."

"But why Katherine? The investments are doing so well."

"I have my reasons."

"What can I do to change your mind?"

Katherine had always liked Andrew physically. She thought about it for a few minutes. Then said, "Sleep with me tonight."

"What?"

"Take me home with you and sleep with me Andrew. You know I always had a soft spot for you."

"I'm in a relationship right now and I don't think," she stopped by placing a finger to his lips.

"Andrew, if you want me to keep my money in the company stock, you'll make an exception."

"Ok. Let me make a call."

Andrew got up from the bar and went outside. He called his girlfriend and left her a message indicating something had come up and he wouldn't be seeing her that night. When he came back in, he said, "We're all set."

"Good. Now let's have a nice dinner and go to your place."

The two ate talking small talk about past things. About seven o'clock, they finished their drinks and desserts and went to Andrews.

"Make us a drink Andrew."

"Anything particular?"

"You decide."

While Andrew was making drinks, Katherine went into his bedroom and undressed.

"Kat?"

"In here," she responded from the bedroom.

He went down the hall, drinks in hand. As he entered the bedroom, she was lying on the bed, naked.

"Join me?"

He took off his clothes and joined her on the bed. The two moved quickly through foreplay until Katherine knew Andrew was ready.

"Do you have a condom?"

"In the bathroom. Let me get it."

When Andrew went into the bathroom, Katherine could hear the front door close. She got up and walked down the hall. As she stood there at the end of the hall, naked under the hall light, a woman closed the door and looked at her.

"Who are you?" the woman asked.

"A friend of Andrew's," said Kat.

Just then, Andrew came down the hall with an open condom in his hand.

"Julie, what are you doing here?"

"I might ask her the same thing Andy."

"Andy?" said Kat kind of laughing.

Julie stood looking at the two standing there naked.

"Katherine is a business acquaintance," said Andrew.

Julie looked down below Andrew's waist, "I can see the business part, now how about the condom?"

Andrew looked at the condom in his hand and put it behind his back. "It's not what you think Julie."

"It's exactly what I think Andy."

She turned, opened the door, and slammed it behind her.

"I guess she doesn't understand business relationships," said Katherine.

"I'm screwed," said Andrew.

"Speaking of screwing, come with me?" Kat said as she took a hold of his hand and led him back to the bedroom.

"I don't think I can do this now."

"Oh yes you can. Give me a few minutes and you'll think differently."

Andrew just lay back on the bed staring at the ceiling in disbelief. Katherine worked her magic and in a few minutes she was on top working at a vigorous pace. Andrew reached climax around the time Katherine did for the third time.

"You'll get over it," she said as she got off him.

"I don't know. She was really pissed."

"Andrew, she's a woman. You have the goods. She'll be back."

"I can't believe I did this just to keep you from selling your 401k company stock."

"Oh, I'm not keeping the account. I just wanted to have sex with you one more time."

"You bitch."

Katherine got up, got dressed and left closing the door quietly behind her. When Andrew got up, he found the wrapper for the condom but couldn't find the condom itself. Katherine had taken it with her.

Chapter 27

Attorney Levine prepared a brief for Tom Bowman's sentencing. In the brief, Attorney Levine summarized the attacks on the victims and referenced recent similar cases. In the referenced cases of battery, the convicted person received anywhere between six months and two years sentence. In the cases of sexual assault, the convicted person generally received a sentence of no less than two years and the most serious situations received the maximum sentence of ten years. Attorney Levine had suggested a sentence of one year for each of the battery attacks and seven years for each of the sexual assault attacks. Since this was the first conviction for Tom Bowman, it was recommended the sentences for the battery attacks run concurrent, the sentences for the assaults run concurrent and both run concurrent with each other.

In total, Attorney Levine recommended Tom Bowman be sentenced to a total of three one year sentences for the battery charges and three seven year sentences for sexual assault. This recommendation would put Tom Bowman in jail for a total of eight years.

Attorney White knew Tom Bowman had no other record and prepared his brief requesting a minimal sentence. He found prior case history in which the convicted person received a suspended sentence for battery where no significant injury occurred. He found similar precedent in previous sexual assault cases where the convicted person received the minimum sentence in situations where penetration had not been proven. At no time during the trial did the prosecution present nor prove Tom Bowman actually had intercourse with any of the victims. Attorney White thought he had a strong position in recommending a minimum sentence. Of all the sexual assault cases referenced, the minimum sentence Attorney White came across was one year. The brief made reference to all the cases Attorney White used to support his argument.

In summary, Attorney White's brief recommended a minimum sentence of one year, suspended after six months.

Early in the week, Judge Benson received the briefs from both counsel. He read the briefs and formulated his opinion.

On Monday afternoon, Captain Tomlinson and Detective Jenkins were informed by the prosecutor's office that the Judge had received the briefs recommending sentences for Tom Bowman. Detective Jenkins had planned on having dinner with Katherine that night. He'd tell her of the recommendations.

As Katherine and Frank were having dinner, he said, "I was meeting with Tomlinson today when we got a call from the DA."

"What was it about?"

"She said the briefs had been submitted to Judge Benson for Bowman's sentencing."

"Do you know what they were requesting?"

"Attorney Levine asked for three one year terms for battery and three seven year terms for sexual assault."

"I like the sound of those recommendations."

"Don't get giddy just yet. Bowman's Attorney asked for suspended sentences for the battery and a one year term for the sexual assault."

"How could he ask for sentences like that?"

"Bowman doesn't have any priors. The court tends to go easy on first time offenders."

"But he might not be a first time offender. What about Sam?"

"Nothing was ever proven in Sam's case."

"What do you think the Judge will do?"

"Even under the DA's recommendation, the sentences are to run concurrent for the three battery charges and concurrent for the three sexual assault charges."

"What does that mean?"

"All the sentences start on day one, not one after another. Bowman would probably serve no more than seven or eight years."

"Eight. I get twenty seven when I add all the sentences up."

"He'll never get twenty seven. The courts just don't work that way."

"We'll see."

"There really isn't anything you can do about it now Kat. It's in the judges' hands."

"We'll see."

Nothing else was said about the sentencing. The two talked about the upcoming trip to Rio.

"Assuming my case gets resolved satisfactorily, what should I plan on bringing with me to Rio?"

"Do you mean clothing?"

"Yes."

"Well, their weather is pretty much the opposite as what we're having. When we are in fall, they're in spring and vice versa."

"Since its September, their weather should be like our March?" Kat asked.

"Well, not like our March, but warmer. Go online and look up the weather for Rio and you will have a pretty good idea of what to pack."

"Ok. Should I pack any fancy clothes for dinner or functions?"

"I think we can get a night out while we're there. I have a few meetings to go to during the daytime. You can go to the beach or site seeing. Then we can do things together at night."

"I plan on packing for four days even though we're returning on Monday."

"That should work."

"Is there anything special you want me to bring?"

"Just having you there will be special enough."

"Oh, Frank, that's so nice. I'll bring something special for our nights in Rio."

"Like what?"

"You'll have to wait and see."

"Now you've peaked my curiosity."

"Why don't you come with me and I'll give you something to look forward to," she took his hand and pulled on it indicating he should follow her. She led him to the bedroom.

After Frank left the next morning, Katherine called the Barnstable Court House. She asked to speak with Judge Benson and was put through to Judge Benson's assistant.

"Judge Benson's office."

"Hello, this is Katherine Sterns. I'd like to speak with Judge Benson if I may?"

"I'm sorry Ms. Sterns, Judge Benson isn't taking any calls right now."

"Oh, is he in court?"

"No, he is in his office reviewing materials and asked not to be disturbed."

"If he is reviewing materials for the Bowman case, I have information he probably will want to have."

"Why don't you tell me what it is and I'll convey it to the Judge."

"I'd rather not. This will only take a few minutes. I'm sure the Judge will want to hear what I have to tell him."

"Hold on a minute. I'll see if he will talk to you."

"Thank you."

Two minutes later, Benson picked up the phone.

"Ms. Sterns, my assistant said you have information I should be aware of in the Bowman case?"

"Yes your honor."

"Well, what is it you want to tell me."

"I'd rather show you."

"This is rather inappropriate Ms. Sterns."

"Mike, can't we drop the formalities. We know each other from our college days and I want to meet with you to talk with you about Tom Bowman."

"I really can't Ms. Sterns."

"It's Katherine and yes you can. Look Mike, it's in your best interest that you meet with me for a few minutes. Remember the night of your bachelor party?"

"Yes."

"I have pictures."

"Pictures?"

"Yes, pictures that you will not want out."

After a minute of silence, Judge Benson said, "All right. Where and when?"

"Meet me tomorrow evening 7 pm at the Route 28 Motel."

"What's the address?"

"Just go east on Route 28 from Hyannis. You'll see it on your right a few miles east of Hyannis."

"All right. I'll be there at seven."

"Come to room 201."

Chapter 28

At seven o'clock prompt Judge Benson knocked on the door to room 201. Katherine answered it.

"Come in Mike."

He came into the room and sat in the one chair in the room. She sat on the edge of the bed.

"Well, what is it you want me to see?"

She opened her purse and took out a photo and handed it to him. He looked at the photo. His expression changed. He was clearly surprised. The picture showed a naked young man lying in a bed passed out. In the background of the picture, a reflection from the mirror on the bureau revealed the naked body of a woman taking the photograph. Benson knew he was the person on the bed and the woman in the reflection was Katherine.

"So what do you plan to do with this photo?"

"Oh nothing. The photo is yours to keep."

"Why would I want to keep it?"

"As a reminder of the kind of pictures I have from that night."

"I was young and in school. What could you possibly want with those pictures?"

"I just want you to do the right thing Mike."

"What do you mean?"

"Tom Bowman. He needs to pay for the things he's done."

"I really can't talk with you about Mr. Bowman."

"But you can and you will."

"Now why would I do that?"

"Because you don't want the other photos to find their way to your wife or the media."

"That's blackmail."

"Not blackmail. Let's call it insurance."

"My wife will understand."

"I'm sure she will. When it comes out that you lied to her when she called the next morning when all the while I was in bed right there with you. I'm sure she will understand."

"You wouldn't?"

"And when I tell her about the time the next semester after you were married when you came to my apartment and had sex with me. I'm sure she will understand."

Mike Benson thought about it for a minute. He hadn't thought about the implications of the photos. Hell, he didn't even know they existed. Pictures like the one she gave him would be hard to dispute.

"So Ms. Sterns, what you're asking me to do is to break the law."

"Not so Mike. I'm just asking you to impose the maximum sentence you can on Tom Bowman. All within your authority as the sentencing Judge."

208

"How can I be assured you will not use those pictures against me again in the future?"

"Look Mike. I'll send you a picture every year on the anniversary of Tom Bowman's incarceration."

"How many pictures do you have?"

"I can't tell you. You'll just have to wait until they stop coming."

"I don't know."

"Oh, you know what has to be done."

"You are a bitter person Ms. Sterns. Why?"

"Wouldn't you want revenge if your wife died under suspicious circumstances and then the person of suspicion came after you?"

"If that's what happened, why don't you just go to the police?"

"The evidence is gone. It sank when the ice broke up."

Mike Benson didn't really understand what she was referring to other than that she was holding Tom Bowman responsible for the death of her husband.

Katherine started to undress. She took off her top and bra.

"What are you doing?"

"How about one more time for old times sake?"

"I can't."

"Sure you can." She undid his pants and pushed them down. She removed his underwear even as he made a feeble attempt to protest. When she touched him, he began to grow.

"See, I knew you could do it."

"But, I......"

He didn't get to finish the sentence. He gave in. He reached down and touched her breast. He closed his eyes and just allowed it to happen. She removed her pants and underwear, stood and led him to the bed.

As she lay on the bed, he got on top, moving without protest. She allowed him to renew his memory of her body for a few minutes and then took control.

"Do you have a condom?"
"No. I don't usually do this sort of thing."
"Mike. You need to be more careful."
"I guess."
"Well, I have one in my bag."

He moved to one side so she could get up. She retrieved a condom from her bag, opened it and put it on him. Then she went back to what they were doing. Mike kissed her passionately. Katherine worked her magic and in a few minutes they were both breathing heavily making love. He couldn't hold out any longer and reached climax. She didn't but faked it.

When done, he lay beside her still breathing heavily.
"Wasn't it worth it?"
"We shouldn't have."
"Oh come now Mike. You got off."
She took the condom off him. She held it up so he could see it was no longer empty. Then she set the condom aside on the nightstand. She pressed her body against his and kissed him.
"I can't believe I did this?"
"Mike, a number of years have gone by since we did this the last time."
"I have never cheated on my wife."
"Oh yes you did. Are you forgetting about the spring semester of senior year after you were married?"
"That really doesn't count. I was young then."
"Adultery is still adultery."
He was silent for a few minutes allowing her comments to sink in.

"Mike, you're smart. I'm sure I can count on you. If Bowman goes away for a very long time, then there can be more of this or not. Your choice."

"I don't want more of this."

"Well, then as long as you do your job, we can both forget this and our college days can be forgotten."

"I think I understand what you're saying."

"I'm sure you do."

Mike got up from the bed and got dressed. He put the photo in his pocket, "I'll see what I can do."

"I'm sure you'll do the right thing Mike."

He turned and left seemingly a much smaller man than when he came in.

Chapter 29

The next week, a preliminary hearing was scheduled for Katherine Sterns. Judge Benson asked each of the parties to be prepared to make their statements and then he would rule about a trial.

Katherine Sterns was seated at the defense table with her attorney. When they all stood as Judge Benson came into the courtroom, Katherine just smiled when he looked in her direction. Attorney Ann Levine was again the prosecutor. Judge Benson asked her to proceed.

"Your Honor, at this time, the people wish to withdraw their case against Ms. Sterns. It seems all of the evidence gathered is circumstantial and all of the victims in the attacks refuse to cooperate."

Judge Benson asked Katherine's Attorney if he had any questions and he did not.

"Then I see no reason to continue. The case against Katherine Sterns is dismissed."

Katherine turned to her attorney, "Steven, exactly what does this mean?"

"You're free to go."

"Can I ever be charged in these attacks again?"

"Not really. The Judge has dismissed the case. It would be difficult for another charge to be pursued. You're free and clear."

"Good."

Katherine Sterns smiled at the Judge. She thanked her attorney and turned to leave. Sitting in the courtroom was a red-faced and mad Tom Bowman. On the other side of the courtroom, Ann Benard, Tina Fletcher, Sue Kent and Linda Sage all stood and smiled. Katherine went over to them and received a group hug.

"Thanks girls for being here for me."

"We take care of our own," was the response from Linda as she turned from Katherine and looked at the other three.

"I'll see you at Sundancers," she said.

"We're going there right now. Why don't you join us?" said Ann.

"I might. First, I have to talk to the good Detective," she pointed to Detective Jenkins seated on the other side of the room towards the back.

"Well, if you can, come by and we can all celebrate," said Linda.

"I'll try."

Katherine turned and walked to the back of the room.

She stopped next to where Captain Tomlinson and Detective Jenkins were seated.

"Didn't have to get you in any trouble now, did we Captain?"

Captain Tomlinson didn't respond but Frank Jenkins said, "I'm glad it all worked out Katherine."

"So am I. Will I be seeing you later Frank?"

"I'll call you."

"Now we can take that trip."

She turned away from them.

Captain Tomlinson said, "Are you taking her with you to Rio?"

"Yes. Her going was contingent on this case being settled. Now that it has been, she's free to do whatever she wants."

"Now that's a scary thought," said Tomlinson as he rose to leave.

"There is only one more issue to be resolved and then I think Katherine Sterns will drop off the radar screen for a while."

"One more issue?" Captain Tomlinson asked as he stopped and turned back to look at Jenkins."

"Yes. Tom Bowman's sentencing."

"Has the sentencing hearing been scheduled?"

"Next week."

"Aren't you traveling next week?"

"My trip starts Thursday. His sentencing is at the end of the week. I expect to be back on Monday."

"Well, hopefully things will settle down once the Judge sets the sentence."

"I hope so."

They turned towards the door just in time to see Katherine exit the room. As she did, Captain Tomlinson said, "That woman is trouble."

"She has her good points and bad," replied Jenkins.

"Frank, you're just talking through your dick," Tomlinson said shaking his head. "If I were you, I'd leave that one alone."

"I think I can keep her under control."

"For your sake, I hope so."

"Want to stop at Sundancers for a drink?"

"No, I have some things to finish back at the station, plus I got to make things right with my wife. I think I'll cut my losses and stick close to home."

"Your call Captain."

"I'll see you tomorrow at the station."

"See you then."

The two law enforcement men left the courthouse. Tomlinson went back to the station and Jenkins to Sundancers.

As he entered the bar, the women were all seated at the high tables adjacent to the bar. They were all making toasts and drinking a lot. Jenkins observed from the bar.

After an hour or so, Katherine left the group and walked over to Jenkins.

"So Frank, you want to go to my place?"

"Maybe."

"Can you spend the night?"

"Maybe."

"If you can't decide, I'm sure I can find someone else in here who wants some of this," and she backed up and ran her hands from the top of her head down past her waist.

"Katherine, I'm not happy with our relationship. You slept with quite a few men during the time I have known you. I'm not sure I should be involved with someone who can't make a commitment."

"I can make a commitment."

"Oh you think you can?"

"Sure."

"Ok, we have the trip to Rio on Thursday. Do you think you can refrain from sleeping with anyone else before we go?"

"I think so."

"Let's finish up these drinks and go to your place."

"Sounds good to me," and she put her arms around him. "Let's go plan the trip," she said in a slurred voice.

"I think you've had too much to drink. Why don't you let me drive you home?"

"That's what I've been saying, let's go to my place."

Jenkins paid the tab and the two of them left in his car.

Arriving at her house, Jenkins got the key to her house out of her bag. He then went around and opened her car door. He picked her up and walked to the house. When he opened her front door, he noticed the neighbor looking out the window at the two of them. Katherine had passed out and Jenkins was carrying her in his arms.

The neighbor watched for another few minutes. Lights went on downstairs and then upstairs. Then the downstairs lights went out and finally the upstairs lights went out. When the neighbor went out to get her paper in the morning, Jenkins's car was still in the driveway.

Frank had carried her to her bedroom and laid her on the bed. He took off her shoes. Then he propped her up and took off her blouse and bra. He laid her back with her head on the pillow and then undid her pants. He slid one hand under her to ease her up and with the other hand he pushed her pants down. Her underwear slid off inside her pants as he removed them. Then he went to the bottom of her bed and gave a light tug on the bottoms of the pants freeing them. He took her underwear out of the pants, folded both and put them on her bureau. Then he folded her top and bra and put them on top of the pants.

Looking at her, he could tell she had a chill as goose bumps appeared on her arms. Her breasts reflected the chill as well. Frank took off his clothes and got into bed next to her. He pulled a sheet and comforter up over both of them and then wrapped her in his arms. Katherine didn't respond. She only turned onto her side facing away from him. He snuggled up behind her. He started to get aroused and pressed against her. When she didn't respond, he said, "What am I going to do with you Kat?"

He stroked her hair and hugged her.

"I can't seem to get past your spell. You are truly a beautiful woman. I wish I could have you all to myself."

He fell asleep holding her in his embrace.

Chapter 30

The next few days were rather quiet. The case against Katherine having been dismissed left Katherine with nothing to worry about. She spent her time shopping and buying things in anticipation for the trip to Rio. Each night, Frank would come over to her house and the two would talk about the upcoming trip. On evening, Frank brought a pile of brochures with him. Katherine had planned to have dinner on her back deck and was out there setting the table when he arrived.

"I've got some things for you to look at for the trip Kiddo," he said as he laid the pile of materials on the table.

"Great. I've been doing some research on the Internet also. I want to make sure we get to Ipanema and Copacabana."

"We're staying at the Caesar Park Hotel at Ipanema. Beach every day."

"I can't wait."

"I'll make dinner reservations for us one night at the Copacabana Palace or at Satyricon's. That's the place Madonna supposedly goes to for seafood."

"I'd like to go to the Copacabana. I've always heard about the famous hotel and now we're going to get to see it first hand. Maybe we could try the other place as well for after dinner drinks."

"Why not? We can see the town."

"I'd like to go see the football shaped rock when we are there, too."

"You mean Sugarloaf?"

"Yes. That's the one."

"You know, there's a cable car you can ride up to the top. It's called the SamBodromo."

"Can we take it?"

"I'm sure I'll have some free time during one of the days down there. I understand the view is spectacular both day and night."

"Great."

Frank held up brochures showing the Copacabana Hotel, Sugarloaf and one of a big stadium.

"You can take a look at these when you get a few minutes. Some of the places you mentioned are in here."

"Thanks."

Katherine went to the kitchen and brought out the steaks. She handed them out the door to Frank and asked him to start them on the grill. She went to the refrigerator, took out two bowls and brought them out. One contained a green salad and the other contained rolls.

Frank opened the grill to find two potatoes wrapped in foil already baking. He put the steaks on the already hot grill. As he turned back to the table, Katherine was looking at the materials he had brought.

219

"What's this statue?"

"That's the Christ the Redeemer statue. It's one of the Seven Wonders of the World."

"I want to make sure we get to see it."

"And what is this stadium?" She was holding up a folder containing a picture of Maracana Stadium.

"That's the place where all the official Olympic ceremonies are to be held. I have to go there during the trip to check things out."

"Can I come along?"

"Why would you want to see an empty stadium?"

"If just to say I've been there."

"I guess you could come along. It might be a boring day."

"How could it be boring? Just think of the importance of such a place and we can say we were there."

"Now you're being a tourist."

"I've got an idea."

"What?"

"Not now. I'll tell you when we get to the stadium."

"Ok. How do you want your steak?"

"Medium."

Frank opened the grill and flipped the steaks over. They had a nice grilled pattern burned into them.

"Steaks will be ready in a few minutes."

"Great. Let me get the rest of the stuff from inside."

Katherine went back in the house. She took salad dressings out of the refrigerator, a butter dish, salt and pepper and a small bowl of sour cream and came back outside. She placed the items in the center of the table.

"Frank, give me the potatoes and I'll get them ready."

Jenkins opened the grill and took the two foil wrapped spuds off the grill. He put them on a plate and handed it to Katherine. She put one on his plate and one on hers. She opened the foil revealing a perfectly cooked baked potato covered with Italian salad dressing and sliced onion. She slit each potato down the middle.

"Butter and sour cream?"
"Sure."

She put both on his and her potato. Frank turned the grill off and put the steaks on a platter.
"We're all set."
The two sat down to a nice late summer dinner. The clouds in the bright blue sky were just starting to show colors of orange and red as Frank made a toast.
"To a good trip to Rio."
"And a memorable one," said Katherine.

They ate their steak, potatoes, rolls and salad along with a few glasses of wine. As they were cleaning up after dinner, Katherine's phone rang. She went into the living room and answered it.

"Katherine, it's Andrew."
"Why are you calling me?"
"Julie has broken it off with me."
"Why, because she caught you having sex with me?"
"Yes."
"She isn't being very realistic Andrew. You guys are all alike. Given the chance to go to bed with an attractive women, ninety percent will do it without a second thought."
"I don't know if that's true or not, but Julie doesn't want any part of me thanks to you."
"Look Andrew. You're a big boy. You knew what you were doing."

"It's really all your fault."

"Go ahead and blame me if you must Andrew. If I recall correctly, that was you inside of me. So, why are you calling me Andrew?"

"I needed to tell you I can't see you anymore."

"Don't be stupid. You liked the sex just as much as I did."

"I also wanted to talk with you again about your decision regarding your 401k stock."

"I already told you. I'm moving the funds to a more secure place."

"Are you concerned about Sterns and Dunn?"

"Sterns and Dunn has nothing to do with it. I have plans for my future and they don't include me owning an interest in any small business."

"You've been getting a decent return on your investment. I think you should reconsider."

"Not a chance."

"How am I supposed to raise a few million dollars to buy out your shares?"

"That's not really my problem Andrew, now is it?"

"It is if I can't raise the funds."

"Look Andrew, if you're telling me the firm isn't worth it, then you've been lying to me all along. I'd think you have a liability issue if that's the case."

"The firm is worth it. It's just that I'd have to go through the steps of raising cash to buy out your interest."

"Then do it. Andrew, you have two weeks to resolve this. I'm going on a trip and I'll expect to hear from you when I get back."

"Can we get together and talk about it?"

"Andrew, I'm not going to sleep with you again."

Just then, Frank had walked close enough to the living room to overhear what she had been saying. When she hung up the phone, Frank said, "What was that all about?"

"Nothing really. Andrew Dunn is having trouble liquidating my interest in the 401k plan Sam had set up when he worked there."

"Is it worth a lot of money?"

"A few million."

"Well, that's quite a bit."

"Andrew says it will take some time for him to raise the cash to buy out my share."

"Is all of your interest in the 401k in company stock?"

"Yes, Sam had put it all in Sterns and Dunn stock."

"Is Sterns and Dunn a public company?"

"No, and that's the problem. He'll have to find a buyer for my Sterns and Dunn stock so that I can get out of the 401k."

"Is there a good market for non-public companies?"

"Sam had told me one time that a company with good books, good management and a strong business is always in demand. I just have to hope Andrew hasn't screwed Sterns and Dunn up."

"Do you know if the company was ever in good shape?"

"Yes. When Sam died, Andrew had to have the firm valued for Sam's estate. I had it audited and the business had quite a bit of cash on hand once Sam's Key Man insurance paid off."

"Does it still have a lot of cash?"

"I don't know. I don't get the reports I used to get when I was an active partner. Now I only get a 401k summary report once a year."

"Why don't you ask for an update?"

"I guess I could. I just don't want to have to meet in private with Andrew again."

"Is that because of him or you?"

223

"What do you mean?"

"Look Kat, I'm not blind. I know you've been with him."

"That was a long time ago."

"And what about last week?"

"I had to meet with him about business, that was it."

"If you say so."

"Frank, you know I've told you I'm not seeing anyone else these days. Can't we just leave it at that?"

"Sure."

She put her arms around him and kissed him.

"Let's go to the bedroom. I need you."

He followed her down the hall.

Chapter 31

On Tuesday, Katherine went to the Barnstable County Court House for the sentencing hearing for Tom Bowman. Judge Benson called the attorneys to the bench for a discussion. It seemed to go on for quite a long time then Judge Benson asked the attorneys to step back.

"The defense counsel has requested a two week delay for the sentencing hearing. I am granting the request and this case will be continued until two weeks from today."

Katherine couldn't believe what she was hearing. How could this be happening? When Judge Benson left the bench, she rushed out of the courtroom. She stopped at the end of the hall just in time to see Judge Benson rounding the corner. She ran after him. As she got to the corner, she saw him enter the second door after the one with his name on it. She quickly walked up to the door and opened it.

Judge Benson was standing by the windows in his office taking off his black robe.

"Ms. Sterns, what are you doing in here?"

"What's going on Mike? I thought we had an understanding?"

"This is just posturing Ms. Sterns. Don't worry. Mr. Bowman is going to jail."

Hearing those words from Judge Benson calmed her down.

"Why the delay?"

"This is nothing unusual Ms. Sterns. The defense has the right to request a delay for good reason."

"And what was the good reason?"

"That's not important. It's merely a procedural matter."

"I want him put away."

"Like I said, don't worry. He's going to jail."

She walked over to Judge Benson. She put her arms around him and kissed him on the lips.

"I can be a very appreciative woman Mike."

"Please Ms. Sterns, this is very inappropriate."

Tom Bowman had been standing outside the courthouse speaking with his attorney when he looked back at the courthouse. He could see Katherine through a window on the first floor talking with Judge Benson. Then he saw her kiss the Judge.

"That bitch."

"What did you say?" asked his attorney.

"Oh nothing," said Tom as he shook his attorney's hand and turned to go to his car. When he looked back at the office window, no one was there. Had he really seen what he thought he saw, or had he just imagined it?

Katherine went home and took out two suitcases and began to pack when her phone rang.

"Hi Kat. How did court go?"

"They didn't sentence him."

"Why not?"

"Some procedural thing. It's been rescheduled two weeks out."

"Are you upset?"

"I was, but now I'm not."

"What settled you down?"

"I met with the Judge. He said Tom is going to jail."

"You met with the Judge?"

"Yes. I followed him to his chambers and talked to him."

"And he saw you?"

"I've known Judge Benson for a long time. That's all I'll say."

"I hope this all goes the way you wanted."

"It will. Listen, I have two suitcases I'm packing for the trip. Do you think two will be enough?"

"We're only going for a long weekend. What do you need other than a swim suit, a dinner outfit and a few casual clothes?"

"Just like a man. A woman needs to be prepared for anything."

"But Kat, it's only for a few days."

"Ok. I'll get by with the two."

"Can I see you tonight?"

"I'm counting on it."

"I'll be over around eight."

"I'm going to Sundancers for dinner with Ann but I'll be home by then."

"Ok, see you then."

Around four o'clock, Katherine changed into a sexy outfit and left her house headed for Sundancers. When she walked in, Ron said, "Looks like Kat's on the prowl tonight."

Dee, looking to the door, said, "She hasn't been in here the past few days. I wonder what she's been up to?"

Katherine took up a stool on the side of the bar nearest to the windows. She ordered a martini. Dee made the drink and set it in front of her.

"Katherine, we haven't seen you in here the past couple of days."

"I've been planning and packing for a trip I'm taking on Thursday."

"Where you headed?"

"I'm going to Rio de Janeiro."

"Really?"

"Yes. Frank has to go there on business for a few days and he invited me along."

"So you and the Detective are going to Rio?"

"He's not going as a Detective but rather as a security consultant to the USOC."

"Why would the USOC want a Dennis Police detective to go to Rio for them?"

"Frank's done it in the past for them so they asked him again."

"When are the Olympics?"

"In 2012 in London and 2016 in Rio."

"That's a few years out. Why start now?"

"He said something about having Olympic security teams overlap in order to share information and be prepared. He's consulting regarding security issues and it apparently takes that long to work it all out."

"It probably takes quite a bit of time since so many countries are involved and the Olympics take place in a foreign country. Didn't something happen at one of the previous Olympics?"

"Frank said there were security issues in Munich, Germany and again in Atlanta during past Olympics and his job is to help plan security so things like that don't happen again."

"Well I hope you have a good time."

"I will. I'm going to the beach and to see the sights."

"Sounds like fun."

"Oh, there'll be a lot of fun also."

Ed Phillips and Kenny Brown had been seated across from Katherine the whole time. Kenny said to Ed, "So, Kat's going out of the country for a few days. We should visit her place when she's gone and take care of her freezer."

"We'd have to break in to her house. What if we got caught?"

"Who's going to catch us. You heard her say she's going with Detective Jenkins. Down where she lives everyone's gone home for the winter. They'd never notice us."

"It's not winter yet."

"No, but the summer residents have already left. We go down there next Friday night and we'll have no problem."

"Friday night? Won't the weekend warriors be back?"

"Even if they are, they'll just think we're someone else coming back for the weekend. Plus, I know where she keeps her spare key."

"Ok. What time do you want to go there?"

"Let's plan on 10 pm. That's late enough for it to be dark and still reasonable for someone coming in for the weekend."

"I'll meet you here for nine. We can have a few drinks and then go check her place out."

"Nine it is."

Chapter 32

Frank Jenkins arrived at Katherine's house a few minutes after eight. When he knocked at the door, it took a few minutes for her to answer. Finally, the door opened.

"What took you so long?"
"I can't get my second suitcase closed."
"Let me see if I can."

She led him to the bedroom. She had two large size suitcases on the floor. One was closed and latched. The other had way too much in it to close. Frank tried to push it closed, but it wouldn't.

"Kat, you're going to have to take some of this stuff out."

"But I might need it."

"As I said, we're only going for a few days. How much do you need?"

He started to take things out of the suitcase. He quickly discovered she had packed nine pair of shoes, two pair of sneakers, four pair of flip-flops and a pair of sandals in the suitcase.

"Can't you get by with less footwear?"

"Not really. I have day shoes, dinner shoes, beach shoes, sightseeing shoes, pool shoes and evening shoes in there. I didn't even add the pocketbooks yet," she pointed to a pile of pocket books lying by the closet door.

"You're going to have to cut back. Just bring two nice outfits and casual clothing for sightseeing and the beach."

"If I only brought things for those activities I could probably only have to take one suitcase."

"Now you're being sensible."

"But Frank, I have to be able to look my best."

"Kat, you always look great no matter what you are wearing."

"You're just saying that because I sleep with you."

"You look even better when you have nothing on."

"Ok. I'll re-pack and see if I can get everything into the two."

"I'm sure you'll make the right choices."

"Go make us a drink and let me work on this."

Frank went into the kitchen to make drinks. He took out the shaker, vodka, olives and two martini glasses. He found a shot glass and measured the vodka pouring it into the shaker. He went to the freezer, obtained ice cubes from the icemaker then he made the martinis. He poured the two and added olives to Katherine's. When he went back to the bedroom, Katherine had both suitcases standing and closed.

"I did it," she declared victory.

"Great. Now here's your drink," he handed it to her and made a toast. "To adventure and Rio."

"I can't wait."

"I have my stuff in the car ready to go in the morning. I'll take your suitcases down and put them in the car."

"What if I want to add something else?"

231

"You're all packed. Leave it as it is. I'm sure you'll look just great."

"Ok. I trust you Frank. I'm going to get ready for bed while you put the bags in the car."

Frank Jenkins took the bags out to the car and had to put them in the back seat, as they were too big to fit in the trunk. When he came back in, he locked the door behind him, turned off the lights and went to the bedroom. Katherine was already under the sheets waiting for him.

"Take those clothes off and come here," she said. "Let's get this party started."

He did as instructed.

The two rose at five in the morning, showered and got dressed. Katherine had made coffee while Frank was in the shower. When he came out, they had doughnuts and coffee and were ready to go by six. The two drove to Logan in anticipation of a 10 am flight. Everything went as planned and by 10:30 they were at 28,000 feet headed to Atlanta for their connecting flight to Rio.

The flight to Atlanta took around two hours. They had an hour and a half layover and by early afternoon, they were in the air again headed to Rio. By the time they arrived at Galeo-Antonio Carlos Jobim International Airport in Rio, it was already dark. It took a little over an hour to get their luggage and clear customs. Both travelers were exhausted but ready to start their vacation. At 9 pm, the two were finally standing at the desk in the Caesar Park Rio de Janeiro Ipanema Hotel. They got the key to their room and followed the bellman to the elevators. Entering their room on the seventh floor, Katherine went out to the balcony. She could hear the ocean and smell the salt air. As she looked left, she could see the city all lit up. She looked right and could see quite a way down Ipanema beach. Frank tipped the bellman and closed the door. He left the bags where they were and went out on the balcony.

Katherine put her arms around him and kissed him.
"We should live like this all the time," she said.
"Remember, I'm here to do a job."
"I know, but isn't this fantastic?"
"We'll have a good time."
"Starting right now," she said as she started to take her clothes off.
"You might want to go inside," Frank said as he motioned to a few people sitting on a balcony a few hundred feet away in another hotel.
"We don't know them."
"Even still, let's go inside."
"Oh Frank, where's your sense of adventure?"
"I have it packed in my suitcase," he said as he went back into the room.
Katherine came inside and continued to strip. In a minute, she was standing completely naked just inside the sliding door. Frank was thankful the room had drapes blocking some of the view into the room. What he didn't realize however was the light coming out of the room made the white cloth drapes pretty much transparent. Katherine put on a pretty good show for the people who had been on their balcony at the adjacent hotel. Little did she know, one man sitting on his balcony alone on the eighth floor of the adjacent hotel held his position and watched intently for a half hour.

On Friday morning, Frank had a meeting at 10 am with the security personnel from the various countries assigned to discuss all of the security issues, so he had made coffee in the room. After taking a shower and dressing in business casual clothing, he gave Kat a peck on the cheek. She rolled out from under the sheets, still naked, and gave him a big hug.

233

"My meeting will only last until one. Then I'll take you to see some of the sights."

She kissed him and walked him to the door. Frank left for his meeting. Katherine looked at the clock. It read nine-thirty. She was up and could see the bright sun through the drapes. She pulled on the cord opening then she slid the doors open to let in the fresh sea air. As she looked up at the building next to the hotel, she saw a man looking in her direction through a pair of binoculars. She quickly ducked behind the drapes and pulled them shut. Katherine was a little unnerved from the incident as she was sure the man had been looking at her from the distance.

She decided she would walk and maybe even jog on the beach before taking a shower. She dressed in her workout shorts and sports top bra, put on sneakers and left their room. When she got to the main lobby, she asked the concierge where the best place would be to walk and jog.

"There's a sidewalk above the beach leading in both directions out of the hotel. You'll see many other walkers and joggers. You can go about a mile to the left before the walk ends or about four miles before it ends to the right," said the young concierge attendant.

"Thank you," Katherine said with a smile.

She exited the hotel and turned right. As she started to walk, she looked up at the building next to the Caesar Park looking for the room where the peeper had been standing. No one was there. She walked past the main entrance of the building and thought about going in to report the peeper but decided otherwise.

Katherine started walking, slow at first gradually increasing the pace until she was walking at a brisk pace. There were many other people out walking, jogging and running. Most of the people exercising were dressed in festive sports clothing. A few people who passed her said "Buenos Dias" and some said "Good morning."

Katherine nodded in return. After forty-five minutes, she turned and headed back in the direction from which she had come. As soon as she turned around, she noticed a man in slacks, dress shoes and a white dress shirt about fifty feet behind her walking at the same pace and in the same direction as she. He quickly turned so she could not see his face. He walked to the edge of the sidewalk by the beach looking out at the water. His shirt was wet from sweating and Katherine wondered how long he had been following her. She decided to jog for a while.

She picked up the pace. After jogging for five minutes, Katherine stopped. She faced the water and walked to a bench at the edge of the sidewalk. As she sat, she looked back and saw the same man standing not too far behind looking out at the water. She got up and started to run. Twenty minutes later, she ran into the Caesar Park. The bellman held the door open. Katherine stopped in the lobby to catch her breath. The young concierge who had told her where to exercise came over to her.

"It looks like you had a good workout?" he said handing her a towel.

"Someone is following me," she said trying to catch her breath.

The young man walked over to the door and looked out. "I don't see anyone standing out there," he said as he came back to Katherine.

"Let me ask Jorge," said the young concierge.

He went outside and spoke to the bellman.

"Jorge didn't see anyone following you," he said when he came back to Katherine. "Can I help you to your room Ms. Jenkins?"

She stood up and looked at the young man. "I'm not Ms. Jenkins," she declared.

"I just thought since you were staying in Mr. Jenkins's room," his voice trailed off.

"I'm here with Mr. Jenkins but my name is Ms. Sterns," she said in a matter of fact tone.

"Is Mr. Sterns here with you?"

"No, my husband died some time ago."

"I'm so sorry for your loss."

"It was some time ago."

"If there is anything you need Ms. Sterns, just call. I'm here to help."

"Thank you. I'm sorry, I didn't get your name?"

"It's Roman."

"Thank you Roman. I think I'm ok now."

"Remember Ms. Sterns, call if you need anything."

"I will."

Katherine went to the elevator and she pressed the button for the seventh floor. When she went into her room, she walked over to the sliding door to the balcony and peeked out. She could see a person standing inside the room where the peeper had been before. The person was too far inside the room for her to be able to make out if it was a man or a woman let alone see any of the person's features. She left the drapes closed and went about her business taking a shower and dressing for the day. She decided to put a swimsuit on and go down to the beach for a few hours of tanning before Frank returned.

She put on the robe hanging in the bathroom over her swimsuit along with a pair of flip-flops. She called Roman to find out where she could obtain a beach towel.

"I can bring one right up for you."

"I'm on my way down now. Can I pick it up in the lobby?"

"Sure. Just come see me and I'll have it waiting for you here."

"Thank you Roman."

Katherine went to the lobby. She walked over to Roman to pick up the towel.

"Ms. Sterns, follow me. I have you all set up on the beach."

"I only need a towel."

"Not someone so beautiful as you Ms. Sterns. We have cabanas."

"I don't think I need a cabana."

"Come see, follow me," he said gesturing to her with his hand.

Katherine followed Roman out the door across the walk on to the beach. About thirty feet out on the beach stood a row of small cabanas. Each had soft flowing sides of white chiffon providing shelter from the sun when not pulled back and privacy when wanted.

"These belong to the hotel," said Roman as he led her to the first one on the end.

Roman showed her where everything was located inside the cabana. It had a cooler with water in it. A small cabinet contained sun tan lotion, towels, visors and sunglasses.

"You have everything one needs at the beach right here!" exclaimed Katherine.

"Yes Ms. Sterns. We want to make sure our guests are comfortable."

"Roman, please call me Katherine."

"Yes Katherine."

Katherine started to take off her robe. Quickly Roman said, "Let me take that, Katherine," he took her robe off her shoulders and hung it on the towel hook.

"Would you like suntan lotion, Katherine?"

"I can do it myself," she said picking up the lotion.

"I'm here to make your stay memorable Katherine. Let me do it."

"Ok then."

She sat in the lounger and laid back. Roman flipped the door to the cabana closed. He put lotion on his hands and started to apply it to her shoulders. He put some on her neck and gently applied some to her forehead and cheeks. Then he moved around to her legs and carefully applied lotion to each leg. As he moved up to her thighs, she slowly spread her legs allowing him to get lotion all the way down on the sides. Next he moved up to her tummy. He applied lotion to his hands and started to spread it.

"Wait a minute Roman," she said as she undid her top and slid it off. "Make sure you put some on the sides."

Roman slowly applied the lotion around her breasts.

"You might want to apply some of the blocker cream here and here," he said lightly toughing her nipples. "That way, you will not get burned in the sensitive areas."

"Why don't you do it Roman?" she said with her eyes closed.

Roman did as instructed. He was gentle. She was firm.

"If you turn over, I'll do your back as well."

Katherine turned over. When she did, she found herself staring at his bulging pants. She reached out and touched him.

"So you like your job Roman?"

"What's not to like Ms. Katherine?"

Katherine withdrew her hand allowing Roman to continue. Roman applied lotion to all of her back and then to her legs. When he was done, he said, "You should be all set now Ms. Katherine."

"How old are you Roman?"

"Twenty-two."

"Let me return the favor."

238

She reached over and pulled his shorts and underwear down. She turned over on her back. Roman joined her. They made love for the next fifteen minutes. When done, Roman retrieved a towel and gently cleaned the two of them up.

"Thank you Roman."

"If you need me for anything else, just pick up the phone and press 88," he said as he retrieved a portable phone and handed it to her.

"How convenient. I'll call if need anything else."

Roman asked her to stand for a minute. When she did, he pulled the chaise lounger forward towards the opening. He folded back the sided and tied them to the cabana. Looking at her he said, "You might want to put this back on," as he handed her the suit top and bottom.

"Thank you Roman."

Katherine sat back down on the lounger. Roman had positioned it so she had privacy yet full sunshine. She sat back, put on a pair of sunglasses and took in the sun. After about a half hour, she turned over and sunned her back for another half hour. She started to get hot when she remembered about the cooler. She got up, opened it and took out a bottle of cold water. Sitting back down, she looked up and saw a man standing in the water just down from her cabana. He had a swimsuit on, sunglasses and an oversized hat. The man was looking up at her cabana. She thought he might be the same person who had been following her.

Katherine got up, put on her flip-flops and walked to the water. She walked right up to the man standing there. Lightly splashing the water as she walked, she said, "Is there something I can do for you?" She asked the man.

"Katherine, don't you remember me?"

239

The sun was behind the man's face. Katherine put her hand up to block the sun but still couldn't make out whom it was. She couldn't believe someone here in Rio actually knew her name.

"I don't know you."

He took off the hat and sunglasses and moved forward. Without the sun behind his head, she gasped, "Charles?"

"So you do remember me?"

"What are you doing here?" she asked in an excited voice.

"I live here."

"Why did you leave Cape Cod?"

"I think you know why."

"So you did do it?" was her response.

"Let's just say I took my fees and got out of town."

"But you stole so much money from me and those other women?"

"I didn't take it all."

"Still, you stole it."

"What are you doing in Rio, Katherine?"

"I'm here with a friend."

"Anyone I know?"

"Maybe."

"Could it be your husband's former partner Andrew Dunn?"

"No."

"Then is it the guy who was with your husband when he died?"

"I'm not going to tell you Charles."

"By the way, I'm not Charles Chamberlin anymore. I go by Wes Donlevy now."

"Why did you change your name?"

"It's just easier this way."

"Easier to avoid being found?"

"Well, that too."

240

Just then, Roman came down, "Ms. Sterns, you wanted me to come and get you after an hour and a half. Mr. Jenkins will be returning soon. You said you wanted to be ready."

"So you're here with Jenkins." Charles said.

"So now you know."

"Is he still a Detective?"

"Yes and he's here on business."

Charles looked around becoming nervous. He started to walk out of the water when Katherine said, "Why don't you come by and have a drink with us tonight Charles or rather Wes?"

"I have other plans."

"I'll bet you do."

Charles kept walking, "See you around."

Katherine walked back with Roman. He assisted her to the hotel and offered to help her to her room.

"I'm all set Roman, but thank you for everything."

She pressed seven as she entered the elevator by herself.

Chapter 33

At ten o'clock, Frank Jenkins met up with Fred Travis at the Olympic Headquarters building in downtown Rio.

"Glad you could make it Frank."

"No problem Fred. My boss and the local politicians are all for participating. I think the politicians figure they can get some political capital by supporting events like this, makes 'em look worldly."

"If they are still in office when the Olympics are held, then they're probably right. It seems everyone wants a piece of the action when the events actually take place. The USOC is very generous with those who support the cause with tickets to the best events and stuff like that."

"I can imagine."

"You'll see as time gets closer. People who you think don't even like you will become your best friend."

"I guess it's all who you know?"

"You got it. Listen Frank; these preliminary meetings are mostly to get to know each other. We will go over the general layout, scheduling and stuff. Actual security issues can be addressed later."

"I get the picture. Anyone in particular you want me to pay attention to?"

"Yeah, any country who sends a security rep and is from the Middle East are the countries needing particular attention."

"I remember. The last time I participated in this detail, we had a family tribal leader representing one of the Middle East countries. Little did we know, the guy was passing security plans along to his people back home along with tickets to specific events. Someone in administration tracking tickets saw the same names showing up too often and questioned it. That was how the breach was finally detected."

"These folks can be clever not to mention how their good intention participation makes you think everything is on the up and up."

"I'll keep my eyes open."

"Thanks. We can talk tomorrow if you see any problems. Just write any concerns you have down and include it in your written report."

"Got it."

"Let's get in there."

The two walked into the large conference room. There were around forty other people in attendance. The OC security head ran the meeting introducing everyone and then walking them through the plans for the next five years and the actual Olympic schedule itself. After an hour, the group broke for an informal lunch where everyone got to mingle while having appetizers and soft drinks. By one thirty, the meeting was over and everyone departed.

Frank arrived back at Caesar Park Hotel by two. Katherine was in the room having just showered. She was drying herself off when he came in.

"Kat, want to take in some of the sights?"

She came out of the bathroom naked drying herself off. "Sure, are you done for the day?"

"I have a cocktail hour to attend to at seven. Other than that, I'm free."

"Can we take the cable car up to Sugarloaf?"

"Sure. It's not far from here. We can take a cab and be there in a few minutes."

"Great. Let me get dressed. I should be ready in ten minutes."

Frank sat on the couch in the living room portion of the suite. From time to time he could see her walk by the door. Each time by, she had added another piece of clothing. When she had finally finished, she came out with a pair of sneakers in hand. She had dressed in shorts with a light floral pattern blouse. She had combed her hair back into a ponytail and donned a visor. She sat on the edge of the couch, put on her sox and sneakers.

"I'm ready," she stated.

Frank looked at his watch. "Wow, exactly ten minutes."

"I told you I'd be ready in ten."

"I don't know any woman who goes from naked to dressed and ready to go in ten minutes."

"I'm really excited to see the sights."

"Ok, then let's go."

They got into a cab and Frank instructed the driver to take them to the Sambodromo. The driver merely responded, "Si."

On the way there, Katherine said, "You're not going to guess who I saw here in Rio today?"

"You saw someone you know here in Rio?"

"Yes."

"Ok, I give up, who?"

"Charles Chamberlin."

"Are you sure?"

"Yup. I not only saw him, I talked to him."

"Where?"

"Well, Roman, that's the concierge person, he helped me get a cabana on the beach. After Roman had helped me apply suntan lotion, I laid out in the sun. I saw a man standing in the water just looking at me. I was curious after a while so I went down to the water to introduce myself and to my surprise it was Charles Chamberlin."

"Didn't you recognize him?"

"He was standing with his back to the sun directly in my line of sight. I couldn't see him clearly at first. Then he took off the big hat and sunglasses he had on and it was definitely him."

"What did he say?"

"He said he's changed his name to Wes Donlevy down here and that he lives here now."

"Donlevy, I remember the name. One of the attorneys I met while investigating the case was named Donlevy. In fact, a Wes Donlevy in Grand Caman had opened one of the accounts we traced. I wonder if it had been Chamberlin all along?"

"I asked Roman to remind me when an hour and a half had expired so I would be ready when you got back. When he came down to the beach, Charles got nervous and left. I think it was the mention of your name actually."

"Did you see where he went?"

"He went up to the sidewalk and walked away from the city," she was pointing to her left.

"I wonder if he lives near our hotel."

"We can ask Roman when we get back. He seems to know everyone."

"Good idea."

The cab came to a stop and the driver pointed to a small building in front of cables stretching over the water up to Sugarloaf Mountain. Frank paid the fare and they got out. They purchased tickets and boarded the cable car. A few minutes later, the attendant closed the door and asked everyone to take a seat. The car began to move in a jerky motion at first and then once the car cleared the wheels at the base, the ride became very smooth.

Ascending to Sugarloaf, they could see out over the water and all along the beach.

"This is magnificent," said Katherine looking all around.

"Look up there." Frank said pointing to the Statue of Christ the Redeemer. "It's called Cristo Redentor."

Katherine looked up. The sun was behind the statue from their vantage point giving it a brilliant glow. In a whisper, she said. "That's amazing."

"Look up ahead, we're coming to the station," Frank said as he pointed to the drop off point on SugarLoaf Mountain.

The cable car came to a jerky stop. The attendant opened the door and asked everyone to be careful exiting the car. When they got out, they could see three hundred and sixty degrees.

"This is an impressive sight," Katherine exclaimed.

"It sure is."

The two spent a half hour at the top before getting back on the cable car heading back down.

"This was fantastic Frank, don't you think?"

"It is impressive."

"I think anyone who comes to the Olympics should get to see these things."

"I'm sure it will be on everyone's itinerary."

"When do you go to the stadium?"

"That's tomorrow."

"I can't wait."

The cable car jerked again as it reached the base station. The two got out. "Can we see something else?"

"I'm going to have to pass Kat. I have to get ready for the cocktail hour I told you about. You can come if you want to."

"No, I think I'll spend the time getting ready for our night out. You're taking me to the Copacabana Hotel tonight aren't you?"

"We have reservations for ten o'clock."

"I want to look my best and it will take me a few hours to get ready."

"Ok, then I'll do the cocktail party then come back and get you for dinner."

"Sounds like a plan."

Frank hailed a taxi and asked to be taken to the Caesar Park Hotel. When they got back, Katherine asked the concierge if Roman was available and he said Roman had just left for the day.

"Looks like we'll have to talk to him tomorrow."

"Let's get up to the room so I can change and you can start getting ready."

They got into the elevator. Katherine pressed seven and when the doors closed, she put her arms around Frank and kissed him.

"I'm so glad you asked me to come along."

"Me too."

When they got to the room, Frank changed. Katherine had stripped to her underwear and bra. She sat at the vanity selecting different kinds of make-up things to apply.

"I'm going to get going. It's a little after six and the party starts at seven."

"Have a good time. I'll be ready when you get back."

He kissed her on the lips, put on his sport jacket and left.

Chapter 34

Jenkins went to the cocktail party. He mingled with the other security people from the other countries. Fred Travis introduced him to the head of the United Kingdom delegation and to the head of the Brazilian delegation. Frank spent quite a bit of time talking with the United Kingdom representative because he figured they were the most prepared since they were hosting the 2012 Olympics. By eight, he was ready to go pick Kat up.

Arriving at their room, he stood in amazement looking at Katherine as he entered the room. She turned a full three hundred sixty degrees allowing him to take it all in.

"Do you like it?"

"What's not to like?"

She looked stunning. She had let her hair down and had ironed it straight. The length came to the middle of her back. The evening dress she wore was black sequins with a deep low cut in the back. He had to check to see if she had anything on below the cut. The dress had a built in bra yielding quite a bit of cleavage. Katherine had put on a fragile gold necklace supporting a diamond cluster in the front. She wore two-carat diamond studs in each ear.

All Frank could get out was "Wow."

"I'm ready for the Palace," Katherine declared as she picked up a tiny purse and took his arm. The two left for their dinner date.

On the way to dinner, Katherine told Frank about the person following her when she had taken her walk.

"Was it Charles Chamberlin or Wes Donlevy?" he asked.

"I'm not sure. I had taken the walk before I saw Charles at the beach so I wasn't even looking for him. In fact, I don't know if the person following me was a man or a woman."

"Too bad you didn't see the person better. Why would Chamberlin be following you?"

"I don't know. I haven't talked to him in a long time and he certainly didn't know I was coming to Rio. It must just be a coincidence."

"I don't know. Like the Captain says, I don't like coincidences."

"How else could he know?"

"We'll see what we can find out tomorrow."

"Ok, then let's not let this interfere with our evening."

Frank looking at her said, "Oh, it won't. He's already out of my mind," Frank was looking down her dress.

"You pig," she said laughing.

They arrived at the Copacabana Hotel. The place was beautiful and very big. Entering the hotel, Katherine held her breath looking up at the ceiling murals.

"This is beyond spectacular," she said.

"Pretty impressive if I do say so myself."

They went into the elegant dining room and were seated by the windows overlooking the city.

"What a view," Katherine said looking out.

"Like I said, very impressive."

They ordered champagne and appetizers. While drinking their champagne, Katherine talked about how helpful Roman had been.

"You have to see the cabanas. They have everything you need for the beach."

"I'll bet."

"Roman even applied the suntan lotion so I didn't have to get messy doing it myself."

"He's a real do-gooder is he?"

"Frank, don't say it like that. Roman only wanted to make sure I was having a good time. He even brought me special cream so that my nipples wouldn't burn."

"I'll bet he even applied it for you didn't he?"

"Yes, how did you know?"

"Oh, I didn't. I just know the type."

"Do I detect a note of jealousy?"

"I just find it convenient. The full service and all."

"It's just what a woman wants. To be pampered."

"Call it what you want. I call it foreplay."

"We didn't have sex." She lied. "Well, maybe not in the traditional sense."

"Would you have if he were more aggressive?"

"Frank, when you go to the doctor, does he give you a prostate exam?"

"Well yeah."

"Do you think of it as sex?"

"No."

"Well, if someone is putting their finger up your ass, don't you think that should be considered sex?"

"I see your point."

"Thank you."

"Ok. I'll let it go. Let's have a nice dinner."

"Yeah, then we can go back to the hotel and screw our brains out."

"Katherine, sometimes you have a way with words."

"Hey. I'm just saying out loud what you're thinking."

"Oh really?"

"Really."

Their dinners arrived. They dined on fresh local seafood and vegetables accompanied by a fine white wine. After dinner, they went to the lounge for an after dinner drink and a little dancing. A piano player offered romantic tunes on the piano in the dimly lit lounge. An hour later and after unchained melody, Katherine said, "I'd like to go back to our room."

"I'm ready as well."

They left the Copacabana Hotel having had a very nice evening. On the way back to the Caesar Park Katherine said, "This has been way beyond my expectation Frank."

"And the evening isn't over yet."

"I'm sure the rest will be just as good."

Frank closed the door to their room and looked at his watch, 1:30 a.m.

"What an evening."

"Do we have any Chambord?" Katherine asked.

"If we don't, I'll call down and have some brought up. I'm sure Roman will help." Frank winked as he said it.

Frank checked the liquor bar. No Chambord. He called the concierge and ordered a carafe. Ten minutes later, there was a knock on the door. He tipped the waiter and brought the liquor inside. He poured two glasses. He took them out on to the balcony and sat next to Katherine. She had been looking off into the distance taking in the surroundings.

"What a place," she said picking up a glass. She sipped it. "This is good."

Frank picked up his and sipped it. "Sure is."

He put his arm around her. She had changed into a nightgown when he was on the phone ordering the drinks. Sitting on the balcony in the cool of the evening, she started to get a chill.

"Let me get you something to keep you warm," Frank said as he got up and went inside.

When he did, Katherine was looking at the building next to the hotel. Her eyes trained on the room where she thought she had seen the person looking at her earlier when the lights in the room she had been looking at suddenly came on. She could see a man in the room. He put something in the refrigerator and then turned out the light in that room. Another light went on in the next room and she could see him pulling the shade down. A few minutes later, the light went out. She couldn't tell if it was Charles or not and didn't say anything to Frank when he came back out with her robe. He put it over her shoulders and sat back down. The two sat and talked for another half hour sipping their liquor. When the glasses were empty, Katherine said, "Let's go to bed."

Frank didn't say anything. He rose, followed her in and closed the door behind him. He pulled the drapes closed and undressed. In ten minutes, the two were embracing each other making love. That went on for another hour.

"I didn't think I could do it more than once," Frank said.

"How many times do I have to tell you Frank, it's not up to you?"

"You've made your point."

"Yes I did."

"How many times did you orgasm Kat?"

"Four."

"Wow. I can't imagine that many in one night."

"That's nothing. The only thing that slows a woman down is dryness or if she's had enough. If not for one of those, a woman could keep going on and on."

"Don't you mean coming?"

"Yeah."

"Let's get to sleep. We have a busy day tomorrow."

"Ok. Do you have any official duties tomorrow?"

"Yea. I have meetings in the morning and I should be done by two."

"Good. I'm looking forward to seeing more of the sights."

"Me too."

He kissed her goodnight. They embraced and fell asleep in each other's arms.

Chapter 35

Frank rose first the next morning. He showered and dressed business casual with dark gray slacks and a short sleeve light blue-collar shirt along with black loafers. Katherine had decided to sleep in.

"Kat, I should be back in a few hours. I'm meeting with the UK delegation today to discuss what they did as preliminary planning for the 2012 Olympics."

"Ok. I'm probably going to the beach for an hour or two. What time do you want me to be ready to go to the stadium?"

"Why don't we plan on going there around 2:30?"

"I'll be ready."

Frank kissed her on the cheek, closed the hotel room door behind him and put the *Do Not Disturb* sign on the handle as he left.

When Frank got off the elevator in the hotel lobby, he walked over to the concierge desk. A young man was sitting behind a computer looking at something when Frank said, "I'm looking for Roman."

"He'll be right back. He's running an errand for a guest."

Frank took a seat next to the desk and waited. After a few minutes, Roman came through the front door and walked over to the concierge station. The young man seated at the desk said, "Roman, this gentleman would like to speak with you."

Roman turned to Frank Jenkins, "How may I help you?"

"I'm Mr. Jenkins. I'm staying here at the hotel. Yesterday, you helped my companion Ms. Sterns get set up with a cabana on the beach."

"Oh yes, Ms. Katherine."

"She said a man she saw on the beach kind of made her nervous. I'd like to ask you if you know the man."

"Ms. Katherine had asked me to come and get her at a specific time. She said she needed to be ready to go sightseeing. When I went to get her as she had requested, she was talking with a man down by the water. As I approached, the man left."

"That's the person I'm trying to find."

"I have seen this person before. I think he lives in the building over there," he pointed to the building next to the Caesar Park.

"Thank you Roman, you've been a big help."

"Anything for Ms. Katherine."

Frank Jenkins walked outside the main lobby of the hotel and looked at the building next door. It was a high-rise condo type building as tall as the Caesar Park. He wanted to stake out the building to see if he could catch Chamberlin but his morning meeting had priority. He would have to come back later.

Katherine got herself out of bed about an hour after Frank had left. She walked to the sliding doors leading to the balcony and pulled the drapes back. The sun was shining and the warmth on her face felt good. She walked out on the balcony dressed only in her nightgown. While the sun was shining, the morning air brought a chill to her. She didn't mind. She looked across the way to where she had observed the peeper. No one was there. She went back inside and called the concierge. Roman answered.

"This is Ms. Sterns. I would like to know if a beach cabana is available."

"Ms. Katherine, it's Roman. The cabanas are all ready. Would you like one?"

"Yes Roman. I'll be right down."

"Come to the concierge desk and I'll be waiting for you."

"See you in a few minutes."

Katherine quickly changed and put on her pink bikini swimsuit. She put on flip-flops and a robe and went down to the lobby. Roman greeted her as she exited the elevators.

"Your cabana is waiting."

"Roman, you are so helpful."

"Anything for you Ms. Katherine."

Roman selected a cabana for her and helped her get everything set up.

"Do you want me to apply lotion?"

"No thank Roman, I don't think the sun is too strong this early."

"If you stay till noon, you will want to put some on."

"I'm going to see the stadium today. I have to be ready to go by lunchtime so it shouldn't be a problem."

"If you change your mind, call me on the phone," he pointed to the portable phone.

"I will."

Roman left and returned to the concierge desk. After he left, Katherine lay on her stomach sunning her back. She dozed off. About a half hour later, she was startled awake by hands applying lotion to her back.

"Roman, I thought I said I didn't need lotion."

"But you do," came a response from a different voice than Roman's.

Katherine turned over. Charles, also known as Wes, was now kneeling over her applying the suntan lotion to her back.

"Charles, what are you doing?"

"Making sure you don't get burned."

"But you already burned me, didn't you?"

"Kat, let's not be so judgmental."

"Charles, you took two million dollars from me."

"I think if you check your account, you'll see it has been put back."

"Tell me you're kidding?"

"No. When I saw you yesterday, I knew I had to do the right thing."

"Well thank you."

"I'm sorry Kat for taking advantage of you. I shouldn't have."

"Charles, I'm glad you feel that way. I really liked you."

"Do you think I might have a second chance?"

"I don't know. I'm here with someone else."

"I know. I saw you two the other night from my room."

"So it was you in the building next door?"

"Yes. I couldn't believe it when I was sitting out there the other night. I looked across the way to the Caesar Park and there you were."

"So it was just by coincidence?"

"Yes. And by the way, you should pull the inside drapes to your room at night. Those thin white drapes are transparent at night when the lights are on in the room."

"So you saw me with Frank?"

"Oh, yes. I saw everything. Now let me get some of this lotion on you or you'll burn."

She lay back on the lounge. Charles reached over and pulled the string holding the chiffon sides open. Katherine had taken her top off and lay back with her eyes closed. He squirted lotion on his hands and began to apply it to her body. He applied some to her face, neck and shoulders. Then he lightly touched her breasts. She sighed. He moved down and applied lotion to her stomach. She raised her mid section up a little as he reached the bottom of her swimsuit. She slid it down and kicked it off. Charles continued applying lotion all the way to her ankles. When he reached the tip of her feet, he stood and took off his suit. Katherine held out her hand taking hold of his, coaxing him to her.

She reached into her bag and retrieved a condom. She opened it and put it on him. The two made love in the cabana for the next hour. Just as they were finishing, Roman opened the door to the cabana, "Some fresh towels for you Ms. Katherine."

Roman turned his face when he saw the two naked in the embracing position. "I'm so sorry Ms. Katherine. I didn't know someone was in here with you."

Roman dropped the towels and left.

"Will this be a problem for you Kat?"

"No so long as Roman doesn't say anything to Frank."

"Do you want me to talk to him?"

"No. I'll take care of it."

"Ok. How long are you going to be here?"

"We head back to the States tomorrow."

"Too bad. I would really like to have seen more of you."

259

"Charles, you have seen all of me today."

"You're right but you know what I mean."

"Why don't you come back to Cape Cod?"

"It might present problems for me."

"Did you return the money you took from the other widows?"

"No. Only you."

"Then you're right. The police will still be after you."

"Even if I return all the money, they will be after me. I have a good life down here and I enjoy the location."

"I could get used to this as well."

"Then why don't you stay a little longer?"

"Like I said, I'm seeing Frank now and I think I have a future with him."

Charles looked down at her naked body, "A future, huh?"

"Charles, this was spur of the moment. I don't do these things any more."

"You just did Katherine. I don't think you can be a one man woman."

"You may be right."

"I'd bet I am."

"Well, don't let Frank know."

"Oh, I don't plan on talking to the Detective any time soon."

"Probably a good idea."

"You know where I am if you ever want to get in touch with me. Let me give you my card."

He took his wallet out of his swimsuit pocket and produced a business card. It read: Wes Donlevy, Financial Consultant. The card had his Rio address and phone number on it.

"Only you would have a business card in your suit and only you would have someone else's name on it. Still doing the Financial Consulting thing?"

"It worked so well back in the states, I set up here doing the same thing. You can't imagine how successful it is."

"With your charm Charles, I'm sure you're very successful."

"You have my card. Call."

Charles kissed her. He stood and put on his swimsuit and left. Katherine retrieved the condom from the wastebasket and put it in her robe pocket. She got dressed and walked back into the hotel. She walked over to Roman, "You didn't see anything today Roman. Got it?"

"I didn't see anything Ms. Katherine."

She turned and headed for the elevators. She had to get ready for sightseeing.

When Frank came back to the hotel after his morning meeting, he went to talk to Roman.

"Did Ms. Sterns come down?"

"Yes. She went to the beach for a little while."

"So she got some sun?"

Roman was getting a little fidgety and nervous, "Yes. She was in her cabana for an hour or two."

"Roman, did you see her talking with anyone on the beach today?"

"No. Yes. I mean no, not that I noticed."

"Roman, why are you so nervous?"

"Ms. Katherine had me say I wouldn't say."

"Wouldn't say what?"

"That she was with someone in her cabana."

"What do you mean with someone?"

Roman held up one hand making a circle with his index finger and thumb. He put the index finger from the other hand into the circle moving it back and forth.

"Are you saying she had sex with someone in the cabana this morning?"

Roman made a facial expression indicating in the affirmative. "Please don't tell her I told her?"

"I won't. And you didn't Roman. You didn't."

Frank turned and walked to the elevators. He went up to the room. Opening the door, Katherine was dressed, ready to go sightseeing. Frank said, "Let me change and we can get going."

He went into the bedroom to get dressed. He opened the top drawer to Katherine's bureau. When he picked up the underwear, he saw a used condom in a plastic bag. "Hmmm." He dressed in shorts, sneakers and a pullover shirt. He walked back into the other room, "So how was your morning?"

"Fine. I went down to the beach for a little while."

"Yes, Roman told me. I saw him when I came back from my meeting."

"What else did he say?"

"Nothing. Just that you had gone back up to the room a little while ago to prepare for the day."

"He didn't say anything else?"

"What else was he supposed to say?"

"Oh nothing."

"Let's get going. It's our last day here and I promised I'd take you to the stadium where the Olympics are going to be held."

"I'd like to go to a bar and dancing tonight if we can also."

"Let's see how the day goes."

262

Chapter 36

Leaving the hotel, the two walk a block and entered the metro station.

"Roman said we can take the metro all the way to Maracana Stadium."

"Is Metro their subway?"

"Yes. It goes to all the main attractions in the city. You'll like it. It's really modern."

They purchased tokens and entered the gate to the train. The place was very clean. The walls were decorated with mosaic scenes of all of Rio's main attractions.

"It must have taken a long time to do all of this." Kat said as she looked at the murals.

"I'm sure it did."

"How long before we get to the stadium?"

"It's four stops once we get on the subway."

The two waited for a few minutes on the platform. A modern looking subway train entered the station from the opposite end and stopped in front of them. The doors opened and they went in. Being Sunday, the subway trains were not very crowded. After another three stops taking a total of about fifteen minutes, the train stopped at the Maracana Stadium station. They got off.

Coming out of the metro station, they were right at the stadium. Katherine looked up at the structure. It was enormous. Frank said, "We have to find the security office. It's next to gate one."

They looked at the hanging signs and could see the metro station entrance was across from gate five. Frank pointed to the left and they could see gates four and three around the bend. They walked in that direction. After rounding two corners, they could see the sign for gate one. Next to the gate hung another sign indicating the security office. They went in.

Frank spoke with the desk officer. He pointed to a door at the back of the office. Frank signaled for Katherine to follow him. They went through the door. It opened on to a ramp leading down to the stadium field. Frank and Katherine walked down.

Upon coming on to the main field, Katherine said, "I can't get over how big this place is."

"It can hold over a hundred thousand," said Frank allowing his eyes to scan the immense structure.

They continued to walk until they were at the center of the field. "You could put four or five Fenway Parks inside here," said Frank.

"Just think, this is where it will all happen in 2016." said Katherine.

"Yeah."

"The pageantry, the costumes, the athletes, it's impressive."

"And you can say you were here."

"You said you have to come back a few more times over the next couple of years and then for a few weeks in 2016?"

"That's right."

"Maybe I could come with you on a few of those trips?"

"Maybe."

"I could get used to this place."

"Just what is it you like down here?" Frank wasn't sure what her next response would be but he was digging.

"I don't know, the weather, the city, the restaurants, everything?"

"Yeah, and the cabanas too?"

"I do like the beach."

"I wasn't referring to the beach," he was really referring to the lotion rubs and Roman's spilling the beans about Katherine and a man in the cabana."

"You're right, I like having everything at my fingertips," she was referring to the amenities, he wasn't.

"Well, you'll have to see if your schedule will allow for you to come back."

"I'm sure it will."

"When we talked about this place yesterday, you said you had a surprise for me when we got here. Well, we're here. What's the surprise?"

Katherine started to undress. "Let's make love right here in the middle of the stadium. Then whenever we see this place on TV it'll have a special meaning to us."

"I don't think so," said Frank as he pointed back towards the way they had come into the stadium. The security man Frank had spoken to when they got to the stadium was standing by the entrance.

"I didn't see him. Maybe we can try again another time."

"Don't count on it. This is a pretty busy place. Let's get some lunch. Then we can plan the evening."

"Sounds good to me. Frank, can we go to that seafood place?"

"You mean Satyricon?"

"Yeah, that's the place."

"I don't see why not. Give me a few minutes to speak with the stadium security. Then we can go."

Frank went back into the stadium security office. After a few minutes, he emerged with a few papers in hand.

"I've got what I came for. Now the rest of the day is ours."

They went back to the metro station. Frank looked up the routes for the trains and saw that the metro would go within a block of the restaurant. They took the subway to the restaurant. When they arrived, Katherine said, "I want to have shrimp and scallops."

"Kind of New England style isn't it?"

"I guess I just want to see what they offer down here that I would recognize."

They got a table by the windows overlooking the water and ordered lunch and drinks. After a good lunch, Frank said, "Where to now?"

"Are any carnival activities going on?"

"Wrong time of the year Kat. Carnival takes place late winter early spring."

The waiter had over heard the two talking about Carnival, "You can go to the district. Carnival is always going on there."

"Where is the district?" Frank asked.

"If you're taking the metro, get off two stations down. You'll be right in the middle of the district."

Frank said, "Thanks."

The two finished their lunch and went back to the metro. They took it two stations down. When they exited the metro station, sure enough, a parade was just passing the station. They followed the crowd.

After a few blocks, the two stopped at a corner bar. The sidewalk outside the bar had tables set up with a few patrons sitting having drinks watching the activities.

"Let's get a martini?"

"Ok, but not too many. We have to fly tomorrow."

"Oh Frank, don't be a dud."

"I'm not. I just know we have hours of flying to do tomorrow and I wouldn't want to do it with a hangover."

"Don't worry. We can work it off when we get back to the hotel."

They had a few martinis and joined in the festivities. Katherine would walk to the edge of the sidewalk from time to time whenever the people throwing beads walked by to get a few. Within an hour, she had a necklace consisting of over twenty strands of beads around her neck.

"Just like Mardi Gras," she said.

"If you say so." Frank said sipping his third martini.

"This has been so much fun Frank. I can't begin to tell you."

"I'm glad you enjoyed yourself," he said tipping his glass in her direction.

"I did. Let's go back to the hotel so I can express my gratitude to you properly."

"I'm with you," he said as he requested the tab. He paid it and they walked back to the metro. They took the subway back to the hotel arriving there just as the sun was setting.

Back in their suite, Katherine opened the drapes and doors to the balcony.

"Come see this sunset Frank. It's spectacular."

Frank came out to the balcony and looked to the west. The sky was a kaleidoscope in colors of red, yellow, orange, blue and purple.

Katherine walked back inside and took off her clothes.

"Come here. I need to show you my gratitude."

Frank came back inside. He was about to close the drapes when she said, "Only close the outside drapes. I want to be able to see the rest of the sunset."

He did as instructed, shed his clothing and joined her on the bed. After fifteen minutes, the sun had gone down and the room became dark. She turned on the light next to the bed and turned her attention back to Frank. She was on top. She took her time making sure she showed him her gratitude. After what seemed like a half hour, they both lay next to each other spent.

"That was terrific Kat."

"Sure was."

She got up and went over to the balcony door. She went out on the balcony naked. When she looked across to the other building, she could see Charles sitting on his balcony looking through his binoculars. She waved, turned and went back inside.

"You shouldn't be out there like that."

"It's our last night. I just want to take it all in."

"Well, now that you have, I think we need to pack. We have an early flight tomorrow."

"Ok."

He put his underwear on and started packing. She packed still naked. Each of them left out the clothing they planned to wear traveling the next day. In a half hour, all three bags were ready to go.

The two called it a night and as the lights are turned off, Katherine could see through the outer drapes just like Charles said he could see in now that the inside lights were turned out. She could still see him sitting on his balcony in the building next door.

They awoke at five in the morning to the alarm clock, showered quietly and dressed. Frank called for a bellman. When someone knocked at the door, Roman was standing there.

"You called for assistance?" Roman said.

Frank pointed to the bags, "We're all set to travel Roman. Can you get us a cab while I settle the bill?"

"Sure Mr. Jenkins."

Roman put the bags on a cart and took them down stairs. He hailed a cab at the door and put the bags inside. He opened the door for Katherine to get in. He wheeled the cart around to the back of the cab and helped the cab driver put the three bags into the trunk.

"I hope you enjoyed your stay Ms. Katherine." he said as she got in. She turned to him and kissed him on the cheek.

"I'll be back Roman."

"I'm looking forward to your return."

Frank was just coming out the door. He overheard Katherine and Roman but decided not to say anything. He handed Roman a fifty.

"Thank you Mr. Jenkins. I hope you and Ms. Katherine come back soon."

Frank Jenkins didn't respond. He went around to the other side of the cab, opened the door and got in. He asked the driver to take them to Galeo-Antonio Carlos Jobim Airport.

269

When they got to the airport, they checked their bags, went through security and proceeded to gate B4. In another hour, their plane taxied down the runway for the flight back to Atlanta.

Chapter 37

While Katherine was in Rio, Ed and Kenny had met at Sundancers on Friday night. The two were sitting at the end of the bar.

"Ed, we should go to Katherine's place and make sure she doesn't have any of our DNA in that freezer of hers."

"I don't know Kenny, that's breaking and entering."

"She's away for the weekend. She doesn't even have to know."

"How would we get in?"

"Like I told you the other day, I know where she keeps her spare key. We could just walk in."

"I don't know."

They had a few more beers. Tina had been on the other side of the bar not getting much action. She walked over to where Kenny and Ed were seated.

"Kenny, want to buy me a drink?"

"Tina, why don't you join me and Ed?"

"I thought you'd never ask."

She took up the stool on the other side of Kenny.

"So what are you two up to tonight?"

"Not much. I've been talking to Ed trying to get him to go with me to Katherine's."

"Why? She's out of the country."

"I know. That's why I want to go to her place. She has those condoms in her freezer and I want to make sure there isn't one in there with my name on it."

"She already owned up to what happened. What are you worried about?"

"I don't want any of my DNA showing up in any of her criminal deeds."

"Do you think she's going to do something else?"

"You never know with Kat. Anyhow, I'm trying to get Ed to go with me."

"You think she has something on Ed over there also?"

"He said he used a condom when he was with her so I'll bet there's one in her freezer with his name on it."

Tina looked at Ed, "If she has one with your name on it, wouldn't you want it out of there?"

"I guess."

"I guess Ed, what kind of response is that?"

"I'm just as mad as you are Kenny. I just don't like the idea of breaking into her house."

"Like I said, we aren't breaking in. I know where the key is."

"Hey, I have an idea," said Tina. "Why don't the three of us go over there and do it in her bed. That would be getting back at her."

"Heck, why don't we just get everyone to come along?" said Ed.

"Don't be silly Ed. Just you, Kenny and me can go there. We could leave the place where she would know someone was there."

"I don't know," said Ed drinking his beer.

"Ed, do you ever live on the edge?" Kenny asked.

"Not really."

"It's time you did," said Tina. "Dee, give us each a shot of Jager."

Dee got them each a shot. When they were in front of the three, Tina said, "Let's do it."

Kenny picked up his shot glass and downed it. Tina did the same. They both looked at Ed. He picked up his and downed the shot.

"Now that's what I'm talking about," Kenny said.

The three paid their tab and got up and left. They all got into Ed's truck. Ed left Sundancers parking lot headed east towards Katherine's house. When they got to her house, he pulled his truck into the driveway. Kenny jumped out and went around to the garage. In a minute he was back with a key in hand. The three of them stood on the front porch while Kenny opened the door. They went inside. Tina flipped on the light switch.

"Do you think that's a good idea?" Ed asked.

"Who's going to see us Ed? It's off-season. How many cars did you see at other houses as we came down the street?" questioned Kenny.

"I guess you're right," Ed said.

"Ed, let's see what she has in her freezer." Kenny said leading the way into the kitchen.

"I'll be in the bedroom when you boys are ready."

Kenny opened the freezer. On the left side, there was a box containing a pile of zip-lock bags. He took the box out. Ed picked up the first zip-lock. He read the name written on the outside in magic marker. "Tommy Anderson."

"Should we take it?" He asked.

"No. If we take all of them, then she'll get suspicious. Just look for any with our names on them."

"Ok."

273

Ed continued to look through the box. He came across one with his name on it. He stuffed it into his pocket. He continued to go through the pile. He came across one with Kenny's name on it. He handed it to Kenny.

"I knew she had one here with my name on it." Kenny said as he put it in his pocket.

"Here's another one," said Ed handing another bag to Kenny with Kenny's name on the outside.

"That bitch," commented Kenny.

Ed continued to go through the pile. "Here's another one," Ed said laughing as he handed it to Kenny.

"What's so funny Ed?"

"You thought she only had one bag on you. This one makes three."

"Well, Kat and I got together a few times as I recall."

"I thought she would have another one with my name on it as well." Ed said as he got to the bottom of the pile.

"Maybe the other one was one she left at the scene of one of the attacks? Or who knows Ed, maybe she thinks differently of you and threw yours out." Kenny commented.

"You're probably right."

"Ed, put those back in the freezer and let's go see what Tina's up to."

Ed put the box of bags back into the freezer. He closed the door and walked down the hall. When he got to the bedroom, Kenny was already taking his cloths off. Tina had pulled back the blankets and was lying on the bed naked.

"Come on in Ed. I can handle both of you at once."

"I don't know. I've never done anything like this."

"Ed, it'll be fun," Kenny said as he took off his underwear. Kenny was ready to go.

"Ed, take those clothes off and come here," said Tina.

As he did, Kenny got on top of Tina and went to work. In a few minutes, he climaxed. Ed had finally taken everything off when Kenny rolled off Tina. She motioned for Ed to join her. He did but wasn't ready. Tina took care of that. She brought him around and got on top. Ed seemed to be holding back as Tina increased her pace. Her breathing became very rapid and she reached climax. He continued to grow. Tina sensed the change in hardness and continued. She reached climax again. By now, Ed was taken completely in. He didn't think Tina could excite him any further than he already was, but she did. Then he exploded. So did she.

"Ed, that was fantastic," Tina said getting off Ed and holding both Ed and Kenny at the same time.

"Ed, you're a stud," Kenny commented.

Ed was kind of shy about it until Tina bent down and kissed both of them.

"I don't know how I was able to hold back for so long." Ed remarked.

"You were probably just a little distracted," commented Tina. "You know, a threesome and all."

The three got up off the bed. The sheet was wet.

"Let's make the bed back up. She'll notice the stain when she goes to clean the sheets and will wonder," said Tina.

"I hope we don't get in trouble for this," said Ed.

"Don't worry Ed. She'll probably think this happened during one of her conquests anyway," said Kenny.

They made the bed up and got dressed.

Tina said, "Lets go back to Sundancers."

"I have to take you back there for your cars anyway," Ed responded.

The three exited the house turning all the lights off on their way out. Kenny put the key back where he found it in the garage. They got into Ed's truck and left the same way they had come in. About an hour and a half had gone by since they had arrived.

They didn't know it but the neighbor across the street from Katherine's had been home when the three went there. The lights to the neighbor's house in the front were all out and the car was in the closed garage so it would have been difficult to tell if anyone was home. As the three got back into the truck, the neighbor's curtains opened just a little allowing her to see out. She watched the three leave just as she had watched them when they arrived. The closing doors to the truck had alerted her to someone at Katherine's house, and she knew Katherine was on vacation.

Heading back to Sundancers, Ed said, "You'll never guess whose name I saw on one of the bags in her freezer?"
"Who?" Tina asked.
"Mike Benson."
"Who's he?" Kenny asked.
"Isn't he the Judge?" Tina asked.
"Sure is," said Ed.
"So, Kat has the Judge in her back pocket," commented Kenny.
"Or at least in her freezer," said Ed laughing.

Kenny and Tina laughed also. When they got to Sundancers, the three were still laughing as they walked inside.
"What's so funny?" Dee asked.
"Just a play on words," responded Tina.
"You three look like kids who just went to the ice cream store." Dee said.
"More like frozen yogurt," Tina replied.
"Good one Tina," said Kenny.

"Get us all a drink Dee, if you would?" Tina asked.

"Sure."

Ed said, "Do you think she'll be mad when she finds out someone was in her bed?"

"I doubt it," said Tina. "Kat has had lots of different people in that bed. I doubt she'll even notice."

"Oh, she'll notice," said Kenny. "I left a condom and zip-lock bag in her bed for her."

"Whose name was on it?" Ed asked.

"Tom Bowman," replied Kenny.

"That will really piss her off," added Tina.

Dee got each of them their regular drinks. The three sat at the bar laughing and joking for another hour.

Chapter 38

Frank and Katherine landed at Logan late in the afternoon. They picked up his car at long-term parking. It took an hour and fifteen minutes to drive back to Cape Cod.

Crossing the Sagamore Bridge, Katherine said, "It looks like the sunset is going to be beautiful."

"Want to stop at the beach on the way home?"

"Sure."

Fifteen minutes later, the two were getting out of the car at Chapin Beach. They walked to the end of the parking lot. The sunset was magnificent.

Katherine turned to Frank, "This was a wonderful trip Frank. What a way to end it. Isn't the sunset breathtaking?"

"Yeah, but darkness brings out all the evil."

"Frank, that's a terrible thing to say."

The two looked to the west. The majestic sun setting on the distant horizon produced a brilliant display of color in the sky as it slowly sank below the black sea. As it did, a cool brisk breeze gave Kat the chills returning her to reality. It was nighttime again, cougar time. She put her head on his shoulder, "Let's go to my place and finish this trip up in style."

They got into his car. When they got to her house, the two went inside.

"Leave the bags right there."

She took his hand and led him to the couch.

When they were finished, he got dressed, "I've got to get going. I'm going to my place to get things ready for my week," he said standing in her living room doorway.

"You're not going to stay the night?" she asked.

"No, I have a busy week and I want to get some things done before it gets too late."

"Ok."

"Where do you want the bags?"

"Put them in the bedroom if you would?"

"Sure."

While he was putting the bags in the bedroom, she went to the kitchen, took out a zip-lock bag, labeled it and put it in the freezer. When Frank came into the kitchen, he said, "It smells like magic marker."

"She took one out of a drawer, "I had a scuff on my shoe and used it to touch it up."

She pointed to what looked like a mark on her black shoe.

"I'm going to get going."

She put her arms around him, "I had a wonderful time Frank. I hope I can go with you again."

"There will be other trips," he said as he returned the kiss. "I'll call you tomorrow."

He let go of her and headed to the door.

Katherine followed him outside and waved as he drove away. She walked down to her mailbox and opened it. She

279

took out the stack of items and turned to walk back when she heard her neighbor from across the street say, "Your tenants didn't stay very long."

Katherine turned to see her nosey neighbor walking towards her with a drink in her hand. "Were you talking to me?"

"Yes. Your guests didn't stay very long on Friday night."

"I didn't have any tenants staying here while I was gone."

"Well, someone was here Friday night. They knew where the key was so I thought they were your guests."

"How many people were there?"

"Three. I think two men and one woman."

"What makes you think they were staying here?"

"The lights went on in the living room, kitchen and eventually the bedroom so I just thought they were guests staying while you were away."

"How long were they here?"

"I'd guess an hour or two."

"What kind of vehicle were they driving?"

"A pickup truck."

Katherine turned and went back to her house. When she got inside, she called Frank Jenkins.

"Frank, someone was here at my house while I was away?"

"Was it a delivery or something?"

"No. My neighbor said three people were in my house Friday night. She said she thought they were guests since they knew where my spare key is kept. She said she could tell they went through the house as lights went on and off from room to room."

"Can you tell if anything is missing?"

"Not that I can tell. Everything looks to be the same way as I left it."

"Well, check carefully. If you think something is missing, make a note of it and then come to the station in the morning."

"Ok. I don't like the idea that someone was here when I was away."

"Isn't that the neighbor you said is crazy?"

"Yeah, but she seemed to be ok when she talked to me just a little while ago although she did have a drink in her hand."

"Just check everything out and call me back if you are still concerned. Oh, and bring that spare key into the house."

"Ok."

Katherine grabbed the key, went back through her house and checked everything. She checked her jewelry. She checked her filing cabinet in her office. Her TV's and computer were still there. She even opened the freezer and saw the box of zip-locks was where she had left them. She didn't think anything was missing or changed.

Finally, she decided everything was in order. She decided to go to bed. She went into her bedroom. She turned the lights on and got undressed. She put on comfortable PJ's. She turned down the sheets on the bed and gasped.

"Oh, my god. What happened here?" she said as she looked at the stains on her sheet. Then she noticed the zip-lock. She picked it up and read the writing. "Tom Bowman."

She picked up the portable phone and called Frank Jenkins.

"Is there a problem Kat?" Frank asked.

"Someone's been here for sure."

"Is something missing?"

"Not that I can tell, but someone has been in my bed."

"Why do you say that?"

281

"I had changed the bed sheets before we left last Thursday and put clean ones on the bed. When I just turned the bed down for the night, I discovered stains on the sheets and a used condom."

"Could they have been there before?"

"No. I am particular that way."

"Bring the sheets in to the station in the morning and I'll have them tested. Maybe we'll get lucky and the lab will identify who was there."

"Can you do that?"

"Sure. I'll tie it to a case."

"Thanks Frank."

"No problem. I'll see you in the morning." She didn't mention that the condom was inside a zip-lock with Tom Bowman's name on it.

Katherine hung up the phone. She changed the sheets and put the dirty ones in a bag. She put the zip-lock back into the freezer. In the morning, she would take the bag to the police station.

After Katherine's call, Frank couldn't go so sleep so he decided to send an e-mail to Captain Tomlinson. In the e-mail, he told the Captain about Katherine's meeting with Charles Chamberlin in Rio. He noted that Chamberlin had changed his name and was now going by Wes Donlevy. He also mentioned the Donlevy name being part of the investigation of the widow crimes the two had looked into in the past. Jenkins told the Captain he would like to add a few extra days on his next trip to Rio to see if he could do something about Chamberlin. He closed the e-mail saying he would come see Captain Tomlinson when he got into the office in the morning.

Frank shut his computer down. He went to his kitchen and got a beer out of the refrigerator. He sat in his living room watching the news on TV thinking about his relationship with Katherine. He was having trouble coming to terms with her inability to stick with just one man: him. Then he remembered seeing the condom in her drawer at the hotel in Rio and made a mental note to check her freezer the next time he was there.

He wanted to see if she still had a bag there with his name on it.

After the news, he picked up the package he got at CVS containing prints of pictures he had taken in Rio. Frank thought to himself about how far picture-taking technology had come allowing him to utilize a disposable camera, drop it off on his way home and then pick up the finished pictures an hour later.

He sat on his couch for the next half hour looking at the pictures of Kat and him taken at all of the sightseeing landmarks in Rio. One picture in particular got his attention. The picture showed Kat in her bikini at Ipanema. He didn't remember taking the picture and wondered just who took it. He kept looking at the picture and remarked, "She sure is beautiful."

Finishing his beer, he decided to call it a night.

Chapter 39

Early the next morning, Jenkins arrived at the station before the morning shift meeting. When he got there, Captain Tomlinson was already in his office. Jenkins stuck his head in, "Morning Captain."

"You're in early."

"I couldn't sleep and I wanted to get caught up."

"I got your e-mail. So, Chamberlin's in Rio?"

"Sure is. How do you want me to proceed?"

"I'll have to get back to you. I'm not sure what the protocol will be given it's a different country."

"I have to go back there in a few months, so just let me know what you want me to do."

"I'll get back to you. How was you trip with Ms. Sterns?"

"She's amazing."

"She sure is," said Captain Tomlinson as he was gazing out his window. Frank wasn't sure what the Captain was referring to.

"So you had a good time?"

"We did."

"Good to hear. You should probably follow-up with Attorney Levine today as Bowman's sentencing is coming up."

"Will do. Anything else?"

"That'll be all for now."

Detective Jenkins went to his office. He went through his in-basket sorting out the important stuff from the junk. A report from Officer Trudy had been in the pile summarizing where things stood regarding Tom Bowman's sentencing. Trudy had written that the DA was going to recommend a total sentence of eight years for Bowman. Even though there were multiple convictions, the sentences would run concurrent all adding up to around eight years. Trudy's report said the judge was entertaining testimony for the sentencing aspect of the trial and had set a cutoff of Friday as the day witnesses could be listed. She wrote that the DA thought the sentencing aspect of the case would only last a few hours at the end of the following week.

Jenkins picked up his phone and called Attorney Levine.

"Attorney Levine, this is Detective Jenkins. I just returned from a business trip and wanted to follow-up with you regarding the sentencing aspect of Tom Bowman's trial."

"It looks like we're all set Detective. I'm recommending incarceration of eight years."

"That's what I read in Officer Trudy's memo. Don't you think you should try for more?"

"Bowman's a first time offender. The law's pretty lenient on first timers. I could ask for more but then the judge might reduce it even further if he thinks I didn't do my homework. I'll stick with what my research indicates is reasonable precedent."

"You're the attorney, I just think he would be getting off pretty easy given what he's done."

"I don't disagree. Bowman may think he didn't do very much, but our laws say otherwise. And as the saying goes, if you're going to do the crime, be prepared to do the time."

"Guess you're right."

"I think I'm on solid ground with my recommendation. The judge can always decide to put the guy away for more time if he wants."

"Does that happen often?"

"Not very often, but occasionally."

"Ms. Sterns wants to see this guy put away for a long time."

"She seems to be a revengeful woman. She was acquitted so she probably thinks the whole blame for everything that happened should fall on Bowman's shoulders."

"She has pretty much said those words to me."

"I hope she can put all this behind her. After all, most of what took place did so with her near or at the center of the action."

"Yeah, I know what you're saying but the judge didn't agree."

"I don't know about Judge Benson. He doesn't usually give up on a case as easy as he did with Ms. Sterns."

"About what? You don't think he will do the same thing to Bowman do you?"

"No. From what I gather, he's going to put the guy away for a while. He has been rejecting much of the arguments the defense has been submitting in the sentencing briefs."

"Well, is there anything else I need to do?"

"Not at this time. Thank you Detective."

"Call me if you want me to do anything."

"I will."

The defense team had been busy during this time as well. Attorney White had called upon Andrew Dunn to ask him a few questions regarding the circumstances of Mrs. Stern's interest in Sterns and Dunn. It just so happened that Katherine had just ticked Andrew off just before she left on a trip and Andrew was only more than happy to talk with the defense attorney. Andrew went to Attorney White's office during the same day that Katherine was returning from her trip. He met with Attorney White and Tom Bowman in Attorney White's conference room.

"Mr. Dunn, can you tell me about the relationship Ms. Sterns has with Sterns and Dunn?"

"Right now, she doesn't have anything to do with the firm. She sold her interest back to the firm some time ago and only has an investment in the form of a 401k still with the company."

"Is her 401k investment worth very much?"

"Yes. It's over a million dollars."

"Quite a big sum."

"Yes. Her husband Sam and I were partners. Sam put as much as he could into the 401k for years. It all went into company stock. As the firm grew, the 401k grew. That's how his retirement funds got to where they are today."

"So you really don't have any problems with her in relation to the business these days is that so?"

"Not really. She came to me recently and said she wanted to liquidate her 401k stock out of Sterns and Dunn and invest the money elsewhere."

"Do you plan on doing it?"

"By law, we have to. It isn't going to be easy, but I'm going to have to find a way."

"Can't you borrow the money?"

"It can take time and she wants her money in a few weeks. I'm racking my brains out trying to find some way to get her to back off a little. Then I would have time to put together a package allowing the firm to buy her 401k out without having to take on much debt."

"What would you do, find another investor?"

"Something like that."

"Can't you reason with her?"

"Have you ever tried to reason with Katherine Sterns? It's her way or the highway."

"I know the type. There must be something you can think of that would get her attention."

"She's so obsessed with this Bowman trial right now. I don't know what would distract her."

"Let's talk about the sentencing part of this case. The defense can call witnesses in order to get the judge to be more reasonable in sentencing. Maybe you know something we could use that would help Mr. Bowman and help your own cause at the same time?"

"What do you mean?"

"Well, you might be able to get the court to consider postponing any action against your firm while you were on the list to testify on Bowman's behalf."

"What could I possibly offer?"

"You'd be surprised what people know and don't know they know."

"I'm willing to help if it gets her off my back for a few weeks."

"Has she told you anything about this case?"

"Sure. She told me she got even with Tom Bowman. I'm not really sure what she meant, but I think she was referring to his conviction."

"How did she get even?"

"One day when I was at her house making drinks, I went to get ice out of the freezer. When I opened the freezer, I saw this box containing plastic bags with condoms in them. They were all labeled with names of men. When I asked her about it, she said they were insurance. I asked insurance from what and she just said insurance to get Tom Bowman."

"That's interesting."

"She also said she had a fool proof way of implicating Tom Bowman."

"Do you know what she meant?"

"No, she didn't elaborate."

"Would you be willing to testify in court as to what you just told me?"

"Sure if it buys me a little more time to raise the funds to buy out her stock."

"Let me list you as a witness for the sentencing hearing. I'll indicate you intend to show mitigating circumstances, which should be taken into account at Mr. Bowman's sentencing. At the same time, I'll tell the judge about Ms. Stern's request for the funds and make it look like she is only trying to hurt your firm. I think he will grant a postponement on that matter."

"How long do you think you can get?"

"Since the sentencing is scheduled for the end of next week, I'll initially ask for a month. We can always extend it if needed."

"I should be able to work out my company issues by then. Yeah, let's do it."

"I'll let you know if anything comes up Mr. Dunn. Thanks for coming in."

"You're welcome. I'll plan on being available for the sentencing hearing next week."

"My assistant will call and let you know the day, time and place."

"Got it."

After Andrew left the attorney's office Tom Bowman and Attorney White talked about the sentencing hearing.

"Tom, I'm going to have to rely on the judge's ability to see Ms. Stern's role in these attacks in order to get a favorable sentence for you."

"Do you think Andrew's testimony will help?"

"I'm counting on it. If we can deflect significant portions of the blame on to Ms. Sterns, I think we can expect a minimum sentence."

"What if the judge doesn't buy Andrew's testimony?"

"Let's not think in those terms. I don't see how Andrew's testimony would be ignored. It may even open up new charges against our precious Ms. Sterns."

"Ok. You're the attorney."

They concluded their meeting with Tom feeling a little better about his chances of receiving a favorable sentence.

Chapter 40

On the next night after returning from Rio, Katherine decided to go to Sundancers for a drink. She walked into the bar by herself. Everyone was there: Ann, Sue, Linda, Tina, Bobby, Kenny, Tommy, Paul and Ed. Katherine took up a stool by the windows sitting by herself.

"What will it be Ms. Sterns?" Ron asked.
"I'll have a dirty martini, extra olives please."
"Sure. Coming right up."

Ron went and made the martini. Once in front of her, she sipped it slowly and said, "Just how I like it."
"Anything else?"
"Not right now Ron. I may get something to eat later."
"Just let me know."
"I will."

Paul Bremmer was on his way to the men's room. He had to walk past Katherine to get there. As he passed by, she said, "Paul, how have you been?"

"Are you speaking to me?"

"Yes. How have you been?"

"Look Katherine, I don't think you should be coming in here with all you've done."

"What are you talking about Paul?"

"Kenny told us about the stuff in your freezer. We all think you had something more to do with all these attacks than you said or got punished for."

"Oh you do?"

"Not only me. Everyone thinks you're trouble."

"Everyone huh?"

"Everyone."

Katherine got up and walked around to where the tables were on the other side of the bar. Her friends and dates were all seated around the tables.

"So Paul says you all think I'm trouble. Is that right?" She said looking directly at Kenny.

Kenny turned to her, "Kat, I really wonder just how far you will go to make sure Bowman gets sentenced to the maximum."

"What are you talking about Kenny?"

"I saw the plastic bag with Benson's name on it."

"So it was you at my house Friday night?"

Ed turned to Tina, "I told you we'd get caught."

"I'm not saying if I was there or not Kat, but I never thought you would sleep with a judge just to make sure you got even with Bowman. Hell, you don't even know if Bowman's story about your husband's death was legit or not."

"I know Kenny. And it's none of your business who I sleep with."

"You're right about that. I tell you Katherine you had us all fooled. Ann, Sue and Linda all felt sorry for you. By sleeping with Bobby, Tommy and me, you made sure none of us would say anything. But you shouldn't have crossed Ed. He told me about your freezer. And yeah, we went to see for ourselves."

Kenny pulled a plastic bag out of his pocket and threw it on the table. It had his name written on the outside in magic marker.

"This belonged to me and I got it back. You're not going to implicate me in any of your deeds."

"You broke into my house without my permission. I can have you arrested for it."

"You can try but I'll deny it."

"My neighbor saw you. She saw two other people there as well. Was it you Ed?"

She turned to the women, "And which one of you had sex in my bed?"

Tina looked at her, "You'll never know?"

"Oh yes I will. I've given the sheets to the police this morning. They said they could have them tested for DNA. Then we'll know."

Ed said, "Oh shit."

"So it was you Ed. Who did you screw in my bed?"

Ed did not answer.

Katherine turned and walked away. As she did, Kenny said, "You'll get yours Kat."

She turned, "Are you threatening me Kenny?"

"I don't threaten Kat, you know me better than that."

"You all heard him."

"Not like anyone is going to come to your defense. Why don't you just leave?"

"I am."

She walked out leaving her unfinished martini on the bar.

Kenny yelled over to Ron, "Did she at least pay her bill?"

"No she didn't," was his reply.

"Just another thing to make Harry's day," added Bobby.

Ann said, "I think Kat has lost it. I still can't believe she set everyone up."

"Believe it," was Kenny's reply.

"What are we going to do about those sheets?" Ed asked.

"Don't worry Ed. I'll take care of it," Kenny said.

The group talked for another hour or so and then disbanded. Kenny went to the bar and paid his tab.

"I've got something I have to attend to," he said to Ron. "I'll be back later."

"See you later Kenny."

Sue said, "Maybe some of us should go over to Kat's and talk her out of pursuing this with the police?"

"She's got the goods on them as well," said Ed.

"What do you mean?" Linda asked.

"I saw bags in her freezer labeled Jenkins and Tomlinson. If I know her, she will use them against our two fine police officers to persuade them to do whatever she wants."

"She had condoms in her freezer from the police?" Ann asked.

"Those were the names on some of the bags."

"Did you see any other names?"

"Sure. Tommy Anderson, Bobby Jones, Tom Bowman and some guy named Andrew Dunn."

"That makes at least seven names when you include Kenny. Eight when you count the one I took out with my name on it."

"Wow," said Sue. "Kat's been real busy."

294

"Busy and calculating," said Ed.

"I don't think anyone should go over there to try to talk to her about anything right now," said Tommy. "She needs more than talking."

"What do you have in mind Tommy?"

"Nothing. I'm just saying we should all back off and see where things go. She'll probably calm down in a day or two."

"I don't know," said Ed.

Chapter 41

Katherine was mad leaving Sundancers. She wondered how everyone could have turned against her. Someone had turned the group. She considered those who might persuade the others against her. She decided to take a ride up to Chapin beach to see the sunset and calm herself. As she looked into the setting sun, she remembered what Frank had said when they were there together.

"Darkness brings out all the evil."

The sunset was breathtaking. Some darker clouds silhouetted in a white outline sat low in the western sky. The setting sun cast an array of red, yellow and orange against a blue sky. A reflection of sunlight danced across the ripples of Cape Cod bay in a path leading to the setting sun. The picture was both beautiful and threatening at the same time.

A light breeze kicked up. Kat's arms were all goose bumps. She went back to her car and went home. She knew everything pointed at Tom Bowman. She had made sure of it. How could everyone change his or her mind?

The obvious person was Tom Bowman. Katherine knew the women would never side with him over her. After all, he did go after Ann and Tina. He admitted to both of those attacks. He said he was outside Sue Kent's house the night when she was attacked and admitted putting something in Linda Sage's drink. Tom was a friend of Ed's but the other guys didn't really know him. There was no way Tom Bowman could have swayed her friends.

The next person she considered was Kenny Brown. Kenny had a temper and if he felt wronged, anything was possible. Kenny's attitude from earlier made him a prime suspect. He definitely had an axe to grind.

Katherine thought about each of the women and one by one ruled them out. The last woman she considered was Tina. Tina so much as admitted she was with Kenny at Katherine's house while she was in Rio. Tina had never really been close to Katherine and had challenged her for different men from time to time. Tina was definitely someone who could be persuasive. It had to be Tina. Katherine was sure Tina was the one who got Kenny all worked up and he in turn got the other guys all worked up.

Katherine didn't think Ann or Sue would take the lead to say or do anything against her. Katherine was a friend with both of them. They did things together outside of going to a bar. She was sure the instigator wasn't Ann or Sue.

Katherine didn't consider anyone else. Tommy was too young and Ed was too shy to take an aggressive posture towards anyone. She never considered anyone else outside of her circle.

Katherine made herself a martini. She went into her living room and turned on the television. She watched the NECN news thinking about the confrontation at Sundancers the whole time. She needed to talk with someone.

"Frank, it's Katherine."

"Is everything ok?"

"Not really. I went down to Sundancers tonight for a drink. Everyone there has turned against me."

"What do you mean turned against you?"

"Well, they were all sitting around at the tables in the bar area talking about me. When I said something to Paul Bremmer, he had harsh words for me. Someone in the group has mounted a campaign to turn everyone against me."

"Aren't you being just a little dramatic?"

"No. Kenny told everyone about the bags in my freezer and now they all think I set Tom Bowman up."

"Well, didn't you?"

"What are you jumping on the bandwagon too?"

"Kat, you did some things to make sure Tom Bowman was found guilty of assault and battery. Everyone knows it."

"But I didn't hurt anyone."

"You might not think so, but hurt doesn't always have to be physical. I think you might have crossed the emotional and mental line with your friends."

"I think they all made it perfectly clear that I'm not wanted back at Sundancers."

"Well, it's a public place. You can go there anytime you like."

"Yeah, and be cursed at or ignored."

"Well, it kind of goes with the territory."

"What does that mean Frank?"

"You used your friends and your relationship with them for revenge against Tom Bowman. I think they see it for what it was."

298

"Isn't there anything I can do about them?"

"Unless someone threatens you or harms you, there really isn't anything you can do."

"What about Kenny, Tina and Ed being in my house. I thing their actions should be considered a home invasion."

"I don't know about home invasion, but you have a point. Let's wait and see what comes from the analysis of the sheets you turned in."

"I don't know if I can wait. Kenny kind of threatened me."

"How did he do that?"

"He said I would get what was coming to me."

"Was he saying he intended to harm you or was he speaking metaphorically? Kind of like karma."

"I don't know."

"You need to be able to make the distinction if you want the police to confront Kenny."

"Oh, I don't want anything like that. Kenny would freak out and who knows what he would do then."

"That would be the kind of behavior the police could do something about."

"I'm not ready to go down that road right now."

"Then you'll have to accept things for the way they are. Why not give it a few days. Bowman's sentencing is only a few days off now and things might settle down once this is all over."

"Ok. I can be patient."

"Look, anything you heard at the bar might be just talk. After all, everyone was drinking and you know how liquor can bring out the worst in any situation."

"You're right. I'll see how things go. Thanks for talking to me."

"Your welcome. Call if you need to talk more?"

"I will."

The two hung up.

Katherine felt better after having talked with Frank. She decided she would go to bed and get a good night sleep. She went to her bedroom, turned down the comforter and sheet and opened the bottom drawer of her bureau taking out a pair of black silk pajamas with a playboy logo on them. She fluffed the pillows and climbed in. She turned the television in the bedroom on to the MTV channel. After a half hour, she turned the TV off and was soon fast asleep.

At sometime during the night, she awoke to a banging sound. It sounded like someone was trying to get into her house. She got out of bed and walked to the doorway of her bedroom. "Whose there?"

She didn't get an answer. Then there was another loud bang. She was sure someone was trying to break in. She went back into her bedroom, closed the door and called Frank. Frank was a little groggy having been woken from a sound sleep.

"Frank, it's Katherine. Someone is trying to break into my house."

"Are you sure?"

"I can hear the banging. Someone is trying to break in."

"Hold on a minute. Let me call the station."

He put her on hold and called the station. He asked the dispatcher to have someone go to Katherine's house and he provided the information. He told the dispatcher he had Ms. Sterns on hold and would stay on the line with her until help arrived. The dispatcher said an officer would be at Ms. Sterns address in a few minutes.

"Kat. I talked to the duty officer and he is sending someone over right away. Stay on the line with me until you hear the officer knocking."

"Ok. Thanks Frank. I know I should have called 911, but I feel more comfortable talking to you."

"No problem. The officer should be there soon."

Frank talked to her for a few minutes about the trip they had taken and about the pictures he had developed. The conversation took her mind off the situation at hand.

"I just heard a car door close out in my driveway."

"That should be someone from the station."

"Should I go outside?"

"Not yet, let the officer look around."

"Ok."

"I'm sure the officer will check everything out for you."

"Hold on. My doorbell just rang."

"It has to be the police. Take your portable phone with you and go answer the door."

"Ok."

She walked down the hall to her front door. She turned the lights on as she walked. When she got to the door, she looked through the glass and could see a uniformed officer standing at the door. She opened it.

"Ms. Sterns, I'm responding to a report of someone trying to break into your house?"

"Thank you officer. I have Detective Jenkins on the phone right now."

"Can I talk to him?"

"Sure."

She handed him the phone. The officer said "Yes, I'll do that and I'll call you if I find anything." Then the officer hung up and handed the phone back to Katherine.

"What kind of sound did you hear Ms. Sterns?"

"Someone was definitely trying to break into the house. It was a banging sound."

Just then, a gust of wind came up and the tree at the end of the porch banged against the side of the house.

"Like that sound?" asked the officer.

"Yes."

"It's just a tree blowing in the wind against the house."

The officer pointed in the direction of the end of the porch. Katherine stuck her head out and could see the branches of the tree hitting the side of the house.

"I'm sorry for having you come out officer. I was sound asleep and the noise scared me."

"Better to be safe than sorry Ms. Sterns. Is there anything else I can do for you tonight?"

"No, I think I'm all right."

"I'll take another walk around your house again just to be sure everything is in order. Then, I'll drive around the neighborhood to be on the safe side but I think you're fine."

"I appreciate your coming over, officer."

"No problem. Have a good night."

"Thank you again officer."

She closed the door and waited for the cruiser to leave. When it did, she turned the lights off and went back to bed. She was still a little unsettled, but was more tired than concerned.

Chapter 42

Katherine left one light on in the kitchen. She returned to the bedroom. Fluffing the pillows again, she slipped under the sheet and comforter. Every now and then, she could hear the same banging sound. Each time, she would reason with herself it was just the tree at the end of her front porch banging against the side of the house. She resolved to do something about the tree in the morning. Eventually, she fell asleep again.

After what seemed like only a few minutes, she awoke again. This time, she thought she heard someone in her kitchen. She lay still for a few minutes but didn't hear anything else. She wondered if her mind was just playing games with her. She pulled the comforter up to her shoulders and turned on her side so she could easily see the doorway. She closed her eyes and went back to sleep.

Katherine was just about entering the unconscious sleep state when she heard the floor in her bedroom creak. Before she could do or say anything, someone had put something over her face. She didn't know who it was or what was going on. She tried to scream but nothing came out. Her mouth was being covered. As her adrenaline kicked in, she tried desperately to breath. She drew in as hard as she could. Her lungs felt like they were about to burst. She was not getting enough oxygen. Then everything went blank.

Katherine had no recollection of what had just happened. She only knew someone had covered her mouth and she couldn't breathe. Then nothing.

Her body finally responded allowing her to regain consciousness. She immediately sat up in her bed. The comforter was lying on the floor along with the top sheet. Her head hurt from an intense migraine. She put her hands to the sides of her head and moaned, "What happened?" She sat in bed with her eyes closed for a few minutes. Finally, she squinted them open.

Her bedroom was too dark for her to see anything. She turned on the light next to her bed and looked around.

"What?"

She reached down and felt between her legs. They were wet. As she felt around, she discovered the bottom sheet had a large wet spot. Peering over the side of the bed, she saw a pile of zip-lock plastic bags strewn about on the floor. Scattered among the plastic bags were used condoms. Katherine picked up the zip-lock bag nearest the bed and read it.

"Tom Bowman."

She recognized the writing. She picked up another bag and read it. "Bobby Jones."

"What the heck?"

Katherine got up from her bed and looked at the clock. It was 4:17 am.

She felt a little cold. Reaching for her robe, she realized she had nothing on. "What happened to my pajamas?"

Looking around the room, they were missing. She put her robe on and went to her kitchen. There on the floor she found the box she had put in the freezer to hold the zip-lock bags. She picked it up. It was empty.

Katherine was groggy. She didn't know why. She tried to remember the events of the night. She remembered the confrontation at Sundancers, the noise at her front door, the police officer coming to the house and her call to Frank Jenkins. She picked up the phone.

"Frank, it's Katherine."

"What time is it?" He asked in a sleepy voice.

"A little after four."

"In the morning?"

"Yes. Frank, someone has been here," she said in a shaky voice.

"Are you sure Katherine? Did the police find anything?"

"No, and yes. The noise I heard was from a tree banging against the house."

"Well maybe it's the tree again?"

"Not this time. Someone was in my bedroom while I was sleeping."

"How do you know that?"

"Can you come over? I have something you need to see."

"Sure, but you'll have to give me a half hour."

"I'll make coffee. I need it anyway as I have a migraine that will not quit."

"Take some Tylenol. You'll feel better by the time I get there."

"Ok. The lights will be on."

Katherine filled the coffee maker with water, put in a new filter and added coffee. She turned it on. Then she went into the bathroom to get the aspirin. She took four thinking it would take four to relieve the migraine. Then she went back into the kitchen to sit and wait for the coffee to be done. She took two cups out of a cabinet putting a splash of half and half in one cup. When the coffee was ready, she poured herself a cup.

She took the cup into the living room. She sat on the couch cupping her hands around the coffee cup taking a sip every now and then. A little while later, she saw a set of headlights turn into her driveway casting light and shadows on the wall through her living room window. The door to the car closed. She heard footsteps on her porch and a light knock. Katherine got up and answered the door.

"Are you all right Kat?" Frank asked as he hugged her.

"No. Someone's after me."

Then she began to sob. He closed the door behind him, led her to the couch and sat down next to her, holding her in his arms.

"I don't know who was here," she said in a shaky voice.

Frank sat back so he could look her in the face to speak to her. As he did, he noticed her robe was undone and open. He could see she had nothing on underneath. It took a few seconds for everything to go through his mind. He finally said, "You said you wanted to show me something?"

"Follow me."

She stood and started walking to the bedroom. He thought to himself, "Why all the drama if she just wanted to get me in bed?"

Walking into her bedroom, she said, "See?"

Frank looked around. He recognized the plastic bags as the ones he had seen in her freezer previously. Two bags were on the bed. He picked them up and read the labels out loud.

"Bobby Jones, Tom Bowman."

He looked around the room at the other bags. He picked one up and read it out loud, "CC." He picked up another one reading it to himself. The bag had the name Frank Jenkins on it.

Katherine sobbed, "Someone was here a little while ago. I was violated."

"I can see that."

"No, I mean sexually. Look at my bed."

He did and saw the recently made stain.

Katherine opened her robe, "When I got up, my legs were all wet with semen. Someone assaulted me."

Frank looked around and saw all the condoms amongst the opened zip-lock bags.

"This is going to be really difficult figuring out who did this."

"Why do you say that?"

"Katherine, you had all these bags in your freezer. I don't see how we could put the blame on anyone for this attack. It may be someone you know, or not."

"Take the sheet to the lab and have them test it for DNA."

"Ok, then what. The report will probably show DNA from all those bags you had in your freezer. So who do I charge?"

"You have to do something Frank."

"I will. Let me collect this stuff and I'll take it back to the station. I'll talk with Captain Tomlinson and we'll determine how to proceed. You may have to buy new sheets soon Kat."

307

"I know and I'd appreciate all you're doing. Let me get you a cup of coffee while you're collecting the evidence."

Katherine went to the kitchen. She made Frank a cup of coffee. While she was gone, he took the garbage bag lining the wastebasket and went around picking up all the zip-locks and condoms. He would put his hand on the outside of the garbage bag having it act as a glove ensuring the integrity of the evidence. The last thing he did was to remove the fitted sheet and roll it up into a ball. He put it in the garbage bag along with the other evidence.

Returning to the kitchen, he said, "You'll have to remake your bed.

"I'll ask the lab to list all of the names on the zip-lock bags. Then you'll have to determine if they're all there."

"What do you mean?"

"Well, if I didn't just pick up all of the bags you had in your freezer, then whatever is on the set of sheets from the weekend might have come from your freezer."

"I didn't think of that possibility. Give me the bag, I'll tell you right now."

"I'd rather not. You could taint the evidence."

"I already touched the bags with Tom's and Bobby's names on them. Plus, the bags will have my fingerprints on the anyway since I put them in my freezer."

"Good point. Ok. Look at the zip-locks and give me the names. I'll write them down."

Katherine picked out every bag and read the name. Frank wrote them down. When she was done, she said, "That's all of them."

"Here's the list. Are they all there?"

She looked at the list, "Kenny's and Ed's are missing."

"I'll bet we find Kenny's and Ed's DNA on the sheets you took off your bed from the weekend."

"Then it has to be them."

"Did you look in your trash when you came home?"

"I had no reason to look there. Wait a minute. When I was at Sundancers, Kenny took a zip-lock out of his pocket and threw it on the table. He said something to me about it when I accused him of being at my house when I was gone."

"So you already accused him?"

"That's when he told me I'd get what was coming to me. He has to be the one."

"I'll take it from here Katherine. Don't you do anything."

"Ok."

"Listen Katherine. You should go to the hospital and get checked out. We may need a report from a doctor if you were raped. Why don't you get dressed and I'll take you there?"

"I'll go first thing in the morning."

"Ok. Tell the ER doctor I need the report right away."

"I'll tell him."

"I'm going home to get some sleep. Why don't you do the same?"

"Thanks Frank. You're a good friend."

"Yeah, that's me."

He walked to the door and picked up the evidence and left. He would bring it in for processing in the morning. At that moment all he wanted to do was get back to sleep.

Chapter 43

In the morning, Katherine dressed but did not shower. She reasoned she had to preserve any evidence that might be on her body. She got into her car and went to the hospital. There she explained to the doctor what had happened the night before and told him what Frank had wanted her to tell him. The doctor said he understood and performed the tests he needed, putting any evidence he found in plastic bags, labeling them and sending them to the lab. The whole process took less than an hour.

On her way home from the hospital, she called Frank's cell phone.

"Detective Jenkins," he said answering his cell.

"Frank, I've just left the hospital. I told the doctor what you wanted him to do and he said you should look for the lab report in a day or two."

"Thanks. Now I'll take the things I took from your place earlier this morning and yesterday and have them tested. Let's hope we get a lead out of all of this."

"What should I do?"

"Nothing. Let me handle it."

"Ok. Will I see you tonight?"

"I don't know. Let me get things going and I'll call you later."

"Ok. Bye."

Detective Jenkins went in to see Captain Tomlinson.

"Captain, you're not going to believe this."

"What do you have Frank?"

"I got a call from Katherine Sterns at a little after four this morning. Someone attacked her at her house."

"You're kidding me?"

"No. And it gets pretty messy from there."

"What do you mean?"

"Well, she had been collecting condoms in zip-locks from the men she had been sleeping with for some time and storing them in her freezer. It looks like someone who knew she was doing that went to her place during the night and sexually attacked her."

"Have her examined and the DNA will prove who did it."

"Not so easy in this case. When I went to her house after the attack, all the zip-locks and condoms from her freezer were thrown around her bedroom."

"You mean someone spread the condom contents all around her place?"

"Yeah, and on her as well."

"Now that's something."

"It gets worse."

"How can it get worse?"

"I have a list here of all of the names from the zip-lock bags she had stored the condoms in."

"Ok. So you have someplace to start?"

"You'll need to sit for this one."

"Give it to me."

Captain Tomlinson sat as his oversized desk chair behind his deck. Jenkins took up one of the side seats and began reading from the list he had in his pocket.

"Tommy Anderson, Bobby Jones, CC, that's Charles Chamberlin, Tom Bowman, Andrew Dunn, Frank Jenkins," he stopped to catch his breath.

"So she saved your DNA as well? You've been seeing her for sometime. You shouldn't be surprised."

"That's not all."

"Who else?"

Frank took a deep breath, "Mike Benson."

"The judge?"

"I think so. How many other Michael Bensons do you know around here? It's just too much of a coincidence."

"And I don't like coincidences."

"There's more."

"What can be worse than the judge?"

Frank took another deep breath and again reading from the list said, "Lou Tomlinson."

"Holy crap."

The enormous impact hit him all at once.

"If that information ever got out all hell would break loose."

"Any more?"

"Katherine said there were a few bags missing."

"Who did they belong to?"

"Kenny Brown and Ed Phillips. She said Brown threw a bag with his name on it at her at Sundancers yesterday. So, she thinks he was at her place when she was with me in Rio."

"Then Kenny Brown is probably the guy?"

"But what if his DNA doesn't show up on the things I'm having tested by the lab?"

"I see your point. This is a real mess."

312

"What do you want me to do?"

"I don't know. I'll need to think about this for a while."

"I have to drop the evidence off at the lab. I'll be back in a little while."

"Come see me when you get back and let's see if we can find a way out of all of this."

"Ok Captain."

Detective Jenkins left the station to have the evidence he had collected analyzed. He told the lab technician he wanted the report as soon as possible and to make it a priority. He wanted it returned with the results from yesterday's sheets. The lab technician said he would get right on it.

Driving back to the station, Frank decided he would stop in at Sundancers to see if Kenny Brown was there. He pulled into Sundancers driveway and parked right near the door. Kenny was sitting next to Ed at the bar having a drink when Detective Jenkins walked in. He saw Kenny and walked over to him.

"Mr. Brown, can I speak with you for a few minutes in private?"

"Sure Detective."

The two walked out on to the empty back deck and sat at a table.

"What can I help you with?"

"Yesterday, you made some threatening remarks to Ms. Sterns didn't you?"

"No. I may have said to her that she will get what is coming to her but I didn't threaten her. Why are you asking me?"

"Someone attacked her early this morning."

"So I'm your suspect?"

"She said you were rather hostile to her yesterday."

"Well I didn't do it. Whatever it was."

"Then can you tell me where you were last night?"

"Sure. I was here."

"How about at four this morning?"

"I was at Tina Fletchers. I stayed at her place last night."

"Where can I find Ms. Fletcher so I can confirm your alibi?"

"She's right inside."

"I didn't see her when I came in."

"She was in the ladies room. Go see for yourself."

Frank stood and opened the door. Sure enough, Tina was seated next to Ed having a drink. He walked over to her, "Ms. Fletcher, Mr. Brown has told me he spent the night at your house last night. Can you confirm his story?"

"Sure Detective. He was there all night. As a matter of fact, we came here from my house together just a little while ago."

"And he was with you the whole time?"

"Yes he was."

Kenny walked up behind Detective Jenkins, "See? I told you so."

"What's this all about?" Tina said looking at Jenkins and Kenny.

"Someone attacked Katherine last night."

"You're kidding?" said Ed.

"And Detective Jenkins thinks it was me," Kenny said sarcastically.

"Well, you did have words with her yesterday Kenny," said Tina.

"Yeah, but I didn't do anything to her. And I was with you all night Tina," he said with a smile. "Can't help you Detective," Kenny added.

Detective Jenkins turned and walked away from the three. As he did, Ed could be heard saying, "So someone got to Katherine."

The three snickered.

Kenny said, "Then someone did what we were all thinking."

"Kenny, that's mean," commented Tina.

"Tina, she's the devil in all of this. It had to backfire on her soon or later."

"I guess."

Jenkins got into his car and left.

Chapter 44

Detective Jenkins went back to the station. He stopped by his desk before going in to see Captain Tomlinson. The message light on his phone was blinking. He picked up the receiver and called for messages.

"Detective, this is Vince Morgan from the lab. I have the results from the Sterns examinations. Please give me a call."

Jenkins called the lab.

"Vince, this is Detective Jenkins. I had a message to call you?"

"I have the results from the ER examination. I thought you would want the results as soon as possible."

"I do, what did you find?"

"There were a number of different sets of DNA. I ran the results through our computers and got matches on some of them."

"What names matched up with the DNA?"

"Let me see." Frank could hear the clicking of keyboard keys. "Ah, here it is. Tommy Anderson, Bobby Jones, Captain Tomlinson, Judge Benson and you."

There was a moment of silence and then Frank said, "You found DNA from the Captain, Judge Benson and me?"

"Yes. You remember a few years ago when the state had a program to put all law enforcement people into a computer system in order to isolate their DNA that might be involved in any crimes from the criminals?"

"Yeah, I remember."

"Well, the data base is now available for use. When I ran the comparisons against the sample taken at the hospital, the computer program automatically checks with the law enforcement database."

"I know I touched the sheets when I picked them up but I didn't think we tainted the evidence."

"This isn't from the sheets. This DNA came from the internal on Ms. Sterns."

Detective Jenkins knew the Judge, Captain and he were positively identified. He would have to talk to Tomlinson.

"Anything else Vince?"

"Yes. DNA from a few other men remain unidentified."

"How many?"

"Three. I stopped the scan after the third one. I thought something must be wrong with the material or the database because three no-hits never happens."

"What if the three were from people not from this State?"

"I guess it might explain it. But I have never had a scan have more than one miss."

"Could there have been more?"

"Yes but they would all have been misses. The search program cycles through the list looking for hits and then retries the unidentified ones. So the misses show last."

"Thanks for the information Vince. I'm going to have to talk with my boss."

"That should be interesting."

"I'm sure it will be."

"Can you send the report to my attention?"

"I'll e-mail you the report this afternoon."

"And Vince. Please don't say anything to anyone about your findings."

"I understand."

"Thanks. Good bye."

Frank Jenkins walked down the hall and knocked on Captain Tomlinson's door.

"Come in Detective."

"Captain, I just got the results from the lab regarding the sexual assault examination Ms. Sterns had at the Hospital. The computers confirmed what was found on the sheets."

"What did you find out?"

"Somehow, whoever attacked Ms. Sterns took all those condoms out of those zip-lock bags and inserted them into Ms. Sterns."

"What pervert would do something like that? I can understand squeezing the contents on her and the sheets to create confusion, but inside?"

"Well, think about it. If the perp squeezed the contents of all the condoms on her in the right place and then had sex with her, it's possible all that DNA went along for the ride."

"I see what you mean. If this ever went to trial, my career and marriage will be over."

"Yours, mine, the judge's and who knows who else."

"What do you mean?"

"Vince Morgan from the lab said there were three other samples, maybe more, that the computer couldn't identify. He stopped the program when he saw three unidentified people. He said the computer has never had three people it couldn't identify."

"What it did identify is enough. You're going to have to talk to Ms. Sterns about this Frank and convince her to drop the whole thing before too many people get hurt."

"I can certainly try."

"Is there anything else you want to tell me?"

"Morgan talked to me for a few minutes about the second set of sheets which were tested. He said the computer matched up the samples he was able to extract from that sheet to Ed Phillips and Kenny Brown. Then Morgan made an off-hand comment that the samples from the sheets and ER exam tied all the guys involved in the cougar attacks together including the investigating officer and judge. He said he couldn't remember ever hearing of a situation where everyone involved in a case had been implicated in a follow-up crime."

"Interesting observation. It's like someone has something against all the men and is trying to implicate all of them."

"Or someone wants to get back at Ms. Sterns and figured throwing so much confusing evidence into the mix would make it impossible to identify the responsible party."

"Could be."

"Frank, speak to her. Make sure she understands the situation."

"I will."

Detective Jenkins went back to his office. He called Katherine.

"Kat, it's Frank. How are you doing?"

"I'm ok. I'm just upset that someone did this to me."

"Listen, I received the reports back from the lab. The results from the sheet you took off your bed when we returned from Rio positively matched Ed Phillips and Kenny Brown."

"I figured as much since those were missing from my freezer and they talked about it at the bar already. While Ed didn't throw it in my face, he didn't deny being there when Kenny did produce one of my zip-locks at Sundancers."

"The DNA found on the second set of sheets matched up with all the bags. You know that information is going to be a real problem for Captain Tomlinson, Judge Benson and me?"

"I know. I shouldn't have kept those three."

"I can't believe you slept with the Captain and the judge?"

"The Captain thing just happened. Mike Benson, the judge, and I go back to college. I knew him back then and hooked up with him again as a result of this case."

"Did you have to sleep with him?"

"It was the only way I could think of that would ensure he did the right thing with Tom Bowman."

"Kat, that's just wrong. The sex is one thing, but using it to manipulate the legal system?"

"As it turned out, Judge Benson said he was sentencing Tom to jail anyway. I just made sure the Judge wasn't going to go soft on me."

"Wow."

The two were quiet for a few seconds allowing the conversation to sink in.

"Kat, the results of the emergency room exam have been completed as well. The lab technician told me the material collected in the ER matched the material on the second set of sheets."

"That would mean someone put all those...." Her voice trailed off and she didn't complete the sentence.

"There is another possibility."

"Like what?"

"If the contents of the things you had in your freezer were squeezed on you in that area and someone had sex with you right after squeezing them out, then the DNA from the condoms might have gotten inside."

"So you think someone took the stuff I had in my freezer, put it on me, then had sex with me and that's how all the other DNA got there? I feel so much better. Thanks."

"It certainly is possible. Plus, the lab technician told me the computer couldn't identify some individuals from the DNA."

"How many?"

"Three."

"The scan originally showed three unidentified individuals, but two of the unidentified matched samples from the bags. Since the bags had names on them, the lab technician assumed the name on the bag indeed identified the contents found inside. So while they weren't in the database, the bags were labeled. Two of the mystery people were identified."

"Who did those belong to?"

"One was from a bag labeled Roman. Wasn't he the concierge in Rio?"

"Yes."

"And you had sex with him?"

"When he went to the cabana on the first day, I saw how excited Roman got when he rubbed lotion all over my body. I couldn't resist. Who was the other person?"

"There was one bag in your freezer without a full name on it. There was something written on the bag that looked like initials. It wasn't a zip-lock like the others but rather one of those clear plastic bags like the ones you put ice in. Do you remember putting something like that into your freezer?"

"Yes. I had two of those bags when we came back from Rio. I put Roman's in a zip-lock and it was the last one I had so I just left the other one the way it was."

"Who did it belong to?"

"Charles Chamberlin."

"So you slept with him in Rio?"

321

"Yes."

"Kat, we were only there a few days. How did you find time to sleep with two other men when we were there? Plus, we had sex every day."

"I know Frank. You've been so good to me. I just can't help myself."

"Katherine, I think you might want to just drop this whole thing. Too many people are going to be hurt."

"What about us?"

"What about us?"

"I know you're hurt by my bad decisions, but I love you."

"Then I would suggest you put all of this behind you and forget about what happened."

"But what about the person who raped me?"

"How do you think it might be proven? Just think about it. Trying to explain collecting those condoms coupled with the attacks on the women and Bowman's testimony. I don't think your case would be credible."

"Ok. I'll think about it. Can I see you tonight?"

"Why don't you meet me at Sundancers in an hour. I'm off duty by then and I could use a drink."

"I'll meet you there in an hour."

Jenkins hung up the phone and took a deep breath. This was not going to be a good night.

Chapter 45

Frank Jenkins got to Sundancers before Katherine. He took a seat at the bar opposite the door. Dee came over to him.

"What will it be Detective?"

"Give me a Bud please."

"Sure."

Linda, having seen the Detective come in by himself, approached him.

"By yourself tonight Detective?"

"I'm meeting someone."

"Not Katherine I hope."

"Why do you say it like that?"

"She's out to get everyone here eventually," said Linda curtly.

Harry Adams had come out of the kitchen and went behind the bar. He was putting extra bills into the register and overheard the conversation between Linda and Jenkins. He pretended to count the bills while listening.

"I'm sure she has her reasons," Jenkins responded.

"Look Detective, she slept with everyone here. She saved the used condoms. She participated in attacking me and the other women and spread her conquests on us. We have a right to be mad at her."

"You're getting yourself all worked up Ms. Sage. Maybe it was you who attacked her."

Harry smiled and continued counting.

The door to the bar opened and Katherine walked in. She walked over to Jenkins and kissed him on the cheek. She looked at Linda, "Hi Linda."

Linda Sage didn't respond. She turned and walked away. Katherine sat at the stool next to Jenkins.

"I'll have a martini Dee."

"Sure Katherine. I'll be right with you."

After making the drink and putting it in front of Katherine, Frank said, "I have something to tell you."

"Is it more bad news?"

"Not bad. Just different."

Katherine took a bigger than normal sip of her drink and sat back on the stool.

Frank took a deep breath, "I'm going to become a Chief of Police."

"No kidding? That's great."

"In Farmington, Connecticut."

"What?"

"I was contacted by a friend of mine some time ago about an opening they had to head up the Farmington Police Department. I went on an interview. When I got back from Rio, I had an offer letter waiting for me."

"So you're going to take it?"

"I am. It's a big pay raise and a promotion."

"Plus it gets you away from me?"

"I'd like you to go with me."

"To Connecticut?"

"Yes. We could start over down there."

"I don't know."

"Will you think about it?"

"What would the people in Connecticut think if you took the job and I moved in with you?"

"I don't think they would think anything was strange if Mr. and Mrs. Jenkins moved to Connecticut."

She looked at him with surprise. "Are you proposing?"

"I'm moving in that direction. I need to get down there and settle in. Then, I'd like you to come down as my fiance."

"So you want me to be your fiance?"

He produced a diamond ring from his pocket and went to put it on her finger. She pulled it back.

"What's wrong?"

"Oh, nothing. I hadn't thought about it this way."

He tried to put the ring on her again. This time, she allowed him to put the ring on her finger. She held her hand up and smiled.

"Mrs. Katherine Jenkins. I like the sound of it."

Frank said to Dee, "Can we have some champagne?"

"Sure, what are you celebrating?"

Katherine held up her hand.

"Wow, that's beautiful."

Harry, who had stayed behind the bar pretending to straighten things up heard the exchange, "Champagne's on me. Congratulations."

The two sipped the champagne, talking, laughing and smiling. After a half hour, they both got up and left.

Sue Kent walked up the bar, "What was Katherine so happy about?"

"She just got engaged."

"You're kidding?"

"No. Detective Jenkins gave her a ring."

Harry added, "And they're moving to Connecticut."

"Really?" said Sue.

"Really," Harry responded.

Sue turned around and yelled to her friends seated at the tables off to the side of the bar, "Guess what?"

She was kind of jumping up and down smiling waiving her hands in circles like a little girl.

Bobby said, "Ok what?"

"Katherine is going to marry Detective Jenkins."

Tina said, "What?"

"Harry heard them at the bar. He brought them champagne to celebrate and yes, she is engaged."

"Oh God," said Tina.

"It gets better," said Sue.

"What could be better than getting Katherine out of the mix?" Tina asked.

"They're moving to Connecticut."

"Really?"

Harry walked over, "Really. I heard them myself. Everyone, drinks are on me."

Harry walked back to the bar and helped Dee set up drinks for everyone. After they had taken care of the patrons, Dee said, "Why are you so happy, Harry?"

"Maybe now my business can get back to normal. Hopefully all this unfinished business is all wrapped up now."

"Has it really affected you that much?" Dee asked.

"You can't imagine."

Harry turned and went back to his office passing through the kitchen as he went. He was whistling a tune, smiling and snapping his fingers.

Antonio came out of the kitchen walking up to the bar.

"What got into him?"

"He thinks he just won the lottery."

"No kidding?"

"Yes, I'm kidding. He really thinks he just got lucky."

"Oh," said Antonio. "Can I get a shot?"

"Sure."

Dee got Antonio his favorite.

Chapter 46

Frank and Katherine went to her house. Once inside, Katherine threw her arms around him and began kissing him.

"You are going to make me a very happy woman," she said.

"I'm going to Connecticut this weekend to look for a place to live. I have to be there on Monday to formally accept the position and meet the department. I expect to be back by mid-week."

"Can't I come to help find a place?"

"I'm only going to look at upscale apartments to start. Once we are down there for a little while, we can start looking for a house."

"You and me in a house together?" She stopped talking and thought for a minute.

"Having second thoughts already?"

"No, I'm just thinking of all of the things I have to do."

"Well, you'll have a lot to do here while I'm getting things set up in Connecticut. I'd expect you'll move down as soon as you have wrapped things up here."

"I think I can do that. Let's go to my bedroom and celebrate the right way."

Katherine showed Frank her appreciation. An hour later, Frank was getting dressed when he said, "Are you going to the sentencing for Tom Bowman in the morning?"

"Yes."

"I'm sure everyone will be there. I'm picking Captain Tomlinson up at his house at nine. I'll see you there."

"Ok. I hope the judge gives him the maximum."

"I'm sure he will get a fair sentence."

"I don't want fair. I want the maximum."

"You'll need to get over this Kat. You're obsessed with Bowman."

"I guess I still hold a lot of resentment."

"I hope you can let it go."

"If the judge does the right thing, I'm sure I will."

"I think we've done all we can. Now it's all up to Judge Benson."

"You're right. I feel I've done all I could."

"And then some," Frank said as he leaned over to give her a goodbye kiss.

"I'll look for you at the courthouse," she said returning the kiss.

"See you then."

He left her house locking the front door behind him. He got into his car and went home for the night.

As planned, he picked up Captain Tomlinson at nine the next morning.

"Thanks for picking me up Frank."

"No problem Captain."

"So you're going to take the job in Connecticut?"

"Yes. It's a promotion and a change of scenery."

329

"Gets you away from all the problems up here doesn't it?"

"Well, not all. I've asked Katherine to go with me."

"Are you sure you know what you're doing with her?"

"I'm sure. She can be just terrific when she wants to be."

"Yeah, I know."

"Not just like that. She can be funny and spontaneous. The kind of things this guy likes in a woman."

"Maybe. Just be careful. She has a storied past."

"I know what you mean. I think she was so affected by the tragic events in her life, it drove her to do crazy things."

"I hope you're right for your sake."

"Me too."

"We're here. Is she coming to the hearing?"

"She said she wouldn't miss it for anything in the world."

"Oh God. I hope she controls herself."

"She promised she would be good."

"Are you sure you knew what she was talking about?"

"I think so."

"Well, sit next to her and keep an eye on her. If it looks like she's going to do something drastic, restrain her."

"Got it."

The two men parked and walked into the courthouse. They looked up Judge Benson's courtroom for the day and proceeded there. They were a few minutes early. Katherine was standing outside the courtroom acting very fidgety. Frank walked over to her.

"Kat, you ok?"

"Yes. I'm just nervous."

"Relax, there isn't anything more you can do."

"I could go see the judge before the hearing starts."

"I don't think it's necessary. The Captain tells me Bowman is going to jail for a long time."

"I hope so."

"Come on. You can sit with me."

"Ok."

The two walked into the courtroom. Tom Bowman was sitting with his attorney at the defense table. Attorney Levine was sitting at the prosecution table. A few more people came into the room and took their seats. Then, the court officer stood and announced, "All rise. Court is now in session. The honorable Judge Michael Benson presiding."

Everyone stood. The door behind the bench opened and Judge Michael Benson entered. He sat down and instructed everyone to be seated with the rap of his gavel. He read a document on his desk and then looked up. His eyes made contact with Katherine in the back of the room and she smiled. His expression did not change.

"Ms. Levine, are you ready to proceed?"

"Yes, your honor," she replied.

"Mr. White, is the defense ready?"

"Yes, your honor."

"Ms. Levine, do you have any witnesses you would like to call to the stand?"

"No your honor. The state is ready to proceed with sentencing."

Judge Benson looked to Attorney White, "Mr. White, your brief indicated you would like to call one witness, a Mr. Andrew Dunn. Is that correct?"

Katherine was stunned. She yelled out, "He can't."

"Order in the court," demanded Judge Benson. "If there are any more outbursts, I'll have that person removed."

Frank grabbed Katherine's arm coaxing her to be seated. He leaned in to her and said quietly in her ear, "Katherine, you have to keep yourself under control."

"But Andrew can't testify. I told him things about the attacks that might affect the outcome."

"You can't do anything about it now Katherine. It would probably be hearsay anyway. Let's see what he has to say."

Katherine could see Judge Benson saying something to his court officer. The officer came down the aisle and stood right next to her. She looked at the officer but didn't say anything. His presence next to her was very clear.

"Go ahead Mr. White and call your witness."

Attorney White called Andrew Dunn to the stand and he was sworn in.

"Mr. Dunn, do you know the defendant?"

"Yes."

"How do you know him?"

"He had been a friend of my former business partner."

"And who was that?"

"Sam Sterns."

"Is Mr. Sterns still your business partner?"

"No, Sam died in a freak fishing accident some time ago."

"Do you know Mr. Sterns is a widow?"

"Yes."

"How do you know her?"

"She became my partner when her husband died."

"So she inherited his interest in the business?"

"Yes."

"Did she play an active role after her husband died?"

"Not in the traditional sense."

"What do you mean?"

"Well, I got to know her personally after her husband died. She agreed to let me run the business so long as we remained close."

"Did she ever express an opinion regarding the circumstances of her husband's death?"

"Yes. She said Mr. Bowman had killed her husband."

"Did she offer any evidence?"

"Yes. She said Bowman told her he had done it all for her."

"How did you interpret what she told you?"

"That Sam Sterns died in some other way than was reported."

"Did Ms. Sterns ever confide in you about the attacks of which Mr. Bowman has been convicted?"

"Yes, she told me she had made a plan to get back at Mr. Bowman and it apparently worked."

"Why do you say it worked?"

"Well, he's been convicted and we're here today for his sentencing."

"So, if I understand you correctly, you're saying Mrs. Sterns orchestrated the attacks of which Mr. Bowman has been convicted?"

"Objection your Honor. The witness is trying to describe something that hasn't been proven."

"Overruled. You may answer the question Mr. Dunn."

"Yes, that's what I'm saying."

"Thank you Mr. Dunn. Your witness."

Attorney Levine stood, "Mr. Dunn, have you ever been romantically involved with Ms. Sterns?"

"I don't know what you mean."

"Have you ever had sex with her?"

Andrew Dunn was quiet for a minute. Then he picked his head up and looked to the back of the room right at Katherine.

"Yes. I have had sex with her."

333

"Can you tell us the first time you had sex with her?"

"She called me when her husband had gone missing and asked me to comfort her."

"Comfort her? What did you do?"

"I went to her house and stayed the night with her."

"On how many occasions?"

"A few times while her husband was missing and then pretty much on a regular basis for some time after his death."

"So you had sex with Ms. Sterns while her husband was missing and then regularly after he died. Is that right?"

"Yes."

"Are you still having sex with her?"

"No."

Katherine stood, "That's a lie. You slept with me a few nights ago."

"Order in the court," Judge Benson insisted, banging his gavel on the bench.

"I'll tolerate no more outbursts."

The court officer turned to Katherine as if to tell her it was time to leave. As he extended his hand to take hold of her arm, Judge Benson said, "If you say anything else Ms. Sterns, the officer will escort you out of my court."

"I'm sorry your honor. It won't happen again."

Attorney Levine turned to Andrew Dunn, "Have you had sex with Ms. Sterns recently?"

"Yes, I forgot. I slept with her recently and I know I shouldn't have. But that bitch was and is putting my back against a wall with my business. She wants my company to buy back the stock her husband had in the company's 401k plan. She implied she would keep the stock if I cooperated. I didn't want to get her mad at the company so I slept with her. Then after we had sex, she reneged."

"Mr. Dunn, you are showing animosity towards Ms. Sterns. We're here to determine the sentencing for Tom

334

Bowman. Isn't it true you have allowed your distaste for Ms. Sterns influence your testimony?"

"No. She's guilty."

"But she's not being sentenced here, Tom Bowman is."

"That's only because she slept with....." he stopped himself and didn't continue. He looked at Judge Benson. The Judge was quick to realize what Mr. Dunn was about to say.

Judge Benson said, "You're excused Mr. Dunn. It's evident you have been deeply affected by your relationship with Ms. Sterns. Your testimony is not relevant to the sentencing for which we are here today."

Attorney White jumped up, "I object. Your Honor can't just dismiss the testimony of the witness."

"Mr. White, it is my opinion that Mr. Dunn has been involved in a questionable relationship with Ms. Sterns both before and after the death of her husband. For whatever reason, Mr. Dunn has an axe to grind with Ms. Sterns and is trying to use this court to get even with her. As such, I cannot allow his testimony to be considered in the sentencing of Tom Bowman. The witness is excused."

Andrew Dunn got up and walked out of the courtroom. Katherine gave him a nasty look as he walked past her. Everyone who stood up sat down and Judge Benson looked to both counsels and said, "Anything else?"

Neither counsel said anything.

Judge Benson took a few minutes reading and turning the pages of documents and notes he had on his desk. He looked up and toward the defense table. "Will Mr. Bowman please rise?"

Tom Bowman stood along with his attorney.

Judge Benson read from a document on his bench, "I, Judge Michael Benson, do hereby sentence Mr. Thomas

Bowman to a term of twenty-five years with no chance for parole for the crimes he has committed in the case."

There was a hush in the courtroom. Then out of nowhere, Katherine yelled, "Yes."

She smiled at Judge Benson. He didn't look at her.

"Sheriff, please take the defendant into custody."

The Sheriff handcuffed Tom Bowman and led him out of the courtroom.

Katherine and Frank got up and left. She was smiling, holding his arm as they left the courthouse.

Outside, he said, "Are you happy now?" Frank said walking her to the car.

"Absolutely. Finally, he got what was coming to him."

"Now you can get on with your life."

They got into their respective cars and left.

Chapter 47

On the way home, Katherine wanted to have a celebratory drink. She pulled into the Sundancers parking lot. She was smiling as she entered the bar. She sat at the bar and ordered a martini and Dee made it for her.

"Life is good today huh Katherine?" Dee asked.

"Sure is. I just came from the courthouse. Tom Bowman was sentenced to twenty-five years."

"Wow."

"He'll be an old man if and when he gets out."

"Is that what you wanted?"

"I wanted more, but he pretty much got as much as the judge could impose."

She sipped the martini and looked around. Everyone who had been at the courthouse who had also gone to Sundancers was looking at her.

Ed said, "She shouldn't be so happy. She played a role in all of this."

"I agree with you Ed," added Kenny.

"She's leaving Cape Cod to marry Detective Jenkins," added Tina. "We won't see much more of her. Thank God."

"Probably all for the best," said Harry as he had been walking by the group when he heard them talking about Katherine.

Harry walked back to the bar and stood in front of Katherine.

"Sounds like everything went the way you wanted it to go Katherine," Harry said looking at her.

"Let me buy you a drink."

"Harry that's so thoughtful of you."

"Dee, get Katherine another drink and bring me one as well."

"Sure Harry."

Dee made the drinks and brought them over to the two. She put them on the bar. Harry picked up his drink and declared, "Here's to getting what you asked for and hopefully to the end of the attack on my patrons."

Katherine picked up her drink, touched her glass to his and took a sip.

Harry said, "Isn't revenge sweet?"

Katherine looked at him with confusion.

Harry added, "Now that this is all behind you Katherine, what are your plans?"

"As you know I'm engaged to be married to Detective Jenkins," she held up her hand so he could see the ring. "He's taking a new job in Connecticut as Chief of Police and we're both moving."

They both finished their drinks in two or three awkwardly quiet sips.

"Good for you," Harry said and he raised his glass again.

"Well, thanks for the drink Harry, I have to be going."

"Good luck," Harry said as she got up and left.

As Katherine was getting into her car, Harry said to Dee and Ron, "Now my business can get back to normal." He was smiling.

"Why are you so happy?" Ron asked.

"She wasn't good for business," was Harry's response.

"She added to the character around here," added Dee.

"She is a character," said Harry. "I'm glad she's moving. I hope she never returns."

Jenkins went back to the station after court. He did some paperwork. Captain Tomlinson stuck his head into Jenkins office, "Well, that worked out fine."

"It was touch and go for a little while."

"Yeah, I thought some things were going to be said where Judge Benson might have had to excuse himself."

"Thankfully it didn't happen."

"I'm just wrapping up here and then I'm headed home to do some packing before I go over to Katherine's. I have to be in Connecticut for a few days. I'll be back in next week to wrap up any loose ends."

"Ok Frank. Good luck with the new job and with Katherine."

"Thanks Captain."

Frank Jenkins carried a box of his personal things to his car. He put it in the trunk and then got behind the wheel. He called Katherine on his cell.

"Kat, I'm leaving the station. You want to go to Sundancers and get a drink?"

"No. I just left there. Harry bought me a drink to celebrate."

"Do you want to do some more celebrating?"

"What did you have in mind?"

"We could go somewhere."

"Or you could just come here."

"Ok. I like your idea better. I'll be there in an hour. I have some things to drop off at my place and then I'll come right over."

"I'll be ready."

Katherine went to her liquor cabinet. She took out the ingredients for martinis. She took two glasses out of the cabinet. She put ice in a bowl along with cold water. She put both glassed in the bowl to chill them.

She went to her bedroom to change. She opened her drawer looking for her sexy black silk playboy pajamas but couldn't find them. Then she remembered she couldn't find them after the attack either. She selected a red and white teddy instead and put it on. She combed her hair so that it hung straight down to the middle of her back. She went back into the kitchen.

When she heard the closing of a car door in her driveway, she took the glasses out of the ice water and poured two martinis. There was a knock on the door. She went to answer it. It was Sergeant Grimes. His expression was priceless as he looked at her standing in the doorway dressed in a sexy teddy holding two drinks.

"I was expecting someone else."

"I know. That's why I'm here."

"What do you mean?"

"Detective Jenkins was killed in an accident about a half hour ago."

"What?"

"He had just left the station to go home when his car was broad sided by a construction truck. The impact was so severe a pavement roller on the back of the truck fell off crushing Detective Jenkins car. He died instantly."

"Oh my God," she began crying hysterically.

Sergeant Grimes went in and closed the door. Katherine had dropped the drinks on the floor shattering glass everywhere. Grimes put his arms around her and held her. He could feel the warmth of her body.

"Everything will be all right," he said to her in a soft voice.

"No it won't," she said continuing to cry.

"Is there anything I can do for you Ms. Sterns?"

"I think I need to lie down."

"Sure."

She walked him back out the door.

"You should get some rest. Call me if you need anything."

"What am I going to do?"

"Get some rest. I'll stop by in the morning."

Grimes left and Katherine went to her bedroom. She took off her clothing and slid under the covers. She cried curled up in a fetal position and eventually fell asleep.

Chapter 48

Ann Benard went to the funeral. Since Frank Jenkins didn't have any family, there wasn't a wake. Everything took place the morning of the funeral at the funeral home. The place was very busy with everyone from the police department in attendance. Office Trudy sat in the front row crying. Katherine sat where family normally sits.

Ann walked up to Katherine, "I'm so sorry Katherine. I know you were going to move to Connecticut with him. Now what will you do?"
"I don't know Ann. I'm at a total loss."

Just then, Sergeant Grimes came up to Katherine and put his arm around her. He said something to her in her ear and she smiled at him. She looked to Ann, "Sergeant Grimes has been good enough to help me out."
"I'm sure he will take care of everything you need."
"Yes, he will." Katherine said, tugging Grimes arm.

Ann turned and left the funeral home. She stopped by Sundancers. She ordered a shot and a martini.

"A little strong don't you think?" Harry asked taking a seat next to her. It was only 11:00 am.

"I just came from the funeral home. You can't believe what Katherine is up to."

"Oh, I could believe anything when it comes to her."

"She got what she wanted from the Judge. Bowman is in jail for a long time. Then she was prepared to marry Detective Jenkins and move to another state with him."

"Yeah, it's too bad he died. I liked the guy," said Harry.

"She's hooked up with someone else already."

"You're kidding?"

"No. She was hanging on to another cop at the funeral."

"It's just another chapter in the saga of Katherine Sterns," said Harry. "She can't help herself."

"You're probably right."

"Oh, I am."

Harry got up and went into the kitchen. Ann sat there in disbelief thinking about Katherine. She asked for another shot. Dee made it and set it in front of her.

"I just can't believe she moved on to another man so quickly," remarked Dee.

A new face walked into Sundancers just as Ann was taking to Dee. He took up the stool next to Ann.

"Bartender, can I get a Bud?"

"Sure."

The man turned to Ann.

"Hi, I'm Wes Donlevy."

"Ann Benard."

"Nice to meet you Ms. Benard."

"Call me Ann."

"Call me Wes."

Harry walked over to Dee, "I guess she's over it also."

"Guess so."

Ann sat and talked to the stranger for about an hour.

"It's getting late. I think I'll go home," she said taking the last sip of her martini.

"Me too. I have a busy day tomorrow."

"It's such a nice day. Have you ever taken a walk on the beach?"

"Can't say that I have."

"How would you like to join me?"

"Sure."

"Then let's go. We can take my car."

"Then I'll have to come back and get my car later."

"You can pick it up in the morning."

Wes smiled.

Ann looked to Dee, "Tell Harry Wes is going to leave his car here over night."

"I'll tell him," said Dee as she cashed them out.

Later on, as the night was finishing up, Harry came into the bar.

"Dee, after you cash out the register, can you put the money in the safe in my office?"

"Sure Harry."

"I'm going to have a drink. Care to join me?"

"I'll put the money in the office safe and then I'll be right back."

Dee went to Harry's office in the building in front of Sundancers. She put the money in the safe. While she was doing it, she saw a pair of black silk Playboy woman's

344

pajamas in the safe. She took them out and held them up to see if they would fit her.

"A perfect match," she exclaimed.

She took the pajamas back into the bar with her after locking the safe and closing the office door.

Harry was sitting at the bar. He had turned off all of the lights except one set under the bar. The place had an eerie glow to it as she pulled out a stool.

"I made you a margarita."

"Thanks. I could use it."

She put the pajamas on the bar.

"What do you have there?" He said as the two sat at the bar.

"I found these in your safe."

"Oh, someone must have left them here during an interview or something."

"Who would wear something like this to an interview? And even worse, how did they get into your safe?"

"I don't know. People are always leaving things in my office. Do you want them?"

"How do you think they would look on me?"

"I don't know. Why don't you try them on?"

"Right here and now?"

"Why not?"

"I don't know Harry."

"What do you mean?"

"If I didn't know better, I'd say you got these pajamas just to get me to take my clothes off."

"What if I did?"

"You could have just asked."

"For you to take your clothes off?"

"No, for a date. Then if things worked out, you'd get your wish."

"Well, I didn't buy those pajamas. I'm not really sure how they got into the safe. Maybe they belonged to one of the cougars?"

"So you say".

Dee undressed and tried on the pajamas. Harry sat at the bar with his drink, smiling.

"You look great."

"With or without the pajamas?"

"Yes and yes."

"That's an evasive answer."

"I like the Playboy logo. Nice touch."

"Well, whoever left these had nice taste."

"Why would someone leave something like that in my office?"

"Stranger things have happened."

"You have a point."

"Hey, maybe someone was getting revenge?"

6768197R0

Made in the USA
Charleston, SC
05 December 2010